MY SEDUCTIVE HIGHLANDER

A SCOTTISH HISTORICAL TIME TRAVEL ROMANCE

HIGHLAND HEARTS
BOOK 4

MAEVE GREYSON

MAEVEGREYSON.COM
Magical Romance SlIpping Through Time

ALSO BY MAEVE GREYSON

HIGHLAND HEROES SERIES

The Guardian

The Warrior

The Judge

The Dreamer

The Bard

The Ghost

A Yuletide Yearning

Love's Charity

TIME TO LOVE A HIGHLANDER SERIES

Loving Her Highland Thief

Taming Her Highland Legend

Winning Her Highland Warrior

Capturing Her Highland Keeper

Saving Her Highland Traitor

Loving Her Lonely Highlander

Delighting Her Highland Devil

ONCE UPON A SCOT SERIES

A Scot of Her Own

A Scot to Have and to Hold

A Scot to Love and Protect

HIGHLAND PROTECTOR SERIES

Sadie's Highlander

Joanna's Highlander

Katie's Highlander

HIGHLAND HEARTS SERIES

My Highland Lover

My Highland Bride

My Tempting Highlander

My Seductive Highlander

THE MACKAY CLAN

Beyond A Highland Whisper

The Highlander's Fury

A Highlander In Her Past

OTHER BOOKS BY MAEVE GREYSON

Stone Guardian

Eternity's Mark

Guardian of Midnight Manor

CHAPTER 1

MacKenna Keep
Thirteenth-Century
Scotland

"Dammit, man! Did ye not think to learn her name afore ye decided to bed her?" Gray MacKenna, chieftain of Clan MacKenna, moved to the edge of his seat as though ready to lunge across the room, wrap his hands around Graham's throat and choke the life out of him.

Graham MacTavish edged back a step whilst rubbing the back of his neck. He stole a quick glance around the room. All eyes were locked on him and it was no small wonder. This was thrice in a fortnight that the MacKenna had publicly chewed his arse over what he had honestly deemed as sound choices at the time that he had made them. But apparently, once again, he had chosen poorly.

Dammit all to hell and back. He scrubbed a hand across his mouth, vainly attempting to wipe away any forthcoming words that might damn him even further. He had never chosen his words wisely, remembering the particular deed in question. Nay. Neither lass had given a hint of their surnames. Why had the one not mentioned her husband was the bloody chieftain of the Buchanans?

Ah well . . . it didn't very well matter now. What was done was done. He squared his shoulders and locked his fists to the small of his back. With his chin lifted courageously, he boldly met Gray's infuriated glare. "I didna take her to my bed. We stayed in the stables."

From the purplish tint of the MacKenna's face and the vein twitching in the man's temple, perhaps that was not the best defense. He better try again. "But ye will be pleased to know, I didna lift any of their cattle—nor a single horse this time."

"I should turn ye over to the Buchanan and be done with ye." Gray expelled a rumbling growl while shooting Graham a murderous look. The sorely annoyed chieftain threw himself back in his chair on the dais. The great meeting hall fell silent, all poised to hear what Graham's punishment would be this time.

Graham's gut tightened. To be turned over to the Buchanans would not be good at all. But if that was the MacKenna's wish, then so be it. A snorting, laugh escaped him as he slowly shook his head. 'Twould be a damn shame to die over that lass and her maid.

The women's shrill tirades and dead aims with clods of dried horse shit on the morning after the quite enjoyable romp had taught him a thing or two—mainly that ye best never get too deep in yer cups when charming the ladies because their druthers could sorely change by the time everyone sobered up the next day.

A soft clearing of a throat drew Graham's attention to the chieftain's wife sitting quietly at her husband's side. Lady Trulie smoothed a hand across her husband's tensed forearm and sat taller in her chair. "Now, now. We can't do that, Gray. You know what would happen if we turned him over to the Buchanans."

She leaned forward the slightest bit, glaring at Graham from the raised platform as though he were a disobedient child. "We understand your need to experience all that you missed while cursed but..." Her face darkened like a building storm. "Dammit, Graham! Pull your head out of your ass and stop endangering the peace and safety of this clan just because you can't keep your britches on and your hands off what belongs to somebody else."

Britches? What the hell were britches? He looked downward. Perhaps the Lady Trulie referred to his trews? In, he had not even removed his *léine* while sampling the sweet lasses, but perhaps now was not the time to get into the particulars.

Graham slightly bowed to her. "I am truly sorry to bring such strife to this clan that has so graciously taken me in. Ye ken my fealty to the MacKenna is true. I would never wish to cause the clan harm nor bring dishonor to the name."

"He wants yer head on a pike, ye ken?" The MacKenna's voice had calmed to a more congenial snarl. He even came close to smiling as he covered his wife's hand with his own. "And I canna say that I blame the man. Ye bedded *both* his wife and his mistress under his verra nose." The chieftain stretched forward and jabbed a finger at the center of Graham's chest. "And perhaps ye didna personally help yerself to any of the Buchanan livestock, but whilst ye were busy dipping yer wick, Angus managed to lead away the Buchanan's favorite pair of roans."

Aye. Well—there was that. Said roans were currently resting quite comfortably in their new stalls in the MacKenna stables. "Perhaps we could return them?" Graham turned and waggled a brow at Angus, who was currently doing his damnedest to stay hidden in the shadows of the gallery overhanging the right side of the crowded meeting room. "If Angus releases them close enough to Buchanan Keep, the pair would surely find their way back to their stable."

Angus yelped as Mother Sinclair came up behind him and latched hold of his ear. She yanked him out of the shadows, jerked him to the center of the room, and firmly positioned him in place beside Graham. With her slight body leaning against her twisted staff, she shook a bony finger in both their faces. "Those who play together, pay together." She stamped her cane hard against the stone flooring, the blue crystal ensnared in the claw of roots in its top sparked with an angry blue-white glow.

Ever so slowly, she ambled over to the head of the room, hitched her way up the narrow stone steps, and eased herself down into the smaller seat beside Lady Trulie's chair.

The thick braid knotted at the base of the old woman's neck shone with a silvery white gleam beneath the flickering light of the torches as she nodded at Graham. "We owe him protection . . . guidance while he adapts. He is wild as a buck deer in rut after being trapped in the form of a dragon and locked to the land around Loch Ness for over three centuries—but he was Ronan's protector, his best friend. And Ronan is now family." Granny Sinclair leveled the softly glowing crystal of her twisted cane until it pointed directly at Graham. "But you keep endangering Clan MacKenna with your thoughtless actions and we don't owe you a damn thing, Graham."

Aye, well, he had not exactly been entirely shackled to the land around Loch Ness. After all, he'd traveled quite freely whenever he'd kept to the sea. Graham forced the memories of those long-ago adventures to the back of his mind, quite thankful that that part of his life was well behind him. He cleared his throat and remained silent. He'd best concentrate on getting his arse out of this current mess—especially now that Granny Sinclair was involved.

Granny's gaze shifted and she aimed her staff at Angus. "And you know better than to pull such stunts against an allied clan. What the hell were you thinking, Angus? You're supposed to keep him out of trouble."

Angus tucked his chin to his chest and anxiously shuffled back and forth in place. Sidling closer to Graham, he shot him a dark, threatening look. "I'll never listen to a single word from yer lying arse again, ye wicked bastard," he hissed under his breath.

Still fidgeting in place, Angus hooked his thumbs in his belt. His face darkened to a ruddier shade as he turned his back on the dais and continued his shielded rant in a huffing whisper. "And if ye wish to return those horses, yer own goat-swiving arse can do it alone. I'll not be going back there. I nearly took an arrow in me tail."

Graham stood taller, rolling his shoulders at Angus's words. He would not let another be held responsible for his own behavior. Best get on with this and find out what his punishment was to be. "Leave Angus be. My actions are my own."

Mother Sinclair's narrow-eyed gaze met with Lady Trulie's. The women smiled in unison—cold, calculating smiles that stabbed a sense of dread deep in the center of Graham's heart. May the gods have mercy on his soul and doubly watch over his arse. He shivered against the sudden eeriness in the air that chilled him to the bone. "Pray speak my fate. I accept whatever ye decide. Never have I shirked my responsibilities, ye ken that well enough."

"It pleases me greatly to hear that. Doesn't it you, my husband?" Trulie turned and smiled at Gray with a slow meaningful nod.

"Aye." Gray flexed his hands then curled his fingers over the ends of the carved arms of his chair. His gaze trailed around the hall, studying the many folks standing along the walls and seated at the long rows of trestle tables. He slowly rose, stepped forward then halted on the last step of the raised stone platform as though he were around to announce clan war.

"After much consideration and consultation . . ." Gray paused, tossing back a quick glance at Lady Trulie and Mother Sinclair before returning his attention to Graham and Angus. "I have decided upon yer punishment since ye seem so incapable of exhibiting the least bit of self-control."

Angus hid his mouth by rubbing the tip of his nose with his fist; his voice dropped to an even deeper whisper, "Oy, ye are doomed straight to hell now, man."

Graham eased a step forward and threw out his chest. "Aye. Am I to be turned over to the Buchanans then—to face the pike or the dungeons?"

"Oh no, my friend." The MacKenna shook his head. "I have decided on something much worse. Ye shall face the severest punishment of all. A life sentence, in fact."

Graham swallowed hard. He didn't suppose he could blame the chieftain. After all, a clan could not very well go to war over the womanizing ways of one individual—especially when that individual wasn't even blood kin. "Aye. I would hear it then. What is this severe punishment I am to receive?"

"Marriage."

The word echoed down the length of the hushed hall as the MacKenna patiently clasped his hands in front of his waist and waited.

Angus snorted out a belly laugh.

Graham whirled around and smacked the back of his hand across Angus's chest, effectively knocking the man's hearty laugh down to a hissing snicker. "*Haud yer wheesht* afore I snap yer neck."

There was not a damn thing funny about what the MacKenna had just proposed. Graham turned back to the chieftain and repeated the dangerous word, "Marriage?"

Gray nodded, his stance visibly more relaxed. "Aye, marriage. Ye need a good woman to teach ye the error of yer ways and keep ye to the proper path."

A trickle of sweat rolled down the center of Graham's back and settled in the crack of his arse. Damn, the room was suddenly too warm, and there wasn't even a fire. He rubbed his knuckles against the small of his back while shifting in place. "And who might I ask is this woman that is prepared to mold me into a better man?"

It couldn't be the Buchanan sweetling or her luscious maid. Those two already shared the bear of her husband—Chieftain Buchanan himself—hence the problem. Saint's bones, he prayed it wasn't her sister. That one had the screeching voice of a seabird and a bloodcurdling scowl to match.

Lady Trulie stood and moved to her husband's side. "You're the perfect match for my sister Lilia—and the twenty-first century is the perfect place to keep you out of sight and out of mind until our allies calm down."

"Oh, holy hell."

"Aye." Gray nodded, his ever-widening smile lighting his face brighter than a newly pitched torch. He lifted his hands to all in the room. "All here bear witness; Graham MacTavish shall be duly matched and wed to my good sister Lilia Meredith Sinclair."

Tankards thumped on the tabletops and a chorus of hearty *ayes* echoed to the dark rafters of the high-ceilinged room.

With her fingers laced into a prim knot at her waist, Lady Trulie descended the steps, slowly approaching Graham and Angus with her long skirts gracefully whispering across the floor.

Damned if he didna feel as threatened as a wee mousie facing down Mother Sinclair's cat.

The lady paused once she reached the men, pulling in a slow deep breath while she studied them. Her head barely tilted to one side and her brow furrowed the merest bit as her eyes narrowed.

Sizing up their weaknesses, no doubt. Graham swallowed hard. No force in all of Scotland or the great beyond struck fear into his soul like that of the Sinclair women. Able to skate back and forth across the strands of time at will and control unexplainable powers, the Sinclairs were the bloodline chosen by the very Fates themselves to break the curse of the vile witch who had shackled him into the form of a dragon by day and a man by night, then bound him to the shores of Loch Ness and the depths of the sea for more than three centuries.

These women were powerful and—lore a'mighty—he had seen each of their tempers flare hot and wicked more than once. From Mother Sinclair down to the MacKenna's wee daughter, Chloe. Berserkers appeared meek as lambs when compared to enraged Sinclair females.

"You and Angus come to the solar. We will go over the details of your trip." Lady Trulie lightly patted his arm, then turned toward the stone arch leading up to the chieftain's private tower. "Come now. Both of you."

"Begging yer forgiveness, m'lady." Angus angled around in front of Graham and held his clasped hands up to her, shamelessly pleading. "Surely, ye dinna mean to send me off into the unknown too."

"Hell of a friend ye be." Graham shouldered Angus aside. "Leave the coward here, m'lady. I shall be fine on my own."

One of Lady Trulie's dark brows arched a notch higher in a

chilling look of displeasure. With a quick shake of her head, she waved both men forward. "*Both* of you. To the solar. Now."

The sound of Granny's staff hitting the floor behind them hastened their steps. Graham cast an imploring look back at the MacKenna bringing up the rear. Surely the man's mind could be changed. Surely, he wouldn't damn a fellow Highlander to the scheming of the Sinclair women.

"On wi' ye, man." Gray nodded once toward the winding stone steps at the end of the hall. "Ye brought this on yerself. The both of ye did." He paused and turned to glance at those still gathered in the main meeting room. "I gladly adopted ye into this clan but I will not continue allowing ye to anger my allies at every border. I have many to protect. I will not risk them for the randiness of one."

"I curse the day I took ye as friend," Angus said in a low hissing growl. He stomped on ahead, his stocky form swaying from side to side with his rolling, short-legged gait.

Graham sucked in a long deep breath and blew it out. "And I curse the day I was born," he muttered, while silently praying the gods would somehow reach down and pluck him out of this damn mess.

CHAPTER 2

"Sit." Mother Sinclair pointed at a short bench against the wall beside the stone hearth. "The both of you."

Graham strode across the room and took his stance in front of the cold fireplace. "I shall stand, thank ye." While it was true, he respected the women and looked upon them with no small amount of leeriness, he would be damned if he sat on a bench like a lad due a scolding. They had already named his sentence. Time to get on with the details of his fate.

Angus huffed out a disgusted *harrumph* then obediently stomped over to the bench and plopped down. As soon as he sat, a golden-eyed, black cat hopped up beside him and sat glaring at him with an unblinking stare. The man edged to the end of the bench farthest from the cat, crossing his legs and turning away as though shielding his man parts from the creature's piercing gaze.

Mother Sinclair chuckled. "Very good, Kismet. Keep an eye on Angus and make certain he pays attention."

The tip of Kismet's long sleek tail flipped faster.

A warm, heavy weight leaned hard against Graham's leg. Without looking down, he leaned to the side and scratched behind the massive dog's ears. At least he had one ally in the room. Lady Trulie's hulking black beast of a dog, Karma, had taken up with him since the first moment he had arrived at MacKenna Keep. Of course, it was probably because the MacKenna's five-year-old daughter, Chloe, had named him her favorite uncle. The dog worshiped the wee lass and considered her word law.

"Stay with me, lad," he whispered down to the dog.

Karma thumped his heavy tail on the floor.

Mother Sinclair and Lady Trulie sat in the cushioned chairs pulled close to the hearth. The band around Graham's chest loosened the barest bit as the MacKenna strode over to the waist-high cabinet filled with bottles, pitchers, and assorted cups and glasses. He wouldn't mind a wee nip if the MacKenna was so inclined.

Gray promptly filled two pewter goblets with the deep ruby contents of one of the pitchers. He carried the glasses to the women then returned to the bar, filled three tankards from an amber bottle, and waved the men forward. "Come. I've whisky for ye both and the feeling ye'll be a needing it."

Angus beat Graham to the bar, snatched up one of the mugs then, after a fearful glance at Mother Sinclair, obediently returned to the bench.

Coward. Graham shook his head at Angus, then purposely sauntered across the room as though he had nary a care in the world. He would do as they bade him but he'd damn sure not sacrifice his backbone in the doing of it. He looped his hand through the handle of the tankard then strode back to his spot at the hearth.

"*Sláinte.*" Gray lifted his glass and nodded to each of the men.

"*Sláinte,*" Graham repeated as he lifted his glass first to Gray, then to the ladies before taking a deep draw. He welcomed the burn of the fiery liquid. It reminded him a great deal of when he had been a dragon and housed burning coals in his gullet. A bitter laugh snorted free as he stared down at his reflection in the bit of whisky left in his cup. At least he could say life had never been dull.

"I think you and Lilia are a wonderful match," Lady Trulie said while turning to slide her goblet onto the small arm table between her and Mother Sinclair's chair. "She is strong-willed just like you. I feel sure there will be sparks."

Sparks? Hell's fire, that was all he needed. Sinclair sparks could singe his arse. Graham finished his drink in one quick gulp, silently wishing there was more. He politely nodded. "And ye ken the lady will be agreeable to this match ye desire?"

"Probably not," Mother Sinclair said. Her soft chuckling echoed in her cup as she took a long slow drink. Merriment gleamed in her eyes as she placed her glass beside Trulie's. "Our Lilia is quite the hellcat. Stubborn. Opinionated. And if she thinks it, you can damn well bet she is going to say it."

But then all mirth faded from her as she reached for Trulie's hand. "But our strong stubborn lass in the future thinks allowing anyone to help her is a sign of weakness . . . of failure. Only a year ago, this isolation and selfish guarding of her insecurities nearly caused her to end her life."

Lady Trulie patted Mother Sinclair's hand then rose from her chair and moved closer to Graham. "We are sending you to the future not only to woo Lilia but to save her from herself. She needs to be loved whether she wishes it or not. She can't survive in this world alone—no matter what century. As an empath, she isn't always able to shield herself from the cruelties around her." Trulie cleared her throat, then turned away but not before Graham noticed the moisture of unshed tears shining in her eyes. An empath? What the hell was an empath? Be the poor lass crippled?

Trulie sniffed and pressed the back of her hand against her mouth. Recovering quickly, she lifted her head and smoothed both hands down the folds of her skirt. She returned to her chair and sank into it, slowly blowing out a deep breath. "And even with the prophetic visions the Fates send her, Lilia does not realize she is in danger."

"What is this danger she faces?" Graham placed his empty tankard on the shelf above the hearth. He could not stomach the thought of a helpless woman facing danger alone. Perhaps *empath* meant the poor lass was under some sort of curse or being hunted down by demons. He understood the feelings of utter helplessness well. Curses did that to a soul. The very idea grated against his hide. Women were to be protected and cherished from such unpleasantness. "What danger?" he repeated.

"The danger of depression—of a dark hopelessness." Mother Sinclair shook her head. "Lilia's blessing from the Fates is also her curse. She is able to see future events—usually dire ones. Sometimes, she can save those she sees in the visions. Sometimes not. And when we say Lilia is an empath, we mean she feels the pain and suffering of the world more than most. She can stand inside a crowded room and feel what every individual in that room feels—be it sorrow or joy or anything in between—and she is not always able to shield herself from others' emotions. Soon, she will be alone. The guardian I sent to watch over her is dying. Lilia must not be left alone. Alone, the darkness of despair could very well overpower her and send her to her end."

Mother Sinclair rose, crossed the room, and thumped Graham on the chest. "But if she is properly wooed and married—the greatest energy of all would help keep her from that darkness."

Graham clasped his hands to the small of his back, fighting the urge to fidget beneath the intensity of the old woman's gaze. "What energy do ye speak of? I have no magic, nor powers to keep the woman safe. I can only protect her with my sword—and would consider it an honor to do so."

He would gladly do that if that was what they wished. He sorely regretted endangering the clan with his behavior. They had welcomed him in and named him as one of their own when he'd declined to return to Draegonmare Keep with his beloved friend, Ronan, and his new wife, Mairi—another of the Lady Trulie's sisters.

The thought of returning to Loch Ness, the land he had been anchored to for so verra long, had rankled his soul. So, the MacKennas had adopted him and bid him stay as long as he liked. His gaze dropped and his heart sank to his gut. He was keenly aware of all that the MacKennas had done for him. And look how he had repaid that kindness.

Mother Sinclair moved forward and rested her bony fingers on his arm, her touch gentler this time. She leaned in close and smiled. "You can protect her with the greatest energy of all. You can protect her with your love and understanding."

He sucked in a deep breath, uncertainty threatening to squeeze the air right back out. Love? Surely, she jested. He was not capable of love. He'd hardened his heart against that fickle emotion whilst he was cursed. After all, 'twas the foolishness of enchanted love that had drawn him to the beauty of the vile witch who had damned him into the form of the dragon. "I will give her my honor and protection. I can guarantee no more than that."

Mother Sinclair wrinkled her nose, resetting her wire-rimmed spectacles a bit higher. Her sparse gray brows knotted in a disapproving frown. "You have one full month." She held up a slightly bent finger, knotted and twisted with age. "Just one full cycle of the moon to win Lilia's heart and convince her to be your wife. The Fates aren't the patient sort—especially since we are blatantly tinkering with their web by attempting to permanently relocate you to the future. They will not permit you an extended stay in a time other than your own without a proper anchor to keep your heart and soul grounded. If at the end of that month, you and Lilia aren't as one, your happy ass will be yanked right back here to the past—and to the Buchanans."

Mother Sinclair spoke as though that were a bad thing. Surely, after a month in the future, the Buchanan Clan's ire would have cooled enough for him to safely return to his life in the thirteenth century. He felt more settled, calmer with the certainty of it. Aye, he would be back here in no time at all. All would be well.

"Nay. I ken what ye are thinking." Gray stepped forward and shook his head. "If ye return to this time, I will be forced to turn ye over to the Buchanan to avoid clan war. His ire toward ye willna be set aside so easily. Ye ken, at the verra least, the man wishes to see ye drawn and quartered. Ye cuckolded him within his own keep and 'tis said his women keep his hatred fanned and well fueled by singing of yer *talents* to any and all who will lend an ear." Gray watched Graham over the rim of his glass while drawing in another long sip. He lowered the mug and slid it onto the cabinet beside him. "The Buchanan has accepted the offer that ye are to be banished from Scotland—forever. It was the only option other than yer head on a pike that came remotely close to cooling the man's rage. Ye can wager his people will be watching and willna fail to report if ye return—no matter how long ye stayed away from yer beloved Highlands of this time. Clan MacKenna can no longer be yer sanctuary."

Well, damn his arse straight to hell and back. But surely the chieftain erred in his thinking. Surely, he could return after a bit of time. Graham stood taller. A Sinclair woman. To wife. May the gods have mercy on his soul. But then, surely, it would not be that bad—not as bad as torture, or even worse—the dungeons. And eventually . . . perhaps he could someday return and reunite his new wife with her kin. Aye, that would be his future.

"I will make certain the woman agrees to be my wife." A growing sense of uncertainty stirred uncomfortably in his gut like a poorly digested meal. Lore a'mighty, what would he do with a wife?

"See that you do." Mother Sinclair returned to her chair and scooped up her goblet in a pale knobby hand. She put the glass to her mouth then paused and instead lifted it to Graham in a toast. "Know this—if you cause my granddaughter any pain, the Buchanan will be the least of your worries."

CHAPTER 3

Graham tightened his belt and checked his sword for the third time since they had gathered in the garden beside the reflecting pool. He flexed his calves, finding some small comfort in the leather straps biting into his muscles. Aye, good. Both daggers, especially the most cherished one that never left his possession, were securely sheathed against his legs. Shield and bow rested on the ground beside him. He would take them up as soon as Mother Sinclair bade him it was time to do so.

The old woman and Lady Trulie had spent the past week preparing—nay, not preparing—it was more like the two women had waged a full-blown attack on him and Angus, training them both for this wretched trip into the unknown. Even little Chloe had solemnly shown him her precious picture book the family kept hidden—the strange book with parchment pages that were oddly slick and smooth and the images colorful and bright that they could not be of this world.

Graham glanced at the tensed faces, shadowed and yet glowing in the flickering torchlight of the night-shrouded garden. Every face clearly reflected the same uncertainty eating at his gut. Heaven help him. He was such a swiving fool. Cursed to forsake all he had ever known because of one woman easily lured from her husband's bed. Lore a'mighty—he would never touch another man's woman again. He swallowed hard, suddenly remembering the real purpose of this trip. Saint's bones, what the devil would he do with a wife of his own?

Graham rolled his shoulders. Every muscle throbbed, tensed and aching. Part of him was thrilled at the prospect of this journey but a bigger part of him cowered at the great unknown leap he was about to make. A huffing laugh escaped him. He supposed he deserved this After all, he had spent the last three centuries yearning for freedom and excitement.

Angus fidgeted beside him, taking up his pack and slinging it across his shoulder, then dropping it back to the ground before picking it up again. He shuffled and circled back and forth in the dust like Mother Sinclair's cat looking for a place to shit.

Graham clapped a hand on Angus's shoulder and squeezed. "Be still, man. Ye are fretting worse than a wormy hound."

"Be still?" Angus glared at him with an incredulous smirk. "Be still he says when we are about to jump into the verra jaws of hell itself and we've no way of knowing if we'll come out alive on the other end of it or not."

"Of course, you'll come out alive on the other end." Mother Sinclair thumped her staff against Angus's shoulder and pointed for him to back up a few steps. "Stand over there so Trulie and I can go over the final details."

Lady Trulie slowly meandered back and forth in front of them, studying them closely as though sizing them up for prey. She arched a brow, cleared her throat, then leaned in close to Mother Sinclair and spoke in a hushed tone. "You're positive they will *both* make it through okay? You know it doesn't always work very well with males."

"Oh, holy hell." Angus flung a hand into the air, then raked his fingers through his already wildly unkempt hair. He whirled around and jabbed a stubby finger into the center of Graham's chest. "This is yer fault, ye randy bastard. I told ye she was not a whore." He jabbed Graham's breastbone again. "I canna believe I am going to die just because ye couldna resist a bit a skirt."

Graham grabbed Angus's hand before he could jab him again and squeezed. Hard. Without releasing man's fist, he turned to Mother Sinclair. "Send me alone. Leave this coward behind. He shouldna be punished for my poor choices."

Mother Sinclair shook her head. "No. The vision clearly showed Angus in the future with you. He must go too—and his ability to stay, if he so chooses, also depends on your connection with Lilia."

"What vision?" Graham's blood ran cold. Not once had they mentioned any visions. He'd heard about the Sinclair women and their gifts of prophecy. This could not bode well at all.

Mother Sinclair scowled down at the ground, slowly marking strange glyphs in the dust with the tip of her staff. "Eliza MacTavish, your blood kin, has cried out across time and space with the last bit of her energy. She has watched over you for centuries, suffering whilst the curse held you prisoner and tied her hands against helping you. But now that you're free, her most heartfelt wish for you is the greatest gift of all. She wishes you to find love and contentment, Graham, and she feels you can find it with my Lilia."

Graham swiped his sweating palms on the wool of his plaid, then opened and closed his fists. The seriousness of this task grew greater by the minute—so many damn people depending on him. He jerked his chin up a notch, bracing himself against the uncertainty and fear churning in his gut. "That is not a vision. That's more a request."

Mother Sinclair clucked like a nesting hen, shaking her head as she turned away. "When Eliza made her energy and wishes known to me—that was when I received the vision. You and Lilia are meant to be. The strength and surety of your match came easily to me across the ages. Rarely do the Fates ever allow me any insight into the lives of those I love, but this time, they were overly generous so I might save my sweet Lilia's life."

"She truly is in danger then?" Graham rested his hand on the pommel of his sword.

"The greatest danger to Lilia is Lilia herself. Remember all that we've taught you about the future." Mother Sinclair turned to Angus who was still fidgeting in the dust. "And I have no idea why the Fates have chosen you but you're going with him so man up and stop your whining."

Lady Trulie stepped forward and looped a leather cord with a softly glowing blue crystal around each of the men's necks. She patted the crystal against Graham's chest and smiled. "A little extra protection while you're both in the time tunnel. Hold tight to these crystals and remember to keep your eyes closed." She turned and took her place beside Granny. "It will be nighttime in Edinburgh too. Hopefully, no one will see you drop from the time cloud. Don't forget to lay low until you get your bearings and figure out where you are. Remember the description of the town and its layout. The high points are on the map we gave you. You should be able to find Lilia easily."

"Lay low," Graham repeated with a hesitant glance at Angus.

"Aye." Angus glared back at him and gave an angry toss of his head. "That means keep yer ugly arse hidden until ye figure out what the hell ye are supposed to do instead of wading into a place and expecting everyone to fawn at yer feet. Ye are not a dragon anymore. Ye are nothing more than a man, ye ken?"

"Surly bastard." Graham shouldered his pack higher on his back then turned and nodded at the two women. "Let's be on with it, then."

Lady Trulie and Mother Sinclair each took a torch from the line of metal sconces built into the stone wall surrounding the garden and carefully lit the ring of dried tinder piled knee-deep around the reflecting pool. The flames spread quickly, eating through the wood and sending showers of sparks up into the blackness of the sky.

"When we say the words, the flames will freeze, the water will turn to a mirror, and the portal will open. When you see us lower our torches, you must jump into the center of the ring of frozen fire. Timing is of the utmost importance since neither of you has a drop of time-runner blood in your ancestry." Mother Sinclair paced back and forth in front of the two men then softly touched the blue crystal of her staff to the crystals each man wore around his neck.

Graham did his best not to flinch against the strange warming vibration of the stone against his chest. The last time he had witnessed the powerful Sinclair magic, the accursed witch, and the darkness she commanded had nearly drowned him. Goodwill or not, he was none too anxious to see the Sinclair powers at work again.

A low humming filled the air as the fire crackled and popped ever higher. The wind picked up, swirling around the reflecting pool with increasing force. Graham strained to see through the debris filling the air, struggling to watch the women and hear their words.

May the gods help and protect me, he silently prayed. The mystical haze filling the clearing shielded the women. All he could make out were their shadowy silhouettes and their musical singsong chanting as they passed back and forth on the other side of the burning ring.

The reflections of their torches and the crackling circle of fire danced and flickered across the water. The din filling the air became louder. The bone-shaking hum finally exploded and the flames solidified into tall, frozen, curving spikes straining upward. The water of the reflecting pool popped, then hardened, its surface turning black as ebony.

Graham tensed. It had to be time. With a glance at Angus, he nodded and crouched with his arms outspread. He watched the torches raised high over the women's heads. The hollow rush of his own blood pounded in his ears. The torches fell. A bloodcurdling battle cry burned free of his throat and he launched forward. A higher-pitched roar sounded behind him as Angus followed.

Spiraling through the darkness, Graham clutched both hands around the amulet at his chest. He locked into a tight tuck and roll around his shield and bow, squeezing his eyes tightly shut against the wind howling in his ears.

A constant stream of high-pitched Gaelic cursing came from slightly behind him and to the left. Angus. Graham hugged his weapons tighter to his chest and clenched his teeth harder. He would save his cursing for whenever they escaped this strange roaring hell.

An ear-splitting pop shook him. He flinched and rolled forward even faster. The ground rushed up at a nauseating speed then he hit with a bone-shaking thud.

"Arse-swiving sons a bitches!" Angus crashed down beside him, rolling out of control across the grassy hillside.

Graham finally stopped tumbling, then slowly teetered to one side and cracked open an eyelid. A gentle breeze wafted through the tall clumps of grass and brushed a calming touch across his flesh.

The stars were not as bright here. 'Twas the first difference he noted. The night not as dark. A strange, orange glow settled across the horizon before fading up into the deep blues and eventually the blacks of the star-spattered sky. What strange magic could it be that made the city at the base of the hill flicker with such an unholy light?

He sat up, propped his shield under his arm, and scanned the city below. Lights. Lady Trulie had said the candles with no flame that lit the night were called lights.

"Think we be in the proper time?" Angus scurried over to him on all fours, pausing every few feet to stretch up and glance around the hillside like an oversized rat. "This time . . ." He paused, his nostrils flaring as he looked around. "This time has an odd stench to it."

"Aye," Graham agreed. This place did not smell of the sweet heather from whence he'd come. "What think ye the stench might be? 'Tis worse than the garderobe cesspit."

Angus shook his head, still kneeling as he peered across the waving grasses covering the hillside. "I dinna ken. I see no carnage nor scrap piles. Mayhap this time just smells like shit."

Graham reached inside his tunic and withdrew the hand-sized leather flask tucked into the fold of his shirt. He uncorked it with his teeth and took a long fortifying swig, welcoming the burn in his gullet. Thank the gods. At least that had not changed in this time. "Here. *Uisge beatha.* 'Twill give ye strength."

"Aye to that, my friend." Angus snatched the flask out of his hand and upended it over his mouth. The golden stream of whisky poured down until Angus uprighted the skin and recorked it. He wiped his mouth with the back of his hand and rolled back on his heels. "There's barely enough in this to properly wet a man's gullet. Methinks we best be finding that pub the old woman told us about."

Graham slowly stood and studied the glaring chaos of lights and noise at the base of the hill. It was a damn sight more confusing than the simple map Lady Trulie and Mother Sinclair had sketched out on the bit of parchment tucked safely inside his belted tunic.

"Aye," he said, snorting at the uncertainty he heard in his own voice.

He attempted to wet his lips even though his mouth had gone suddenly dry at the prospect of diving headlong into the melee below. He shook free of the indecision and foreboding like a dog shaking free of the rain. Enough of this. He waved Angus forward. "On to the pub."

CHAPTER 4

Edinburgh, Scotland
Twenty-first Century

Three perfectly white crisp tickets slowly rose behind the screen of her laptop, bouncing back and forth just beyond the edge like dancing cardboard puppets. A teasing singsong voice kept time with the hopping tickets. "Lookie what I've got!"

"I'm busy, Vivienne. Go pester Alberti." Lilia rubbed the corners of her weary eyes, then resettled her black-framed reading glasses back in place. She had to get the marketing campaign nailed down for store number three before the projected grand opening. Something fresh. Something new. Something spectacular. Those words haunted her every waking hour, even bleeding over into her dreams—they constantly hummed in the back of her mind like a demented mantra.

Carefully targeted marketing plus word of mouth around her all-natural line of cosmetics and skincare had boosted sales and built a large enough following to easily support a third store but nothing could be left to chance. It had taken a full year to recover from the gross error she had made when she trusted the wrong person to help her make her dream a success. She had to make sure this was right—absolutely perfect.

She closed her eyes and thumbed her pounding temples. After countless hours of staring at the computer and studying demographics, she very much doubted she would recognize something fresh and new if it bit her on the ass.

Maybe that should be store number three's angle: *Want your sweetie to nibble you straight to ecstasy? Vanilla-scented argan oil will guide your sexy bee straight to the honey pot.* She massaged her aching neck. Coming up with unique marketing and ad campaigns sucked balls.

"Here. Drink yer coffee, my wee grumpling. Have ye bothered eating today or do I need to bring ye a biscuit?" Vivienne slid a steaming bright pink mug toward her, then plopped down in one of the art deco steel chairs, wiggling in the seat until the black leather padding squeaked in protest.

Lilia curled the chunky ceramic mug between her hands, breathing in the blissful caffeine-infused aroma. Vivienne knew her well and took excellent care of her. Thank the Fates for the day that Vivienne had burst into the first natural-beauty boutique Lilia had opened. The way her friend's shriek had split the air that day, Lilia had thought someone was trying to kill her. But then she had spotted Vivienne's hair and face and understood completely.

Lilia immediately suspected a botched home color job as the culprit. She had never seen quite that shade of greenish purple before—except maybe in a Godzilla B-movie. Vivienne had also sported an inch-wide stain of bile green crawling down out of her hairline. The lizardy shade had striped her forehead and zigzagged down the back of her neck as well.

It had taken nearly two full teacups of Lilia's stash of whisky at the shop to calm Vivienne enough to get the details of what concoction she had used on her hair. After several hours, when Lilia was done, Vivienne's porcelain complexion was free of monster-green stains and her chicly spiked *do* was her now trademark, electric fuchsia.

Vivienne had sworn love and loyalty to Lilia that day and even though that had been barely two years ago, it was as though they had been the best of friends for a lifetime.

Vivienne tapped the glass table with a perfectly manicured nail. "Ye've wandered away on me again, pet. I said we've some of those delightful cinnamon biscuits left from the preview party for the coconut oil line last night. Want I should reheat one for ye?"

"Believe it or not, I actually had a scone this morning." Lilia drew in a deep breath, struggling against the darkness and stress squeezing her heart until she thought it would surely crumble. "Eliza seemed a bit more stable today so I had breakfast with her."

"Oh. Well . . . that's good then." Vivienne paused; her mouth pursed downward in a sympathetic frown. "I am so sorry, lovie," she whispered. Her deep brown eyes glistened with unshed tears. She cleared her throat and nervously fluffed her fingertips through her short, spiked hair.

Lilia took another sip of the strong black coffee. Vivienne's unconscious habit of spiking her bright hair into an even wilder bush of abandon somehow consoled her. Vivienne only fiddled with her hair when extremely upset or royally pissed off. By the somber hue of her friend's aura and the echo of sadness emanating from her, Vivienne was just as upset as she was about Eliza's worsening condition.

"So, what are the tickets for?" If she didn't change the subject, she and Vivienne would both be bawling. She saved the PowerPoint chart, then powered down the laptop. Enough planning for store three for one day.

Vivienne's face lit up and she excitedly patted both hands on the table. "Ye know Fringe Festival starts tonight. And look—" She grabbed up the tickets, fanned them out, and waved them under Lilia's nose "The Highland LARPers are putting on a special performance. The tickets were sold out in just under an hour but I scored three of them so you and I and Alberti can go and do a bit of *covert surveillance*." Her voice had deepened to the deliciously wicked tone it always took whenever Vivienne was in full plotting mode. She excitedly bounced up and down in her chair as though prepping for liftoff. "We'll totally win the competition against them later this fall. There'll be no stopping us at the Grand Highland Games if we can study their bit of swordplay and horsemanship and plan our attack accordingly." Vivienne pointed both index fingers at Lilia. "Ye could win the title of Grand Swordsmanship Champion two years straight! A pair of trophies would balance out a shelf quite nicely." Vivienne squealed and patted the table again. "Wouldn't that be banging hot?"

LARPing, or Live Action Role Playing, had been Lilia's saving grace when, just over a year ago, she had nearly lost her constant battle against the crippling darkness of depression. Gifted—or cursed depending on the viewpoint—with prophetic visions and painfully, fine-tuned empathy, life got overwhelming fast.

Drugs hadn't helped, and neither had therapy—especially when she couldn't exactly be totally honest with the doctor when it came to her family history. If she had told the psychiatrist she was the youngest member of a family of time-traveling women, born in thirteenth-century Scotland, then whisked to the future by her grandmother to save her life, the doc would've surely locked her in a padded cell and thrown away the key.

But the intense physical workout and the strategic planning involved in their LARP war games and swordplay competitions had helped—that and Vivienne and Alberti's close watchful care.

Vivienne had introduced Lilia to Alberti after the infamous screaming match she'd had with her former business partner David Sommers over some unexplainable entries in the company's accounts. Vivienne had never trusted or liked David but as Granny would say *the man could charm a dog off a meat wagon* and knew how to double-talk better than any politician. Whenever Lilia had lowered her shields and scanned David, she had never come up with any sense of guilt from him so she had liked him and taken him at his word. Of course, now she knew he never felt any guilt because the bastard hadn't possessed a conscience.

But then Vivienne had brought in Alberti. She'd known him since college and anyone Vivienne recommended was fine in Lilia's book. A savvy businessman, financial whiz, and even a licensed physical trainer on the side, Alberti had jumped at the chance to invest in Lilia's beauty business—a business that for all intents and purposes should be thriving but, strangely enough, seemed to be losing money.

Thank the Fates for Vivienne and Alberti. Not just for being business partners but also for being non-judgy confidants and friends. They knew and unconditionally accepted the parts of her heritage she had risked sharing. And if not for those two, she would've gone off the deep end and drowned in her sorrow a long time ago.

A sharp clap startled Lilia back to the present.

"Ye are worse at yer wandering today, pet. Did ye not sleep last night? If ye are going to get lost in yer thoughts, snag a juicy moment of going up against the wall with some delicious hunk instead of that dark shit that puts the shadows 'neath yer eyes." Vivienne scooped up the coveted tickets and waved them under Lilia's nose again. "Come on, ducks. Ye know a bit a swordplay always cheers ye up. Say ye'll come."

Lilia plucked the tickets out of Vivienne's hands, leaned back in the plush office chair, and slowly swiveled back and forth. "The Highland LARPers, huh?"

"Aye." Vivienne patted her hands on the table in rapid-fire drumming. "We'll have a grand evening of swords, archery, and horsemanship and then we'll be off to the pub to toast our warmongering genius at strategizing the perfect coup for the upcoming battle this fall!"

"Have you told Alberti?"

"Has she told Alberti what?" Alberti, tall, slender, and attired in his usual state of impeccable fashion perfection, leaned through the partially opened office door. "What debacle has Vivienne embroiled us in this time?"

"Piss off, Berti." Vivienne affectionately extended her middle finger with a casual flip of her hand. Only Vivienne could turn a rude hand gesture into a sign of endearment.

Alberti rolled his eyes, ignoring Vivienne with a sleek dark brow arched directly at Lilia. "Have you forgotten we have a meeting with the zoning commission today and—as heaven is my witness—please tell me that is not how you intend to wear your hair?"

Lilia fingered the heavy blonde braid hanging down the right side of her neck. The tethered tip of the long ponytail nearly brushed her lap. "What's wrong with a braid? I just re-blonded everything so I'm trying not to stress it out by taking the flat iron to it."

"Re-blonded? Seriously . . . " Alberti smoothed a hand across his perfectly styled black hair with just enough graying at the temples to sex him up a notch. "Be that as it may, at least coil it into a neat chignon. Much more professional than a braid and a great deal less . . . " Alberti waved a hand in the air, struggling to find the words. "A great deal less Viking opera or queen of the Valkyries."

"Show him the tickets so he'll get off my ass about my hair." Lilia slid the tickets across the table toward Vivienne. She stiffly rose from the chair, stretching her arms high in the air and twisting from side to side. Damn, she had sat hunched over that computer too long.

"This'll throw ye in a tizzy, Berti." Vivienne skipped across the room in her spike heels, waving the tickets in the air. "Ye'll have to leave work a bit early this afternoon to make sure they've sauced up our costumes good and proper. We canna go to a show like this in dreary old street clothes. After all—'tis the start of Fringe, ye ken?"

She popped the tickets into his hands, then hugged herself around his arm, excitedly bouncing them both with every word. With an innocent smile, she almost purred as she batted her false eyelashes up at him. "And this time could ye make certain my outfit is a bit less whorish?"

Alberti's gaze slid from the tickets to Vivienne, his expression shifting from *interested* to *skeptical* with a twitch of a brow. "A bit less whorish?"

"Aye." Vivienne bobbed her head.

"Have ye looked in the mirror today, dearie?" He wrinkled his nose, quietly emitting a disapproving *hmph* as he took in Vivienne's leopard print spike heels then swept up her black leather leggings to her extremely low-cut silky-white tunic. He leaned a bit closer, lowering his voice. "And ye have camel toe, lovie—I mean really, Vivienne."

"Ass!" Vivienne smacked Alberti on the shoulder, then toddled away, all the while yanking her leggings away from her crotch.

Lilia snorted out loud, nearly blowing the last sip of coffee out her nose. Life would be so unbearable without these two. Rubbing her stiff neck with one hand, she moved out from behind the long glass table. "Play nice, you two, or I'm going to sit you in the corner and make you touch noses until you get along."

She couldn't believe she had just said that. Lilia's heart hitched a double-thump then plummeted nearly to her stomach. Granny had always used that threat when the four sisters got into a spat over something infinitely stupid.

Damn, she missed them. Visiting through the fire portal kept them all in touch but it was nothing like really being there and it had been so very long since she'd had the time to jump back for a proper family get-together.

"Now now, lovie. I ken that look. Shake them away. Dinna let those dark demons take hold." Vivienne hugged her around the shoulders and pulled her close. "Berti and I still think ye should take a wee bit of time off. We'll take care of the shops. Why don't ye jump back and visit yer family for a spell? 'Twould do ye a world of good."

"I can't." Lilia blinked hard, forcing the tears back where they belonged. "I can't leave Eliza. I just don't think she has that much time left." Dear, sweet Eliza, the woman Granny had sent to watch over them when she'd decided to stay with Trulie in the past.

Eccentric, bawdy, and a force of nature, Eliza had quickly taken up residence in the Sinclair girls' hearts. But now Eliza was dying. At ninety years old, she had opted out of the recommended therapy to try and rid her lungs of the cancer. She'd said there were a great many things on this earth worse than dying, and having your loved ones watch you with pity in their eyes was one of them. She'd opted to slip away with as much dignity as she could without going through the tortuous regimen of chemotherapy and radiation and the resulting side effects.

Lilia had begged and pleaded with Granny, Trulie, and Mairi to come to the twenty-first century long enough to rid Eliza of the damn cancer with the healing touch the Fates had given them. But they had all three sadly declined and Lilia knew why. She had received the vision too. Eliza had reached the end of this life's path. It was time for her to move on.

Vivienne hugged her again then sadly turned away. "We'll be here for ye, pet. We'll not let ye face this alone. Will we, Berti?"

"Absolutely not." Alberti strode across the room, took hold of her shoulders, and steered her toward the door of the private washroom at the back of her office. "Now come. Let's see if we can do something about that hair before our meeting. We can't have the zoning committee thinking they're dealing with Rapunzel, now, can we?"

"LORE, I love Fringe. It fills the city with such energy." Vivienne swept her way into a street dancer's arms, whirling and dancing across the cobbled street with him, her dark cape swirling out behind her.

"She's going to break her neck in those boots." Lilia looped her arm through Alberti's as they hurried across the crowded avenue. All traffic was blocked from this part of the city. Edinburgh Festival Fringe was twenty-five days devoted to the arts. The world's largest art festival. Held every August. Fringe welcomed the world to Scotland and Edinburgh gladly dedicated its streets and venues to it.

Alberti straightened his own cape at the throat and nodded. "Perhaps I should've had the cobbler go with three-inch heels rather than four. Her swordplay was a bit off this evening. The heels quite possibly threw her balance."

The Highland LARPers had graciously invited Alberti, Vivienne, and Lilia into the ring to join their show—after all, Lilia currently held the title of Grand Champion when it came to medieval swordsmanship. Lilia smiled. The evening had been freaking phenomenal.

She squeezed Alberti's arm and watched Vivienne completely mesmerize the street dancer with her moves. "You definitely got the leather corset just right. Shamus didn't stand a chance against Vivienne's boobs. She disarmed him in the first round. I don't think he knew what hit him."

Lilia smoothed a hand down her own tight-fitting leather armor. Thank goodness Alberti had designed her costume a bit more on the conservative side and along the lines of a female Viking warrior. Lilia snorted as she flipped her long braid back over her shoulder. He'd said her long blonde hair had inspired him.

"One must always accentuate the subject's best traits." Alberti grinned, his chest puffing out a bit farther in his own black leather suit fashioned after the armor he'd seen the character Loki wearing in an action-adventure movie. Tall and lean, Alberti was well-muscled but he was no broad-shouldered Viking god.

Lilia nudged Alberti with her hip as they meandered down the sidewalk. "Your outfit definitely caught Randolph's eye and I saw you checking him out too. You better be careful. You know how jealous Thomas can be."

"Thomas knows I am true to him." Alberti waved Vivienne over. She'd discarded her street dancer and was standing on tiptoe, moving in a slow circle searching for them. He pulled Lilia out of the path of several exuberant drunks and held open the door to the pub. "He also knows I will never stop admiring other men until the day I die. My heart may be bound to him but I have not been struck blind."

"Is this the best or what?" Vivienne jostled her way over to them and they squeezed into the crowded pub.

Lilia nodded. She pulled Vivienne forward, sandwiching her between herself and Alberti as they climbed the dark narrow steps up to their usual gallery table overlooking the main room of the pub.

Frank, the owner of the pub, was totally besotted with Vivienne's plentiful curves and would do anything to catch her heart. Vivienne exploited this infatuation to the fullest but Lilia couldn't really condemn her for it. She had also overheard Vivienne explaining quite clearly to Frank that she would never be his, especially since he had just married his fourth wife. Vivienne might toy with poor Frank to benefit herself but at least she was honest about it.

Lilia slid into the chair in the corner, propping her thigh-high boot on the lowest rung of the railing hemming in the gallery. This was a good spot. It was dark so she didn't have to overly socialize and her back was against the wall.

"I'll go down and get the drinks. As busy as they are tonight, Rabbie will never make it up here." Alberti unbuttoned the cape at his throat and draped it across his chair. He pointed at Vivienne. "Vodka?"

"Aye." Vivienne bobbed her head, bouncing in her seat in time with the thumping beat of the music blaring up from downstairs.

"Lilia?" Alberti turned to her.

"Sparkling water with lemon."

"Lilia," Alberti said in the chiding tone of a mother scolding a child.

"I don't need alcohol tonight." She cleared her throat and sat straighter in the chair. "It's been a rough week with Eliza and the alcohol makes me weaker against the darkness—and there's a lot of darkness vibrating through this many people."

Alberti's mouth tightened and he agreed with a quick nod. "Very well then. I'll be right back."

She hated being the downer. Lilia swallowed hard and sucked in a deep breath. "I'm sorry," she directed at Vivienne.

Vivienne draped an arm across her shoulders and squeezed. "Dinna fret, lovie. Ye ken we love ye no matter what. We'll all get ye through this. Just ye wait and see."

Lilia pinched the bridge of her nose and squeezed her eyes tightly shut. "Don't make me cry. Come on, Viv. Tell me something that will make me laugh."

"I dinna ken if it will make ye laugh but ye have to get a look at this pair what just walked in." Vivienne pulled Lilia closer to the railing and pointed down toward the door. "Now *those* are some authentic Highland warrior costumes. Wait 'til Alberti sees them. He'll be ogling the big one for sure." Vivienne propped her chin on her hand that rested on the railing. "Alberti can have the big one. I believe I'd rather have a ride on the short, stocky lad.

He walks as though he's got quite the prize hanging under that kilt."

Lilia snorted out a laugh. Thank goodness for Vivienne and her ability to chase away the blues. She scooted her chair closer to the railing and searched the room below. There they were. A strange sense of *déjà vu* tingled across her. She knew those colors. Had seen them many times while talking to Granny and her sisters through the fire portal. That pattern decorated the walls of MacKenna Keep. Those men wore the MacKenna Clan tartan.

Both men slowly worked their way across the room to the crowded bar. Vivienne was right. The short stocky guy walked with an unusual swaying gait. His *don't make me kick yer ass* attitude triggered a smile. The man reminded Lilia of a barrel-chested bulldog marching guard around his favorite bone.

But it was the other man who piqued her interest even more. A full head and shoulders taller than most in the room, he held himself as though ready for an attack at any moment. "He must be a body-builder or a bouncer or something. Check out the man bun holding back his hair and damn . . . get a load of those arms." Lilia leaned forward to keep him pinpointed in the crowd while he made his way through the pub. "Call me crazy but there is just something sexy about a long-haired man with a close-cropped beard."

"I wonder how old he is?" Vivienne scooted closer. "His hair's as dark as the devil's thoughts but his beard's got some silver peeking through it." Then she made a sound that could only be described as a predatory purr. "But that body of his is nothing but top-shelf prime. A most decidedly delicious hunk of well-aged beef, if I do say so myself."

Alberti reappeared with the tray of drinks and slid them onto the table. "Here we are, ladies. And what are we gawking at?"

"The short one's mine." Vivienne pointed over the railing at the pair of men below.

Alberti stretched, gazed down into the room, then thoughtfully pursed his lips. "Hmm . . . a bit wooly around the edges, wouldn't you say? But my goodness, they do look authentic." He moved closer to the railing, sipping his drink as he peered closer at the men. "And look at their weaponry. We must go down and speak with them. I must know their supplier."

A shout rose up from the crowd below, followed by a loud banging on the bar.

"Oh shit. Frank's gone and got out his bat." Vivienne stood and bent over the railing, scowling down at the crowd below. "And it's our two lucky pennies. If we're to find out where they bought their gear, we best get down there and save them from Frank."

A cold sweat peppered across Lilia. Heart hammering and struggling to breathe, she slumped back in the chair and closed her eyes. No. Not now. She didn't need a vision now. Unfortunately, the Fates didn't listen.

A dull roaring resembling the hollow growl of a gale-force wind, drowned out all other sound, spinning her into a smoke-filled darkness. Metal on metal clashed through the din. Pain—a hard impact against the center of her back—knocked the wind from her lungs. Strong hands gripped her arms, pulling her to her feet. *"Daren't ye die! I love ye, Lilia. I swear to the gods I love ye and will never let ye go."* A hard-muscled chest pressed against her cheek. A shaking, hesitant touch brushed along her jawline then gently stroked her hair. *"I beg ye. Ye must not die. I canna live without ye."*

She struggled to see through the darkness. Why the hell wouldn't the vision show the face belonging to that voice—the deepest, richest baritone . . . no, not a baritone but a bass—a voice smoother and sultrier than any she had ever heard.

She pushed away from the chest, reaching up to touch the face she couldn't see. But then he was gone and she was falling, spiraling down into the bottomless darkness.

"Lilia!" Vivienne shook her hard, her pert little nose nearly touching hers. "Lilia, talk to me this verra instant or I'm having Frank ring for the ambulance."

Lilia pushed herself up in the chair, blinking away the last of the vision. "I'm fine. Fine . . . I just had a dizzy spell. That's all." Alberti and Vivienne were well aware of her time-runner ancestry and the empathic and aura-reading abilities that came to her as part of the package. But she had never told them about the visions. She never spoke to anyone about the curse of those damn visions.

"Come on. We must go. Alberti's using his gift of diplomacy to cool Frank's temper but we best go and help. This situation could verra well require the use of cleavage." Vivienne pulled Lilia to her feet, then stood with both hands extended as though ready to catch her if she teetered off balance. "Are we good then, lovie?"

Lilia took in a deep breath and nodded. No. She was not good but she could sure as hell fake it. "All good. Let's go." She waved Vivienne toward the narrow stairs.

They scurried down the steps, worming their way through the throng of bodies milling around the room. Lilia pushed her way ahead of Vivienne, homing in on Alberti's distinct droning on and on about the proper handling of customers and the utmost care one must always take to preserve one's image. If sorely pressed, Alberti was quite capable of physically defending himself. After all, he was a licensed trainer and a self-defense instructor in his off hours from their beauty company. But Alberti also loved being the center of attention and hearing himself talk. If given the choice, he much preferred besting his opponents with endless prattling and the slow excruciating death of boredom.

"The sons a bitches expected to pay wif false money. Look at those coins. Happens every year. The damned lot of ye what dress up and do yer little playacting during Fringe think ye can dupe ole Frank wif yer fake money." Frank bounced the bat atop the scarred railing of the bar with a loud threatening thump. "I ain't a having it, I tell ye. I ain't a being made the fool."

"Our coin is not false!" The short, stalky MacKenna Highlander bumped his chest forward, his meaty hands fisted and raised for the fight.

Vivienne slid her way in between Frank, Alberti, and the enraged object of her interest with a smile and a pat against the short man's puffed-out chest. "Leave this to me, sweets." She spun on her four-inch heels, bent forward slightly, and aimed the loosened ties of her gaping leather corset at Frank while holding out her hand. "Gimme the bat, dearie. We mustn't have folks thinking we're not excited to have them visit us during Fringe."

Lilia worked her way around to the side of the other man, the brawny tall specimen she had admired from the gallery. He seemed much calmer than the shorter fellow. In fact, gauging by the feelings he was projecting, he was amused by the entire situation. She leaned in close and raised her voice to be heard above the music, the crowd, and Frank. "I think we should ease our way outside. Vivienne knows how to handle Frank. Once he gets stirred up no one can deal with him but her. Come on. There's another pub around the corner. My friends and I would love to find out more about your weapons. How about if we buy you and your friend a round of drinks?"

Deep, gray eyes darker than a stormy sky and oddly flecked with bits of fiery gold, turned to her. One burly brow notched a bit higher, directly parallel with the lifted corner of his lopsided mustached smile. The man backed up a step, allowing his gaze to sweep from the scuffed toes of her thigh-high boots, up her curve-accentuating leather armor to the top of her braided hair. "Looking for weapons are ye? Why? Are ye in some sort of danger, lass?"

A shiver of recognition rippled through her. *That voice.* It was the voice from her vision. Lilia fluttered a hand to her throat and swallowed hard. "Uhm . . ." She struggled to kick her brain into gear and say something other than *uhm*. How the hell could she hold an intelligent conversation with the owner of the voice who had only moments ago sworn he loved her and couldn't live without her?

The man leaned in closer, his dark eyes crinkling at the corners and amusement filling his face. "Aye?" he prompted.

"Come out from behind there, ye bastard. I'll shove that wee stick of yers straight up yer arse until ye choke on it." The shorter Highlander bounced forward, doing his damnedest to push through Vivienne and Alberti's locked arms.

"If ye would be excusing me for just a wee moment, lass." The owner of the mesmerizing voice from her vision politely bowed then turned around and grabbed the shorter man by the scruff of the neck. "Come, Angus. We will take our money elsewhere."

"Nay. That bastard insulted me. Called me a thief. I'll be damned if I leave without showing him what for." Angus locked both hands atop the bar railing and hooked the heels of his boots into the foot rungs close to the floor. "I'll not leave without a fight, Graham. I'll not do it, I tell ye."

"Aye." Graham grunted and yanked Angus free of the bar. "Ye will do it and ye'll be a doing it now." He grappled Angus closer, muttered something against the side of his head, then shoved him toward the door.

Angus staggered sideways, all the while looking back. Lilia glanced first at Angus then turned and followed his line of sight. What had Mr. Honey-Voice told him? She looked back at Angus once more then turned back again and it all became clear. Angus's attention was focused on Vivienne. Or rather her currently upended leather-covered derriere as she bent over the bar, wrestling the bat away from Frank.

Lilia hurried forward, waving for Graham to follow. A quick glance back assured her that Vivienne and Alberti were now following close behind Graham. Vivienne was grinning from ear to ear as she waved Frank's bat overhead and dance-walked to the song blaring from the speakers. Lilia shook her head and chuckled as she pushed her way out the door into the cool night air. Leave it to Vivienne to transform a barroom brawl into a dancing conga line.

Angus was stomping up and down the sidewalk, pausing every now and then to shake his fist toward the pub, then grab his crotch and shake his kilt-covered parts in a very clear message to Frank and his place of business. He whirled around, bent over, and was just about to bare his ass when Graham caught up with him and thumped him on the back. Angus straightened with an angry jerk; his narrow-eyed glare fixed on Graham.

Lilia patted Angus on the shoulder. "Ignore Frank. Fringe always gets his panties in a wad."

Both of Angus's dark wooly brows arched clear to his tousled hairline. "Panties?"

Before Lilia could respond, Graham stepped forward with a polite bow and an extended hand. "Forgive us, mistress. We are not usually so uncivilized. I am Graham MacTavish and 'tis an honor to meet ye." He motioned toward the glowering man just behind him. "And this be Angus MacKenna."

"Did you say MacTavish?" Lilia paused mid-reach of taking Graham's hand. This was the first time since she had moved to Edinburgh that she'd run across any MacTavishes other than Eliza. Perhaps Graham was a yet-to-be-discovered relation.

Graham kept his hand extended and bowed again. "Aye. MacTavish. Do ye ken the name?"

She slid her hand into his calloused palm. Bits and pieces of smoldering erotic scenes flashed through her mind and pulsing energy surged into her, heating her to her core. She quickly jerked back and curled her fist to her chest. "Sorry. Guess I built up some static electricity inside the pub." Static electricity, her ass. That warm tingling jolt packed enough psychic sexuality and cosmic energy to blow her socks off and trigger the orgasm of the century. What the devil was that about?

Graham's eyes flared wide. With a stiff jerk, he stared down at his hand, then rubbed his thumb back and forth across his fingertips. "Stat . . . What did ye say?" He took another step forward and held out his hand again.

"Static electricity," Lilia repeated. Dare she touch him again? Surely the blood-warming zap had just been a fluke. Probably because she'd just had one of her visions. Some kind of weird residual stuff. That was it. Her energy was stuck on wide open and her amps were humming into overdrive. She just needed to calm down.

She pulled in a deep cleansing breath, rubbed her thumb across her fingers, then firmly clasped Graham's hand. The seductive energy surged into her again, warming, melding, and sensually buzzing through every particle of her being. She knew this man and recognized him at the most basic level of her existence. But how in the world could that be possible? She had never met him before.

"I ken who ye be," he said in a hushed tone. "Lilia Sinclair." He ran his thumb across the top of her hand then reverently lifted it to his lips.

She pulled her hand away and pressed it back to the tightly laced bodice of her leather corset. "You can't know me. We've never met." She eased a step back, the back of her hand still burning from the addictive touch of his mouth. "I'm sure I'd remember it if we had ever crossed paths."

Graham closed the distance she had just put between them, his brow furrowing as he bent closer and studied her. "Aye. I shouldha seen it straightaway. Ye have the look of yer grandmother around yer eyes."

Vivienne bounced over to Angus, Frank's bat propped on her shoulder as though she were next up to the plate. "I'm Vivienne Sands and I must know where you got that exquisite shield. I absolutely adore the pattern."

Angus's mouth sagged open but no words came out. The man was powerless against Vivienne's overflowing leather corset bobbing mere inches from his nose. He pulled the shield out from under his arm and handed it over. "Here. Ye can have it."

She snuggled even closer to him, stroking her fingers across the perfectly round shield decorated with row upon row of brass brads. "So lovely."

Eyes still locked on Vivienne's bountiful chest, Angus emitted a strained squeaking noise and nodded. "Aye," he finally whispered. "That it is."

Forcing her gaze away from poor Angus, Lilia struggled to breathe against the suffocating conviction that she had just walked into a trap. Graham and Angus were from the past: hence the authenticity of their attire and the confusion in the bar. "Why are you two here? Who sent you?"

"Lilia!" Alberti sauntered up to the group, his cloak neatly folded over his arm. "It's Fringe, love. You know they're here for the festivities." He held out his hand to Graham. "Alberti Peebles. It's a pleasure to meet another true artist who insists on historically accurate weapons."

"The weapons are accurate because they *are* historical." Lilia squared off in front of Graham and lifted her chin, doing her best to ignore the thudding pound of her heart against her heavy leather armor. Never had anyone affected her so . . . so . . . deeply and she didn't care for it at all. "Did Granny send you . . . or was it Trulie?"

"Both." A dark scowl replaced Graham's amiable expression of only moments ago. "Chieftain MacKenna, the Lady Trulie, and Mother Sinclair worry after ye. They feel I can help protect ye." He clapped a hand on Angus's shoulder and pulled him away from Vivienne's bustline. "Angus was sent along with me because he too appeared in yer grandmother's vision."

Alberti and Vivienne shared a worried glance then moved to stand on either side of Lilia. Her knotted hands trembled and the pounding of her heartbeat thumped in her sweat-dampened palms. She didn't need this right now. She was already in emotional overload dealing with the impending loss of Eliza. Vaguely, she felt Vivienne squeeze her shoulders. "Come on, pet. I'll take ye home. Ye are far gone weary. Alberti can see to the men and find them a place to stay. We dinna have to deal with this tonight."

Graham held up a hand, stepping closer and blocking the path Vivienne had turned Lilia toward. "Stay." His dark eyes narrowed and his extended hand slowly curled closed then dropped to his side. "I beg ye stay and speak with me for just a wee bit. I mean ye no harm— I swear it." Then he straightened, chin lifted and chest expanding as though shielding himself from what he knew would be her refusal. "Surely ye ken yer family would not send a danger to ye."

That was a fair point. Lilia eased out from under Vivienne's protective hug, giving Graham a quick aural scan before shoring back up the shields that kept the world's emotions from driving her insane.

What lovely colors he emitted and such a unique aura. Swirls of passionate reds vibrated into spiritual purples then flickered out into rich loyal blues. Even though his aura was laced with strange, inexplicable sparks of what appeared to be golden shooting flames, Graham was safe, emanating the strongest and highest traits of each color spectrum she had come to know and respect. And Granny and Trulie had sent him. She could at least hear what he had to say.

She gave Vivienne their long-ago agreed-upon signal that everything was okay for the time being: the stand-down wink and nod. "Why don't you and Alberti take Angus across the way for drinks while Mr. MacTavish and I have a chat?"

"Are ye certain, pet?" Vivienne fixed Graham with the look that Lilia had affectionately labeled *the stink-eye curse of Vivienne.*

"Hmpf." Graham jutted out his chin and returned Vivienne's warning scowl with a dark look of his own.

"I'm sure," Lilia said, pointing across the brick street to a lantern-lit grouping of tables. "Head on over to Lottie's Close and save us a table. We'll be there in a bit."

Angus's countenance visibly brightened. He wet his lips and agreed with a quick bob of his head. "Aye. I could use a pint or three." He hooked his thumbs into his belt and rolled to the balls of his feet in a quick bounce. "Take yer time," he said to Graham.

"Very well then," Alberti said. Ever the leader, he deftly herded Vivienne and Angus toward the outdoor bar. With a backward glance at Lilia, he raised his voice to be heard over the boisterous crowd enjoying the mild summer evening. "I will have my phone on the table. You know what to do if need be."

Lilia reached down into her cleavage, pulled her phone out, and waved it at Alberti. "Gotcha." Alberti would rally every able-bodied officer in Scotland and not a few friends to save her if she speed-dialed him for help.

Returning her phone to her nature-made cleavage-holster, Lilia turned back to Graham's wide-eyed stare. The poor man looked as though his eyes were about to explode out of his head. She patted her chest. "I don't have pockets in this outfit. It's the only place I can carry it."

"Aye," he reverently whispered as his gaze dipped back down to the designated spot between her corset-plumped breasts.

"Let's walk while you tell me what this visit of yours is about." Lilia motioned for Graham to follow her out into the street. The sidewalks were too crowded to allow any semblance of a conversation. The cordoned-off brick stretch of the Royal Mile leading to Edinburgh Castle would serve much better. It was still crowded but not as impassable as the walkways in front of the shops and pubs.

He extended his bent arm for her to take, frowning when she refused with a shake of her head. "Why don't you start by telling me about Granny's vision," she said. The man could play the ancient gallant all he wanted—they were staying on topic.

With a sound that could only be described as a cross between a guttural *harrumph* and an irritated growl, Graham fell into step beside her, visibly paring down his strong, long-legged stride to keep her from having to break into a hopping lope to keep pace with him. "I wasna privy to the details of yer grandmother's vision. I dinna ken what the woman saw other than the fact that I was needed here—by you."

"By me?" Lilia repeated, her irritation prickling when Graham's only response was a curt nod. "So, what are you? A miracle worker or a healer?" She flinched at the bitterness in her tone. She hated being the shrew with an innocent bystander but the only thing she needed right now was someone who could help Eliza.

"Nay. I am neither," he said, his voice rumbling patient and deep as he walked along beside her, seemingly nonplussed by her tone. "But I do ken the way of things and what must be done to survive. I can help ye battle the darkness that oft attempts to overtake the light."

Something in his eyes as he spoke touched a deep part of her soul. She forced herself to look away, break his hold. But then she just as quickly looked back and locked into his gaze. She couldn't help herself. There was so much . . . so much what? She didn't know what she saw in his eyes but she needed it—badly.

"I ken verra well just how cold and wicked the darkness can be," he gently assured. "Ye need but trust me, lass."

Darkness. Funny he should say it that way. Lilia struggled to keep from warming to Graham but her deepest instincts refused to listen to common sense, mocking her with the futility of building any semblance of separation or dislike for the man. The unseen vibrations emanating from him reassured her he was genuine—he cared and she might as well stop trying to harden her heart against him. She shook herself free of the annoying inner voice. She didn't care if the man had a heart of gold. She had to keep him at a distance—a safe distance—at least until she figured out why Granny sent him.

"So, you came here to take me back as soon as Eliza dies?" That had to be his angle. Lilia stopped walking, turned to him, and forced herself to lower her shields. She needed the raw truth of it all and the only way she could trust a single word this man said was to take a chance and set her sensors on wide open to read his feelings.

He stopped walking and faced her, widening his stance as he clasped his hands behind his back. "I didna come here to return ye to the past. I came here to stay wi' ye—to learn yer ways and do my best to help ye and protect ye."

He was telling the truth—at least most of the truth. She didn't miss the thin wavering of uncertainty vibrating at the deepest level of his aura. "What are you not telling me?" She could plainly tell he wasn't lying but he wasn't telling her everything he knew about what she'd asked either. "Graham?"

He didn't say a word, just resettled his footing, lifted his stubborn chin a notch higher, and smiled.

Fine. So, that was how he was going to play it. An *I ain't telling and you can't make me* attitude was the quickest way to piss her off. She spun around and started back down the street to the outdoor pub where Alberti and Vivienne waited. No more games and dancing around the details with a heart-stirring man she had just met—a man she was inexplicably drawn to and suddenly missed now that he wasn't walking beside her.

"Ye canna run from me, lass," Graham called out above the noise of the crowd.

She huffed out an irritated growl but didn't bother looking back. He had it all wrong. She never ran. Granny obviously hadn't warned him who he would be dealing with. She didn't give a rat's ass if it was August. She was heading back to the house to crank up the wood-stove and Granny was going to give her some answers. Granny had meddled and manipulated Trulie, Kenna, and Mairi into returning to the thirteenth century to find their Highland husbands. She had too much going on right now to be next up on Granny's playlist.

CHAPTER 5

"I am not leaving ye alone. I know ye are ... different." Vivienne shrugged as she plopped down on the overstuffed settee in front of the floor-to-ceiling bookcase. "I don't care that ye are odd as an American two-dollar bill. Weird shit doesna frighten me; ye should ken that well enough by now. Ye are my friend, pet. I worry after ye." She plumped a pillow behind her back and crossed her ankles on the arm of the chair.

Lilia shoved crumpled paper up under the crisscrossed sticks then took a long-stemmed match, struck it, and dotted the flame along the edges of the wad. The yellow flame took hold, melting into the thin sheets and dancing up into the bits of wood. She pulled out the silver knob, opening the damper as wide as it would go until the delicate yellow flames became a roaring white blaze. "I think the world of you, Viv, but I don't want to run you off when you realize I am not batty—all the *weird shit* I've told you about is real."

And she didn't want to lose Vivienne's friendship. If not for her and Alberti, she'd either be locked up in a psych ward by now or pushing up daisies in the local cemetery. She ran a thumb along the white scars on her wrist. They'd found her that night after she'd finally signed the papers to prosecute her lowlife business partner

David Sommers for embezzling and identity fraud. That son of a bitch. She had trusted him, called him friend, and the bastard had nearly ruined her.

Her *true* friends, Alberti and Vivienne, had found her crouched in front of the television, drunk as hell, covered in blood and sobbing her heart out at the evening news and all the pain her battered emotional shields had allowed to attack her soul.

Neither Alberti nor Vivienne had ever mentioned that night again. That night when she had finally given up—and they'd saved her and stayed beside her through everything. Dammit, she didn't deserve friends like them. She was a freaking time runner, for heaven's sake. An ancient bloodline blessed by the Fates. She should be able to handle everything alone.

"So, what is this fire portal thingy like? It sounds a bit like some sort of cyber-meeting webcam-type deal. Is that what it is, lovie?" Vivienne stretched forward, unzipped her boots, then kicked them off onto the floor.

"That pretty much describes it. As soon as I get a good bed of coals built up, you'll see." Lilia added more tinder to the base of the fire, shoving in more slivers of wood to keep the blaze roaring until the bigger chunks caught. Maybe it would be easier to confront Granny and Trulie with Vivienne at her side.

"Sounds nifty. I'm going to pop into the kitchen and fix us a spot of tea." Vivienne paused at the door to the parlor. "Or do ye want something a bit stronger? Espresso laced with a splash of booze?"

Lilia chewed on her bottom lip, halfway tempted to build up her courage with some highly caffeinated alcohol. She finally shook her head. "No thanks. Conversations with my grandmother are best handled stone-cold sober."

The fire popped and hissed. The heated air roared up the flue until the cherry-red cast iron stove almost glowed. Lilia pushed open every window in the sitting room. A warm August night was not the best time for a fire portal call.

As Vivienne entered the room bearing a tray with cups, biscuits, and tea, Lilia took the cast iron shovel and scooped away a small pile of ash-coated red coals. Cupping her hand just above them, she gently blew against the chunks of orange and red until they sparked and popped with renewed life.

"Hear me, show me, open and know me." After saying the words, Lilia tossed the spade full of coals back into the fire. The crackling flames disappeared as a wavering dark window slowly opened and blotted out all else within the stove.

"Bloody hell," Vivienne said as she set the tray on the coffee table in front of the settee and knelt down to stare into the woodstove.

"You opened the fire portal to curse at me? Lilia!" Granny's face flickered into view and gradually her sitting room at MacKenna Keep sharpened into focus as well. "I raised you better than that, young lady."

"It wasn't me. It was Vivienne." Lilia leaned to one side and pointed back at Vivienne, now sitting on the settee with her mouth hanging open. "Meet Vivienne Sands. She's the friend I told you about. Remember?"

Granny's face softened with a smile and a nod. "It's my pleasure to finally meet you, Vivienne, and I can't thank you enough for being so good to my granddaughter."

Vivienne blinked as though waking from a dream and weakly waved a hand in the air. "She's my friend. Think nothing of it."

"I met some friends of yours today, Granny." Lilia leaned a bit closer to the portal. "Graham and Angus. Do those names ring a bell?"

"Sarcasm is a very unattractive trait, child, and snarkiness is just plain ugly." Granny appeared to sit taller in her chair as Trulie came into view just behind her.

"We sent them to check on you, sis. We know Eliza doesn't have much longer." Trulie settled down beside Granny, concern and compassion shining in her eyes. "We're worried about you."

"I'm fine." Lilia battled to swallow the aching knot of sorrow lodged crossways in her throat. She took a deep breath, blinking hard and fast against the threat of tears. They had no idea how badly she was hurting and if she had her way about it, they would never find out. Emotional pain was her burden to carry—her legacy. She had to protect her family from the emotional mess she was inside. She cleared her throat. "So, who are these two you sent to check on me?"

Granny's face brightened as Chloe bounced into view. She pulled the five-year-old child up into her lap and pointed at Lilia. "Say hello and tell Auntie Lil thank you for the newest picture book she sent to you through the portal."

Chloe bounced and waved until her dark ringlets quivered like silky springs. "I thank ye, Auntie Lil. When will ye come to see me again? I want ye to see my new horse and watch how Oren helps me ride it."

"I'm not sure, sweetie. Perhaps very soon." Lilia narrowed her eyes at Trulie, who refused to meet her gaze.

Trulie helped Chloe down from Granny's lap and led her to one side. "Wave goodbye to Auntie Lil. It's time for our nightly walk in the gardens with Oren before you go to bed. Granny and Auntie have a lot to talk about."

Chloe waved as she bounced out of the room. "Bye, Auntie Lil! Loves ye bunches and bunches!"

"Bye, sweetie pie! Auntie loves you too!" Lilia waved, then tensed on the edge of her chair. "All right, Granny. Out with it. Who are Graham and Angus and why did you send them?"

Granny wrinkled her nose, then resettled her wire-rimmed glasses a bit higher. "What did they tell you?"

"What difference does that make?" Lilia wasn't stupid. Granny was stalling and trying to calculate her next move. Lilia leaned in close again. "Care to clue me in on this vision you supposedly had?"

Granny's chin lifted the barest bit as she leaned back in her chair and folded her arms across her chest. "I'm worried around you. Eliza will be gone soon and you will be all alone." Granny pulled a white square of linen from her sleeve and pressed it against the corners of her eyes. "And I feel in my heart . . . " Granny paused, wet her lips, then took a deep breath. "I feel certain you are meant to stay in the future. I don't believe your destiny lies in this century with us. But I worry about you being there alone. You're different, Lilia. You have always been . . . special. The world hurts you to your core but you won't allow anyone close enough to help you bear the burden."

"She's got you nailed, lovie."

Lilia jerked around and mouthed *Shut-up* at Vivienne.

Vivienne stuck out her tongue and shook her head.

Granny chortled and snorted. "Oh, I like you, Vivienne. I'm so glad you're Lilia's friend."

Vivienne sat up straighter on the settee. A wicked grin lit up her face. "Why, thank ye, Mother Sinclair. Lilia is the sister I never had."

"You're avoiding the subject. Why did you send Graham and Angus?" Lilia leaned forward and blew on the coals. The connection through the portal was wavering. She needed to hurry and nail Granny down.

"To watch over you, gal. Just to watch over you." Granny leaned closer to her side of the portal, so close that Lilia swore if she reached out she could touch the wrinkled silk of Granny's cheek. "I swear to you, Lilia. I didn't send them to bring you back or trick you into anything. Those two brutes are just a pair of plaid-wearing guardian angels sent to watch over you." Granny's smile wavered as she blew Lilia a kiss. "Let go of your pain, Lilia. You are not meant to walk this world alone and bear the weight of your gifts by yourself. Channel your empathy, my sweet child. Remember your lessons."

The portal darkened and Granny's face faded from view. "I love you, gal. Never forget that. You are much loved by us all."

CHAPTER 6

Graham shoved aside the flimsy material hanging over the window and stared up into the ever-lightening night sky. Just as he thought. Dawn soon. Time to be about the day —especially since his days here could very well be short and numbered if he didn't win Mistress Lilia's heart and convince her to marry him.

He rubbed his thumb across his fingertips, remembering the eerie tingle when she had slid her tiny hand into his. Saint's bones, he'd hardened as soon as they touched and been filled with the urge to grab her up into his arms and never let her go. *Mine,* his heart had cried out. *Mine, forevermore.*

Scrubbing his fingertips through the beard curling along his jaw, Graham turned from the window. He had never felt such before. It was quite unsettling and he was not so sure he liked it. An arranged marriage to keep his head from the pike and atone for his sins was one thing. But love? He shuddered the thought away, stomped across the room, and kicked Angus's booted foot. "Up wi' ye now. 'Twill be dawn soon."

Angus barely twitched from his sprawled position across a pile of pillows scattered across the floor. Without opening his eyes, he unconsciously scratched his belly, then his hand slowly slid back down to his side as a high-pitched snore whined free of his slack-jawed mouth.

"Angus!" Graham kicked the bottom of the man's boot again, hard enough to jolt his entire body.

Angus rolled to a crouched position, unsheathed both daggers, and flashed them back and forth. He jerked around, glancing around the room. "Who attacks?"

Graham blew out a weary sigh. Why the hell Mother Sinclair had saddled him with this great numpty was beyond reasoning. "No one attacks." He headed toward the closed double doors at the end of the room, waving for Angus to follow. "It will be dawn soon. We must be about the day."

Angus straightened from battle readiness, returned the daggers to their sheaths, then stretched with a bone-cracking yawn. He glanced around the room, absentmindedly scratching his arse as he waded free of his pillowed nest. "Reckon they have any food in the house? I've not eaten since we left the keep."

"I dinna ken." Graham pulled open one of the double doors and looked up and down the hallway. "I'm not even certain where the kitchens might be in this place."

Angus lifted his nose and sniffed. "I dinna smell any food." He pushed past Graham and stepped out into the hall, looking both ways as he rubbed at his crotch. "Where did he say the garderobe was? I need to piss."

Graham meandered down the hallway, scowling at the row of pris-tine white doors all firmly closed. "We came in there." He pointed at a set of burgundy double doors with ornate ovals of what looked like plates of colored jewels centered in each panel. The wood floors of the hallway gleamed beneath the yellow light of the strange orbs that looked as though someone had sliced a cannonball in two and magically stuck it on the wall then magically lit it from within. "Alberti and the man called Thomas went up there last night." Graham nodded toward the staircase with the rich mahogany railing. "Perhaps the garderobe is up there?"

Angus shook his head and yanked open one of the narrow doors lining the hallway. "Nah. Last night he pointed to one of these doors. I'm certain of it." He shook his head, closed the door, and moved to the next one. "Nothing but clothes in that one." He pulled open the next door then tilted his head to one side and scratched his jaw. "Reckon this is it?"

Graham peered over Angus's shoulder. "Lore a'mighty. That there be the biggest chamber pot I do believe I've ever seen." He shoved past Angus, stepping into the tiny, tiled room. Easing forward, he leaned over the great white porcelain bowl half filled with water. "This must be it but I daresay whoever went here last must not have been verra healthy. Look how clear their piss be."

"What be that silver handle for?" Angus tapped a finger on another white porcelain bowl, this one waist-high and built into a cabinet with silver knobs and spouts to boot.

"I dinna ken." Graham tapped the cool bit of metal behind the oversized chamber pot with one finger. Nothing happened.

"Hit it harder." Angus nodded toward the porcelain bowl on the floor. "It wiggled a wee bit. I think ye need to hit it harder."

"Harder, ye say?" Graham squatted down beside the bowl, studying the silver handle from every angle. He hooked two fingers atop the metal piece and pushed down hard.

The huge chamber pot came to life. Water whooshed and gurgled, swirling in a tempest until it disappeared with a hollow *glug glug glug*. Graham quickly rose and stepped back. "Saint's bones, did ye see that?"

"Aye," Angus replied, his voice filled with awe. "And look. The water returns. It rises as we speak."

Graham leaned over the pot, watching the slowly rising water. "Amazing."

"I am not pissing in that thing." Angus hiked up his kilt, stood on tiptoes, and leaned over the waist-high porcelain bowl built into the cabinet. "I'll piss here—looks to be much safer."

"I dinna blame ye, lad." Graham clapped a hand on Angus's

shoulder. Any magic that sucked away water with such a fury could very well be a danger to a man's cock.

The thumping of footsteps overhead and down the stairway caught Graham's attention. He left Angus to his business, squeezing behind the man to step back out into the hallway. Strange place, this future. It would take him a lifetime to discover all that had changed.

Hair disheveled and still buttoning his shirt, Alberti emerged from the stairwell. "Good morning, Graham. You're up bright and early today." He padded barefoot down the hallway, motioning for Graham to follow. "Come with me, my good man. I'll have a spot of coffee ready in no time. Or do you prefer tea?" Alberti turned, a dark brow arched, waiting for Graham's response.

"Ale, if ye dinna mind." He had no idea what coffee was and the only time a man drank tea was when he was ailing. Graham squared his shoulders and lifted his chin. Surely the man didn't think he looked unwell.

Alberti frowned as he finished buttoning his shirt and yanked it wrinkle free. "Ale? Hmm . . . I'll see what I can find." He disappeared through a strange door that swung back and forth as though toyed with by spirits.

Graham followed. Raising a hesitant hand to the strange door, he clenched his teeth and pushed through it. The door swung back and thumped his arse once he walked through. He glared back at it, waiting for another attack from the wicked spirits. The door calmly settled in place. His fists relaxed at his sides. Aye. Just as well. Alberti had been a kind host. It would be a shame to destroy a part of his home.

Alberti hurried past him, pulled open the swinging door, and thumped down a strange-looking leg at its base that propped it open. "There now. As soon as Angus gets out of the loo, he'll be able to hear us here in the kitchen. I do hope the man is not unwell. I couldn't help but notice the toilet keeps flushing."

The toilet keeps flushing. Recognition dawned. Graham stuck his head back into the hallway and bellowed, "Angus! Leave the wee chamber pot alone and get yer arse out here."

Angus emerged; his face lit with amusement. "That there garderobe is damn fine. The spring running through the chamber pot carries away whatever ye put in it."

"Oh dear heavens. Pray, what did you put in it?" Alberti rushed down the hallway, stopped at the bathroom door, then sagged against the door facing. "Thank heavens. It's not clogged and overflowing."

"I merely spat in it." Angus shrugged, then wiggled a finger round and round. "'Tis like a whirlpool in the ocean. Everything goes round and round till it disappears."

Alberti rolled his eyes as he hurried back into the kitchen. "I'm sure you gentlemen are famished. Come." He hurried the men over to the narrow oval table waiting in the center of the room. "Have a seat and we'll get you fed before I leave for work."

Graham lowered himself into one of the cold uncomfortable chairs, nodding for Angus to do the same. He balanced his forearms on the hard smoothness of the table, frowning down at his reflection. Was there not enough wood in this century? Most of the furniture of this time appeared to be made of metal and this hard, clear substance that the Sinclair women had said was called glass. Mother Sinclair and Lady Trulie had not mentioned a scarcity of trees. He rubbed his hand across the tabletop. Lore a'mighty, they needed this substance back at the keep. 'Twould keep the winter winds from passing through the windows yet still allow the rays of the sun to light the rooms much better than oiled parchment.

Alberti set a tall glass of amber liquid in front of each of the men. "It's not exactly ale but it's the closest thing I've got."

"Thank ye kindly." Graham nodded as he took a hesitant sip. He held the liquid in his mouth, breathing in to appreciate the warmth of the alcoholic fumes. Aye. This would do quite nicely.

A square plate piled high with odd-looking breads followed. "Here you go, gentlemen. Enjoy some of Edinburgh's finest pastries."

Graham selected one of the lightly browned triangles, brought it to his nose, and sniffed. Yeasty. Buttery. Sweet. He took a hesitant bite, nodding as the flaky pastry melted in his mouth. "Verra fine. I thank ye again."

Alberti smiled, poured some steaming black liquid into a white mug, then joined them at the table. His long slender fingers tapped thoughtfully around the perimeter of his cup. He was obviously struggling against some sort of inner turmoil.

"Out with it, man." Graham shoved the rest of the pastry in his mouth, chewed twice and swallowed. He washed it down with a deep draw from his glass. He had no time to waste this morning so the man needed to spill whatever was troubling him. Graham needed to convince Mistress Lilia to be his wife. Precious time was a wasting.

"Lilia is my dear friend." Alberti's eyes narrowed and he leaned forward. "I don't know why you are here but I will have you know that I won't stand idly by and allow her to be upset or hurt."

Graham frowned. Confusion pushed him to the edge of his hard seat. "Are ye making a claim on the lass? 'Tis my understanding she is not betrothed to anyone." Had Mother Sinclair erred? Was Lilia already taken? Now what the hell was he going to do? He couldn't very well return to the wrath of the Buchanan but he couldn't remain in this century unless he was bound to Lilia. And what about the fire when they touched? He squirmed in the chair at the memory. Nay. He would not let her go so easily out of his life.

Scowling over the rim of his coffee cup, Alberti remained silent overly long. He took several sips before lowering the mug and setting it on the table. "Lilia isn't engaged . . . or betrothed to anyone. Why would that matter to you? Last night, you stated you'd been sent here to watch over her. Do be gracious enough to explain."

"I mean to marry the woman."

Alberti clattered his mug back to the table. "Marry? Surely you can't be serious. The two of you just met."

Graham stood, planted both hands on the table, and leaned across it. "Are ye challenging me then?" He'd not been in a good fight in quite some time. The thought was not entirely unpleasant although from the looks of the narrow-shouldered man, it would not be much of a tussle.

Rising from the table, Alberti set his cup down into the sink then turned and leaned back against the counter. "If it comes to protecting my friend, yes—I will challenge you. I will not stand idly by and see Lilia hurt. But if you're speaking of vying for dear Lilia's hand, trust me; the woman is quite capable of dismissing you herself."

Straightening, Graham hooked his thumbs in his belt. "I would never hurt the lass but I do mean to marry her. I've been charged by her family to keep her safe and the only way I can stay in this century and do so is if I am bound to her by blood."

"By blood," Alberti repeated, a dubious expression wrinkling his nose. "What the devil do you mean when you say *bound by blood*?"

Graham tapped on his wrist. "Bound by blood. We cut our wrists, mix our blood, and say the oath. Do ye not do that anymore?"

"Not . . ." Alberti glanced over at Angus, still sitting at the table, totally oblivious to the conversation and calmly shoving pastries in his mouth until his cheeks bulged. "...usually."

"Saint's bone, man." Graham reached over and thumped Angus on the back. "Ye've had enough. Come. We must be going." He'd wasted all the time he was going to waste talking to this Alberti person. The man didn't ken a damn thing about the ways and how things had to be.

Angus quickly stood, scooping up more pastries and tucking them into the folds of his plaid. "Thank ye kindly for the food and drink." He bobbed his head at Alberti then scurried out into the hall-way. His delighted chuckling echoed back into the kitchen as the toilet flushed again.

Graham bowed his head and pinched the bridge of his nose. Keeping Angus MacKenna in tow was like fostering an ill-behaved lad. Leaning against the back of the chair, he wearily shook his head. "Kindly show me the way to Mistress Lilia's home. I give ye my word I mean the lass no harm. I hold the MacKennas and the Sinclairs in the verra highest esteem. I'll thank ye to take me to her."

"Very well." Alberti scooped a ring of keys off a hook by the window then motioned Graham toward the hall. "Her home is a few blocks over. I'll finish dressing then give you both a lift there on my way to the shop."

CHAPTER 7

Graham shoved the door of the hideous monstrosity open and rolled out to the blessed stability of the ground. He crouched on all fours on the hard sheet of stone stretched in front of Lilia's house.

Great sucking gulps of the early morning air helped settle his churning innards—some. May the gods help him. His stomach groaned out a nauseating gurgle. What the hell had the world come to—forsaking horses for such unholy wagons surely fashioned by the devil himself?

Angus stumbled free of the metal chariot, his face drawn and pale as he echoed Graham's unspoken thoughts, "I canna believe they gave up horses for such a thing as that."

Alberti grinned as he rounded the beast, jingling the keys in one hand. "There now, chaps. Your first ride in an automobile wasn't all that bad, now, was it?"

If he wasn't so feckin' ill, he'd knock that grinning bastard on his arse. Instead, Graham sucked in another lungful of air and huffed it out his mouth. May the gods strike him dead afore he ever had to ride in such a thing again.

The house door rattled and the hinges squeaked. Graham lifted his head and blinked. *Damned, if she isna an angel descending from the verra heavens themselves.*

Her long white tunic was belted at her waist while her silky blonde hair tumbled across her shoulders. Barefooted, Lilia scurried down the front steps and crouched down beside him. The soft weight of her hand on his shoulder nearly made him groan aloud. He breathed in another deep breath, forever memorizing the delicate sweetness of her scent. Damn, she surely *was* an angel sent to save his battered soul.

She wrinkled her nose, sympathy flashing in her green-eyed gaze. "Bad first ride in the car, I see. I saw your exit through the window. Here. Inhale this oil of peppermint. It will help settle your stomach."

Graham thumbed the cork free of the small glass vial, put it to his face, and breathed in—deep. The bile burning at the back of his throat gradually calmed to a tolerable level. "Thank ye, mistress." He passed the tiny glass over to Angus. "Breathe it in, lad. It helps."

Angus grabbed the bottle and snorted in a deep breath. "From now on, we walk. Or find a horse. Never again will I get in such a contraption."

"Agreed." Graham nodded and turned back to Lilia's concerned gaze. "Thank ye for the healing oil. I feel much better." Or maybe it was the mere sight of her smile that had settled him and made him whole.

He slowly rose, then held out a hand to help Lilia to her feet.

She cast a dubious look at his hand then quickly rose without touching him.

Disappointment weighed heavily in his chest. She didn't wish to touch him. She feared the strange connection they had discovered last night. *Aye.* He supposed he couldn't fault her for being a wee bit leery. Mother Sinclair's words rang clear in his mind. *Lilia thinks allowing anyone to help her is a sign of failure. She's a stubborn hellcat.* Well . . . stubborn hellcat or not, Mistress Lilia was meant to be his. And he intended to make damn certain that it came to pass. The surety of the thought surprised him. Aye, he wanted this woman. Wanted her for his very own.

"Come inside. I've got some coffee made and Vivienne is attempting to bake some scones but I wouldn't get my hopes up about those if I were you." Lilia gathered her robe higher above her bare feet and padded up the walkway ahead of them. When she reached the top of the stone steps, she turned back. "Alberti, are you coming inside or are you going straight to check on the shops?"

"Straight to the shops, lovie." Alberti cast a pointed gaze at Graham and Angus then turned back to the car. "Call me if ye need me. Or have Vivienne give me a ring. I can be back here at a moment's notice."

The man called her *lovie*? In front of him? Graham glared back at Alberti. He'd tend to that insult later when Lilia was not around. "She will not be needing the likes of ye. I can assure ye of that well enough."

He didn't know what it was about that man but he didn't like him. Alberti acted as though he had some sort of rights over Mistress Lilia. The fool best get that thought out of his head this very second. Graham stomped up the steps past Lilia, slid his hand past hers to the door latch and pushed it open for her. "Allow me, mistress."

Lilia's eyes narrowed. "Don't think you can be snarky with my friends then sugarcoat it with chivalry. I'm not stupid."

Again, Graham breathed in the sweet fragrance of her, steeling himself against the urge to bury his face in the silky tresses tumbling around her neck. Memorizing aromas was a carryover from his days as a dragon. Even if struck blind, he would know Lilia by her unforgettable scent. "I'd never be foolish enough to think ye stupid." And he wouldn't. He'd been around the other Sinclair women enough to know that ye damn well best be on yer toes whenever they were around.

Lilia gave him a look that nearly made him laugh out loud. Aye and for sure. Mother Sinclair didn't lie. This one was a hellcat. He could see it in her eyes. "Yer family sends their love and they truly did send me here to watch over ye."

"I'm fully capable of taking care of myself, thank you very much." Lilia led the way down the hall to the small kitchen. She unhooked four cups from under the cabinets and lined them up beside a strange gurgling machine steaming on the counter. "And you can tell them that when you and Angus go back."

Stubborn as she was beautiful too. She'd soon find out he could be a mite stubborn as well. "Angus and I will not be going back. Ye best learn that straightaway." He eased closer and lightly tapped a finger across the top of her hand. "We are here. To stay. With yerself."

She blinked up at him, her green eyes so wide and dark he thought he'd surely drown in their depths. He leaned in closer, mesmerized by her parted lips, their soft pinkness bidding him to steal a wee taste of her seductive sweetness.

"Crap on crackers!" Metal clanged, a heavy door slammed, and smoke filled the far end of the kitchen.

Whirling out of Graham's reach, Lilia scooted across the room. "Are you all right? What did you do?"

Vivienne bobbed up and down between the stove, the floor, and the sink, plucking up black smoking bits of bread with a set of tongs and flinging them into the sink. "Run some water on those damn things before they burst into flames." She waved the tongs at Graham and Angus. "Open the windows and the doors before the fire alarm goes off."

"What the hell is a fire alarm?" Angus yanked open the back door and propped it ajar with a brick.

"I dinna ken." Graham studied the latch of the kitchen window for a moment, thumbed it free then shoved the window open. He grabbed a towel and fanned away the smoke.

"Well, shit." Vivienne tossed the tongs in the sink and scowled down at the ruined bread. "So much for a homemade breakfast." She wiggled a finger at Angus then jerked her head toward the door. "Come on, handsome. How do ye feel around coming with me? We'll run and fetch breakfast for everyone."

Angus visibly swallowed hard then wiped his palms on his plaid. "When ye say run . . . do ye mean *run* or are ye suggesting we travel in one of those gut-wrenching monstrosities?"

Vivienne laughed as she scooped the strap of her purse up over her shoulder. "The bakery is just around the corner and it's a beautiful day. We can walk."

Angus's face lit up and he bobbed his head. Gallantly extending his arm, he politely bowed. "Aye then, allow me, m'lady. 'Twould be me honor to escort ye."

Giggling as she pecked a kiss on Lilia's cheek, Vivienne winked at Graham. "We won't hurry back. I'm sure you two have a lot to chat about."

Graham nodded. Wise lass, this woman was. "Aye. That we do."

As Vivienne and Angus left the kitchen, Lilia shot Graham a *go to hell* look that made him laugh out loud. He held out a hand and nodded at the table. "Come now, lass. Let us sit and get to know one another better."

She pointedly brushed past his hand and returned to the cups she'd lined up on the counter. "How do you like your coffee?" She pulled a pitcher free of the strange silver machine and poured the ominous-looking black liquid into two of the cups.

"Coffee?" Graham repeated. The stuff looked like pitch, a bit on the watery side but pitch just the same. He pulled out a chair from the table and eased down into it. "I canna say that I've ever had such a drink."

Lilia set two steaming cups on the table then yanked open the door to an enormous silver box filled with an unearthly light and racks full of colorful items. Some things he recognized—most of them, he did not.

She emerged with a tiny pitcher no bigger than her hand. She set it on the table beside a matching covered bowl and metal spoon. "Then you're in for a treat. I'll doctor your coffee like Granny used to do mine when I was a little girl."

Graham watched with interest as she poured what looked like cream into the black liquid, turning it a swirling, rich caramel color. Then she added two heaping spoonfuls of a granular-looking powder and stirred. She smiled as she slid the cup toward him. "Try it. It's just like Granny used to make."

Graham cautiously sipped the steaming concoction, pleasantly surprised at the sweet creamy taste. He returned the cup to the table in front of him. "Verra nice, indeed. I thank ye." The silence of the kitchen stretched into long uncomfortable minutes. Lore a'mighty, what should he say to win her? He knew how to charm his way into a lass's bed but he'd be damned if he knew how to claim a woman's heart. Perhaps if he spoke about her family. Aye—that be it.

"Yer wee niece Chloe bade me tell ye that Master's Jamie, Caeden, and wee Rabbie dinna deserve any presents from ye this year. She said the lot of them are wicked little beasties that deserve nothing more than having their arses tanned." Graham's heart warmed at Lilia's quick bubbling giggle. Lore, the sound of the woman's laugh was sweeter than a Highland spring trickling down the mountain.

"Need their arses tanned?" Lilia chuckled even more before taking another sip of coffee. "Did Chloe really use that term or are you embellishing?"

Graham placed his right hand over his heart. "I swear to ye the wee minx used those verra words. She's none too fond of her little brother, Rabbie, nor her two cousins since the day they made off with her favorite doll and tossed it down the garderobe."

"They're not even three years old yet. Wasn't Coira watching them?" Lilia went to the cabinet and pulled out a yellow box. She slid her finger around the edge, pulled back the lid, and slid it onto the table. "Shortbread cookies. Perfect with coffee."

Graham chuckled. "I think poor Coira is stretched a wee bit thin of late managing that herd of lively bairns." He pulled free one of the cookies, studied it for a moment, then popped it in his mouth. *Not bad.* He pointed back at the box. "Ye've a fine cook able to bake such treats."

"Store bought." Lilia waved a hand across the opened box of cookies. "I don't cook and neither does Vivienne—obviously." She leaned her chin against her fist and smiled. "Tell me more about everyone back at the keep. I miss them. I haven't been able to hop back in quite a while and the fire portal just isn't the same as being there." She quickly looked down into her cup but not before Graham noticed the sheen of unshed tears glistening in her eyes.

"Why do ye stay here . . . in this time?" He had always wondered what had kept the last Sinclair woman from joining her family in the past.

She frowned down at the table, one finger lightly tracing the rim of her cup. "Have you ever just *known* something was supposed to be a certain way? I mean . . . just felt it in your heart without really knowing why?" She stared at him with a troubled look, brow furrowed and eyes pleading for him to understand.

"Aye." He reached over and smoothed a forefinger lightly across the back of her knuckles, silently wishing he could brush away her troubles just as easily. "I have. Much like our being together." He knew damn good and well she'd felt that same energy the first time they'd touched. That energy that said both their souls had been matched long ago and were destined to be reunited.

She drew in a deep breath, staring down at his finger lightly stroking her hand. "I'm not talking about us. I think I'm meant to stay in this time. Granny even said she felt it." She ducked her head and pulled her hand away, taking a quick sip of her coffee then shrugging as she lowered the cup back to the table. "And anyway, I know for certain I can't leave here until Eliza moves on."

"Tell me about this Eliza." Graham scooted his chair closer, reclaimed her hand and brought the cool softness of her fingers to his lips. His heart soared, then pounded harder when she didn't pull away this time. The tingling jolt of their earlier touch was gone but the warm soothing connection—the deep knowing in his soul—still held strong. *Aye.* This woman was meant to be his. He had never felt anything like it.

A sad smile pulled at her mouth as her gaze dropped and seemed fixed on something only she could see. "Eliza MacTavish has been my guardian angel, my confidante, and my source of sanity for a long time now." Lilia's voice broke and she hitched in a shaking breath as she closed her eyes. "And I can't imagine life without her. I don't know what I'm going to do when she dies."

Graham rose and knelt in front of her. "Ye will not be alone. I will see to it that ye are never alone. I swear it, ye ken?" His heart ached at the pain in her eyes. He reached and gently cupped her face in his palm, smoothing his thumb across her cheek. She shed no tears. Such strength . . . such fear to be seen as weak. He inched closer, sliding his fingertips into the silkiness of her hair. She still kept her pain inside and refused share it. "Let me in, lass. Let go of yer pain. I can ease yer troubles if ye'll but let me in so I can take the pain away."

"I don't even know you," she whispered, blinking hard and fast against the moisture shining in her eyes.

"Ah . . . but ye do." He drew closer still. "Ye need only search yer heart and yer memories. Our souls met before time began. We merely need to rekindle the memories for our hearts to know each other again."

She abruptly drew away, rising quickly from her chair. Avoiding his gaze, she hurried over to the silver machine holding the pitcher of coffee and added a bit more of the steaming dark liquid to her already full cup. "After my morning visit with Eliza, I'm going to meet Alberti and Vivienne at the center—a workout arena that Alberti owns. We have to practice our battle for tomorrow night's competition and then we plan to relax with a friendly paintball war. You're more than welcome to come with me and join in if you'd like."

So that was how it would be. He had no idea what the hell she was talking about but he kent for certain she was changing the course of their conversation and running away from whatever demons only she could see. He slowly rose and hooked his thumbs in his belt, determination clenching his teeth until his jaws ached. The lass thought to avoid anything that made her feel. Aye—well—she would soon discover he would not tolerate being avoided for very long. "I fully intend to stay at yer side. Wherever ye go, I shall follow."

Her eyes narrowed above the rim of her cup as she took a sip.

Graham chuckled. Good. She recognized his challenge.

Mother Sinclair and Trulie's advice floated through his mind. If he was to firmly take hold of Lilia's heart and conquer her world, he needed to embrace the ways of this time. Alberti had descended from his chambers smelling of soaps and oils. Before they'd left his house, the man had ensured his black hair was well slicked back and neatly combed.

As Lilia avoided his gaze and busied herself plucking the chunks of wet black bread from the sink and dropping them into a round metal bin, Graham inconspicuously turned his head to one side, lowered his nose and sniffed. *Humpf.* He had smelled worse but he definitely didn't smell as though he'd bathed in quite the while. Best see to cleaning up before he followed Lilia around her day.

Mother Sinclair and the Lady Trulie had gone into great detail regarding quite a few things of this time and cleanliness was one of them. In fact, just before he and Angus had jumped into the portal, Mother Sinclair had firmly lashed a pack to both their backs with the instructions that the items contained in the bags were to be used once they found Lilia and settled in. As she'd tightened the straps across his shoulders, Mother Sinclair had winked and said Lilia was going to love the clothes she and Trulie had obtained.

Graham glanced down at his tunic and plaid, wondering what sort of attire the Sinclair women had selected for the enticement of Lilia's affections. Mother Sinclair had said something about a shopping spree across the centuries. He worried about what the old woman had meant by such.

"I'm going to hop upstairs and get cleaned up." Lilia dried her hands on a bit of brightly striped linen then hooked the cloth through a metal ring hanging beside the sink. "Once Vivienne and Angus get back, we'll figure out the details of the day."

Lore a'mighty, she sounded like Cook parsing out the day's chores to the kitchen lads and maids. Graham stepped forward with a decisive nod. If this was to be a battle of the wills, the lass would soon discover she was sorely outplayed and her heart was to be his prize. "Angus and I will be a needing our things—our packs. Would yer friend Alberti be so kind as to bring them here so we can clean up as well?" He lifted his chin and took another step forward. "After all, I wouldna wish to shame ye as I accompany ye around yer daily tasks."

Lilia leaned back against the counter with a dubious look on her face. "I can call Alberti and ask him to bring your packs by once he's finished opening both stores. But I'm a little confused. Why didn't you just clean up at Alberti's since you're staying there?"

"Two reasons, lass." Graham closed the distance between them. "I needed to be here with ye and didna wish to tarry." He reached out and smoothed a wandering curl away from her cheek. Such silk. He had known from the first moment he'd seen her that her hair would feel like the finest silk. "And I'll not be a staying another night at Alberti's."

She shifted and caught her breath. Did he imagine she leaned forward the slightest bit? Dare he move even closer? Aye . . . he dared. Else how would he ever win a taste of her tempting mouth? He laced his fingers into her hair, barely brushing the soft curve of her cheek with his thumb. Lore help him, she shook him to his very core. He leaned in and brushed his lips across hers.

The soft weight of her hand settled on the center of his chest. But she didn't push him away and for that he was sorely glad. He nibbled gently at her lower lip then kissed her again, firm and possessive yet still chaste and careful. He daren't push her further. Not yet. He would win her bit by bit, gentling her skittish heart like calming a fearful colt.

Graham stepped back. His heart and hopes lifted at the lovely color riding high upon her cheeks and the swift rise and fall of her chest. Aye, he had done well enough for now. Best allow the seeds he'd planted time to set down roots and take firm hold.

"I'm . . . I'm going to call Alberti." She pushed around him, scooped up the small square oddity . . . the phone . . . she'd kept tucked in her corset the night before, and hurried to the kitchen door. "I'll have him bring your things."

Graham nodded. "I thank ye, lass—for everything."

CHAPTER 8

"I suppose they did need a bath." Vivienne tore a bite-sized chunk off the bagel on her plate, smeared a dollop of clotted cream across it, then pointed it at Lilia. "But ye must admit, even though they were a bit gamey—their wild and wooly look was sexy hot." She leaned back in the chair, grinning as she popped the morsel in her mouth and chewed. "There's nothing hotter than knowing a man's best bits are a mere thin plaidie away."

Lilia had been quite aware of Graham's *bits* when he'd kissed her. Even though he'd not pressed against her, nor touched her except for his mouth and his hand in her hair, she'd been keenly aware of every square inch of him. She huffed out a silent laugh. Every square inch of him—uhm... right.

She pushed her untouched plate to the center of the table and folded her hands in front of her, patiently waiting until Vivienne had scarfed down the last bit of her breakfast. When Vivienne finally refolded her napkin and tossed it to the center of her empty plate, Lilia asked, "So are you coming with us to visit Eliza or are you just going to meet us at the center?"

"I'd never noticed it before but Alberti is right." Vivienne scooped up the plates, slid Lilia's untouched bagel back into the box, then set the dishes in the sink.

"What?"

"Whenever ye dinna wish to talk about something ye completely ignore it and change the subject."

The pound of heavy footsteps thumping down the back staircase echoed into the kitchen. Angus bounded around the landing, grinning broadly as he slicked a hand back across his still-damp hair. Chest puffed out and flexing his muscular arms, he sauntered over to Vivienne. "Tell me, lass. What do ye think?"

Lilia bit her bottom lip and rubbed the end of her nose to hide her smile behind her hand. Angus reminded her of a hormonal schoolboy determined to shed his virginity with the lovely Vivienne. He marched back and forth in front of her, strutting first one way then the other so she would benefit from a full panoramic view of his well-fitted jeans and tight gray T-shirt.

Vivienne grinned as she winked and squeezed one of Angus's bulging biceps. "Verra nice, indeed."

Angus's chest swelled even more, his face glowing as though someone had flipped his light switch to high beam.

"Where is . . ." Lilia lost the ability to speak as she turned back to the raised landing at the end of the stair.

"Aye?"

Totally climbable, ripped abs seemed even—Lilia closed her mouth and swallowed hard, struggling to recover from the exquisite example of male hotness right in her own kitchen.

Hard ridges of muscle shimmered and teased beneath the silky black tee stretched tight across Graham's chest. Black jeans showcased the rest of his body. The material hugged his hips and thighs and the lovely bulging package in between. The man looked like he'd been poured into his clothes and polished to sculpted-god perfection. Where the devil had Granny learned to dress a man like that?

Graham stepped down from the landing, lifting his hands as he turned. "I've no idea why the woman selected black but this is what yer grandmother stowed in me pack. Will it do for the day's errands?"

"Uhm . . . " Lilia rubbed her thumbs across her fingertips, her hands itching to trace and explore.

"Lass?" Graham moved closer, his heavy, black biker boots thumping with each step. "Does this suit ye?"

"If it doesn't, she's a feckin' daftie."

Lilia turned away from Vivienne, hid her fist against the small of her back and saluted Vivienne with her middle finger. She inhaled a deep breath and weakly waved at Graham's attire. "You look . . . fine."

Graham smiled a seductive, knowing smile, one that glinted pure mischief clear to his eyes and promised so much more. "'Tis well and good then. Shall we be on about our day?"

On about their day. He really did mean to accompany her everywhere she went. A wicked idea sprouted. "Do you want me to put the oil of peppermint in my purse or are you going to keep it in your pocket?" She lifted her keys off the hook beside the door as she tucked her purse into the crook of her elbow.

The phases of realization, abhorrence, and downright fear flashing across Graham's features gave her a victorious rush. Ha! She had one. Unable to resist the temptation, she rattled the keys again and smiled. She was okay with his tagging along to the stables, the center, or the paintball field but her visits with Eliza were private. A glance at the time backlit on her phone told her she was already late. She should've been to the hospital and had their morning visit a long time ago. She nodded at the garage door. "Well?"

Graham's Adam's apple skittered up and down his throat as he swallowed hard, his unblinking stare locked on the keys. "Could we not walk?"

Lilia shook her head. "No. The hospital is too far. Especially with some of the streets blocked off because of Fringe. I'll have to take a longer route." A belated pang of sympathy softened her resolve—a little. Poor guy. He was already getting a little green around the gills and they hadn't even gotten out of the kitchen. She'd be generous and give him an easy out. No sense in being *overly* cruel. "The center and the stables are only a few blocks away. If you and Angus want to walk over there and wait for me, I'm sure Vivienne wouldn't mind escorting the two of you."

Vivienne looped her arm through Angus's then beamed her best smile at Graham. "Absolutely. There's no finer way to walk through the streets of Edinburgh than with a handsome man on each arm."

Graham's scowl deepened, his mustache twitching as he appeared to be gnawing on the corner of his lip. His gaze slid from Lilia to Vivienne then back to Lilia again. He sucked in a deep breath than noisily blew it out. "Nay. I canna go with Mistress Vivienne and wait. 'Twould not be honorable. I must pay my respects to Mistress Eliza."

A sense of protectiveness for her ailing guardian flared. Lilia lifted her chin and shook her head. "That is really not necessary." She fisted the ring of keys so hard, the bits of metal chewed into her palm. "She might not even know you're there. Her sleep is . . . uhm . . . deeper . . . these days." More like drug-induced to give her a brief reprieve from the pain, but some things were just better left unsaid.

Shuttering away that thought, Lilia spun around and headed to the door leading to the garage. She locked her focus on the worn brass doorknob, squeezing it hard as she struggled to get a grip on the new wave of despair threatening to overtake her. Her hand shook until the metal latch softly rattled. Tensing against losing control, she forced her hand to still. Graham needed to back off. "I'll meet up with everyone at the field in a few hours," she said without looking up.

Before she could pull open the door, Graham's calloused hand covered hers and held her fingers firmly in place. His warm breath tickled across her nape as he leaned in closer. "I said I'll be a going with ye, lass. Ye'll find I always keep to my word." He gave her hand a gentle squeeze and barely nuzzled the tickling softness of his short beard across the back of her neck. "Yer Mistress Eliza will ken I am there. I feel certain of it," he whispered.

She closed her eyes, concentrating on slowing her breathing and praying Graham couldn't hear her pounding heart.

"Let me in, lass," he coaxed in an even lower whisper. The raw huskiness of his voice stroked her, imploring her to give him a chance. "I'm here for ye. I swear it. All ye need do is give me a chance. Ye have nothing to fear, ye ken?"

Staring down at their clasped hands around the doorknob, Lilia gave in to the slightest glimmer of hope as Graham's emotions washed across her like a warm gentle caress. The tensed knots in her shoulders lessened the barest bit. Maybe she should let Graham visit Eliza. Maybe, even in her current state, Eliza might rouse enough to know he was there and find some small comfort in knowing Lilia wasn't alone anymore—even though she had just met the man and he'd probably be hopping back to the past again very soon.

Lilia nodded. "I can give you *for now,*" she forced out in a strained whisper. "That's it."

Graham pressed a soft kiss to her shoulder. "I'll take *for now* and make it *forever.* Ye'll see."

"For now," Lilia repeated a bit louder, reinforcing the phrase more for her own peace of mind than for his. "Now let's go."

CHAPTER 9

"You okay?" Lilia wafted the oil of peppermint under Graham's nose as he butted himself back against the side of the car, bent forward, and sucked in a series of deep shuddering gulps of air. "I was hoping this ride would be a little better for you but evidently I was wrong."

Holy crap, she had never seen anyone so prone to motion sickness. Her sister Kenna had always been queasy when they had jumped across the centuries but she'd never been this bad with cars. Poor Graham had turned a sickly shade of green as soon as she started the engine and gotten worse at every turn. Thank heavens they'd only driven across town. The poor man would've heaved himself to death if he'd had to ride any farther.

He scrubbed his hand across the sheen of sweat covering his brow, grabbed the vial of scented oil, and fisted it under his nose. Snorting in a deep inhale, he closed his eyes and held it. His greenish pallor morphed into a vein-popping red, much like a time-lapsed video of a ripening tomato. He blew his breath out hard. "I will be—" He shuddered, swallowed hard, and inhaled another deep whiff of the peppermint. "Fine."

She leaned against the car beside him, wishing there was some way she could make him feel better. Poor guy. The perfect specimen of a hot hunky Highlander taken down by technology. "You wait here and keep deep-breathing that peppermint oil, I'll be right back."

Graham didn't open his eyes, just kept sucking in wheezing gasps over the glass vial as he waved her away.

Snagging her purse out of the car, she hurried out of the parking garage, jogged across the street, and tested the door of the local pharmacy. No luck. It was nearly lunchtime and the drugstore always closed for an hour at noon. So much for the idea of getting Graham some motion sickness pills. The way the poor man reacted to riding in a car, he needed something a hell of a lot stronger than oil of peppermint.

She glanced up and down the street, hoping to spot a store that might carry the medicine—maybe a place of business she had somehow overlooked during her daily visits to the hospital. Still no luck. None of the stores lining the busy avenue would carry what Graham needed.

Maybe the tiny shop in the lobby of the hospital? She'd only been in there once to buy Eliza a small vase of her beloved roses, but if she remembered correctly, there had been one wall dedicated to daily necessities. Back across the street she jogged. She didn't bother stopping to check on Graham. She could hear his retching groan echoing through the concrete tomb of the parking garage.

Hurrying through the quietly shushing doors of the entrance, Lilia slowed her careening pace to a much more respectable walk. No matter how old she got, Granny's voice would always be in her head telling her to mind her manners. A pang of loneliness slowed her even more. It had been too long since she'd last jumped back for a visit. She missed them all so much.

Her heart lifted a bit at the brightly lit interior of the gift shop and the glass door propped wide open for customers. Thank goodness. The pink-coated volunteers were there today and the store was open. Now to find poor Graham some drugs. She went straight to the cluttered square of glass countertops hemming in the cash register and an elderly volunteer deeply engrossed in the daily paper's crossword puzzle.

"Excuse me?" Lilia shifted her weight from side to side. She didn't want to be rude but Graham needed help and she needed to get him stabilized so they could get up to Eliza's room without him gagging his way through the hallways.

The silver-haired matron peered up from her folded paper, her ink pen frozen in space mere centimeters from the black and white squares of the puzzle. "Aye? Can I be a helping ye then?"

"Do you have anything for nausea?" Lilia fished her wallet out of her purse and waited.

"Nausea, ye say?" The elderly lady pushed her glasses up higher on the bridge of her nose and, in painstakingly slow motion, tapped the nib of her black ink pen against the blocks of the puzzle in front of her. "First off, I need to ask ye a question. Four letters. Strongest power in the world. Ends with an 'e.' What say ye?"

Lilia curbed the urge to drum her fingers on the glass counter. She needed to be polite and respect her elders or Granny would reach through time and tan her hide. "Uhm . . . I'm not sure. Now about nausea cures, do you have anything? More specifically, something for motion sickness?"

"Ends with an *e*," the volunteer repeated, frowning down at the crossword puzzle, her arthritic fingers slowly tapping against the paper.

Holy crap. Was this old woman serious? Lilia bit her tongue to keep from raising her voice. She had to mind her manners. Granny would somehow know it if she didn't. The answer easily came to mind—thank heavens—maybe if she helped volunteer finish that damn puzzle it would speed things along. "It's *love*."

"Eh?" The old woman peered up at her, her thin silvery brows drawn together in a confused scowl.

Lilia pointed down at the puzzle. "Four-letter word. Strongest power on earth. Ends with an e. It's *love*. L-O-V-E."

"Well, look at that. So, it is." The little old lady blocked the word into the squares with a happy chortle. As soon as she'd written the

last letter, she laid her pen on top of the paper and patted it with a
contented swat. Sliding off her stool, she toddled over to the cluttered
wall behind the counter and snatched down several pale blue packets. She deposited them into a tiny paper bag and handed it over to
Lilia.

Lilia smiled at the kindly volunteer and took the bag. "How
much?"

"Oh, not a thing, dearie." The little old woman struggled to
resume her perch on the wobbly stool and took up her pen.

Frowning down at the bag, Lilia opened it and looked for some
sort of price on the packets of pills but there weren't any numbers to
be found. She leaned over the counter, lowering her voice as she
looked around. "I don't want to get you in trouble. I know these can't
be free."

The old woman looked up from her paper and winked. "Trust in
the power of love, dearie. 'Tis the greatest power of all." Then she
returned to her puzzle, softly humming under her breath as she
slowly filled in the rest of the squares.

What a weird old lady. "Well . . . okay then . . . thank you for your
help." Lilia tucked the bag into the crook of her arm and backed out
the door.

"Think nothing of it, dearie." The old woman glanced up from
her paper and smiled.

Lilia stopped by the alcove filled with vending machines, popped
in the required change, and pushed the button for ginger ale. Perfect.
Ginger ale and anti-nausea pills. Pair those with the peppermint oil
and Graham should soon feel a lot better than he did right now. She
snatched up the bottle from the machine and hurried back to the car.

Graham still leaned against it, bent over with both hands propped
on his knees. He didn't appear to be retching anymore but remained
extremely pale. In fact, against the backdrop of his inky black shirt,
he looked ghostly white.

"Here." Lilia twisted the cap off the bottle of ginger ale and fished
one of the pill packets out of the brown paper sack. "This will make
you feel better. Swallow these then sip at the ginger ale."

"Ginger. Ale?" He scowled at the bottle as though it held poison.

Lilia ripped open one of the packets with her teeth and shook two pills out into her palm. "Here. Put these in your mouth then wash them down with this."

Graham frowned down at the pills, then lifted his leery gaze to her.

"Just do it." She shoved the pills into his mouth and handed him the opened bottle.

He obediently took a swig and swallowed, then held up the bottle, glaring at it with a narrow-eyed expression while he smacked his lips. "That is not ale."

"*Ginger* ale," Lilia stressed, doing her best to keep from laughing. The poor guy had probably never come across such a sweetly fizzy beverage before. "Sip it. It will help settle your stomach."

Instead, he took a long draw off the bottle then thumped his chest and belched.

Lilia couldn't help but giggle at the surprised look on his face. "It's the carbonation. Sip it slower."

He stood straighter, settling his stance as he squared his shoulders and took another deep draw from the ginger ale. "So, this elixir stops the illness caused by the wicked machine?"

"It helps." Lilia took one of the pill packets from the paper sack and fanned it in front of him. "But these will help even more." She frowned at the fine print on the back of the packet. "But they might make you a little sleepy." Hopefully, he'd eventually get used to traveling in a car and would get past the motion sickness. His previous pallor was already giving way to a healthy ruddiness.

Graham finished off the ginger ale, then handed the empty bottle back to her. Rubbing his stomach, he pulled in a deep breath. "'Tis much better now. I dinna feel the need to retch my insides out."

"I'm glad." She stuffed the medication into the car's glove box, then scanned the parking garage for a recycle bin. Not seeing one, she twisted the cap back on the ginger ale bottle and tucked it into the crook of her arm. "I'll just get rid of this inside. I think I saw a recycle bin beside the gift shop."

Graham arched a brow, looking at her as though she spoke in a language he didn't understand. And he probably didn't understand the concept of recycle bins and gift shops. Lilia wondered just how much Granny and Trulie had briefed the poor man on the ways of the twenty-first century. She waved him forward. "Come on. I've made Eliza wait long enough."

Eying the massive brownstone building attached to the parking garage, he held out his arm for her to take. "What did ye call this place?"

Reluctantly, she relented and hooked her hand through his arm, falling into step beside him. Her heart double-thumped. Maybe the twenty-first century could learn a thing or two from the past—such gallantry had become almost nonexistent. She nodded at the bronze dedication plaque mounted beside the double glass doors. "This is a hospital and long-term-care facility."

At his puzzled look, she hurried to explain. "In this time, whenever anyone is seriously injured or ill, they stay here at the hospital where a staff of doctors and nurses do their best to help them heal and survive."

"And long-term-care facility?" Graham repeated the words as though reciting foreign items off a menu.

"That's where some people stay . . . permanently." Lilia frowned at her own explanation, struggling to come up with the right words. "The elderly, the disabled or terminally ill stay in long-term care until they either get better . . . or die." She sadly shook her head. "It depends on their situation."

"What of their families? Why do they not care for their own?" He slowed as they approached the massive sliding glass doors.

"Not everyone has a family who can provide twenty-four/seven care." She tugged him forward. "It's complicated, Graham. I don't know how to explain it any better."

He acknowledged her attempt at explaining with a curt nod, then stepped on the oversized black sensor mat in front of the hospital doors. The wide double doors whooshed open; the light over the entrance flashed a spinning red and white. Graham jumped back, his eyes widening even more as the doors shushed back to the closed position and the light stopped blinking. "What the hell kind of magic is that?"

Lilia bit the inside of her cheek to keep from giggling at his bewildered expression. She needed to be nice. After all, this was his first visit to the twenty-first century. She gently pulled him forward. "Automatic doors." She pointed first at the black mat then up at the tiny silver boxes fitted on either side of the door. "Motion and weight sensors in the mat and those two little—" She flipped her hand, searching for the correct terminology. They weren't really cameras but she wasn't quite sure what to call them. A frustrated huff escaped her as she pointed at one of the sensors. "Those little boxes see when someone walks up to the door and that along with your weight on the mat triggers the doors to either open or close." There. Good heavens. Who knew explaining automatic doors could be so freaking complicated?

Graham's disbelieving narrow-eyed look slid from the boxes atop the doors, down to the mat, and then back to her. "Magic?"

Sure. Why not? Lilia nodded. "Yes. Magic." Since she was neither an electrical nor an architectural engineer, magic was a much easier explanation.

Gingerly easing forward, Graham stepped onto the center of the mat, flinching when the doors quickly slid open. His jaw hardened into a determined line as he squared his shoulders then hurried through the doors, whipping around to watch them as they bounced shut. "Amazing," he said under his breath. He stepped back on the mat, staring at the doors as they slid back open.

"Wait 'til you see the elevator." She pulled him off the mat in front of the door so they'd stop opening and closing. "Wait here while I drop this in the recycle bin."

"Aye." Graham nodded without looking at her, still staring down at the wide black doormat, then up at the doors. He tapped his toe on the mat and made the doors open again.

She rolled her eyes. What a way to keep a thirteenth-century Highlander occupied. She hurried across the smooth marble floor of the lobby, turning at the first wide hallway to access the common area housing the gift shop and vending machine alcoves.

As she lobbed the soda bottle into the recycle bin beside the door of the gift shop, a strong cheery "G'day to ye" rang out from within the tiny store.

A young girl, dark hair pulled back in a neat ponytail tied with a bow that matched her pink volunteer's smock, was busily flitting around the shelves, dusting them with a feather duster.

"Good day to you too," Lilia answered, wondering where the sweet old lady had gone. Odd time of day for a shift change. Even for volunteers.

Oh well. Maybe the old lady couldn't handle an entire shift. Lilia shrugged and hurried back to the main lobby. Graham was cautiously circling an oversized marble fountain sculpted into the shape of a huge orb with water bubbling from its center.

She waved him over to the set of steel doors at the opposite side of the room of the small waiting area filled with uncomfortable-looking chairs and decorative urns of plastic plants. "Come on. I'll even let you push the button." She chuckled at the memory of fighting with Mairi and Kenna to be the one who always got to push the button whenever the family happened across an elevator.

"Push the button?" Graham flexed his hands as he gave the steel doors a stern up-and-down look.

"Right there. The one with the arrow pointing up."

Graham shoved his fisted hand against the button and held it.

She patted his muscled forearm. "You don't have to hold it down. You just push it so it lights up, then let go. The elevator will be here in a minute."

A bell sounded and the steel doors slid open with a bang.

"Saint's bones." Graham backed up a step. "'Tis a burial cairn made of steel."

"Yeah . . . elevators kind of creep me out too but we won't be in it very long." Lilia latched on to his elbow and pulled.

"In it?" A look of disbelief arched his brows higher. He locked his legs and refused to move forward.

"Come on. Before someone else on another floor pushes the button and it leaves." Lilia pulled him in the rest of the way, patting his chest as she led him to the back of the elevator. "I get to push the button this time." She jabbed a knuckle against the seventh floor button then took a stance beside Graham. The doors slid shut and the elevator took off.

"Son of a bitch!" He splayed his hands against the wall on either side of him and lowered himself into a defensive crouch.

She rested a hand on top of his arm. Poor guy. She didn't like elevators either and she knew how they worked. "It's okay. We're almost there."

The elevator jerked to a stop, the bell dinged and the doors slid open. Graham rushed out into the hall, glancing back at the thing as though it were a beast that had just spit him out. His eyes grew even wider as he looked around and realized it had transported them to a different place. His voice shaking, he drew closer to Lilia. "Where the devil are we now?"

"Seventh floor." Lilia took his hand and gave him a reassuring squeeze. "Eliza's room is down this way." Her heart went out to him as his nostrils flared and he jerked a leery look all around. "Disinfectant." She wouldn't add that the sickening aroma of death also filled the air.

An efficient-looking older woman dressed in bright flowery scrubs and clutching a steel clipboard to her chest met them just as they passed the nurses' station. "Good day to ye, Miss Sinclair. I thought ye'd already been by for yer morning visit wi' Mistress Eliza. She didna mention ye'd not been in yet. Ye ken how she always fusses when ye stay here longer than she deems fit."

Dear stubborn Eliza. Bound and determined that Lilia wasn't going to waste a precious minute of life sitting at the hospital waiting for her to die. "I know. She always tries to run me off as soon as I get here."

Lilia pulled Graham forward with an apologetic shrug. "I'm afraid we ran a bit late this morning. How is she? Has there been any change?" Even though her mind knew the odds of Eliza improving were nil, her heart couldn't help but hope.

Compassion softened the nurse's face as she barely shook her head. "Och, no. No change at all. But she does seem to be resting a wee bit easier today. I believe the new medication is controlling her pain a great deal better now that we've put her on the timed IV and she doesna have to ask for it. She's none too happy about it—too strong-willed for her own good, that one is. Ye must convince her 'tis not a sign of weakness to allow us to ease her troubles."

Lilia swallowed hard, battling the choking knot of emotions lodged in her throat. "I'll do my best but you know Eliza. She thinks she's supposed to take care of everyone else—not the other way around." She nervously hitched her purse higher on her shoulder and gently pulled Graham forward. "We'll pop in and sit with her a bit. Even if the meds have her groggy, hopefully, she'll know we're there."

The nurse nodded with an understanding smile. "I'm sure she will, dearie. I'm sure she will."

Lilia reluctantly led the way into Eliza's room, bolstering her trembling wall of control as much as she could. It always broke her heart to see Eliza so still, so small—a faded weak shadow of the vibrant soul she had once been.

Lilia bit her lip. Her dear friend seemed paler today but the nurse was right—the stubborn old woman appeared to actually be resting rather than fighting the endless pain. The deep lines of pain that had been etched across her drawn face were somehow softer.

Graham eased into the room beside Lilia, his movements silent and reverent in the hush of the low-lit area. He scowled at the monitors mounted around the head of the bed, his eyes narrowing at the plastic bags of liquid hanging from the IV poles and the tangle of tubes disappearing into the padded tape cuffing both of Eliza's pale thin arms and the port embedded just below her collarbone.

He moved closer to the bed, his head tilting to one side as he peered closer at her face. He bowed and made a polite dip of his closely cropped beard, one hand fisted to the center of his chest. "It is my honor to meet ye, Mistress Eliza. Graham MacTavish at yer service."

Lilia's heart hitched as Eliza's eyelids barely fluttered and twitched. Her beloved guardian, fragile and worn from her battle, was making a valiant effort to rise from the depths of her drug-induced sleep. One of her mottled hands shifted atop the coverlet, her knobby fingers trembling as she lifted them in what appeared to be a weak acknowledgment that they were there. Her thin lips moved but no sound managed to escape.

Lilia slid her hand beneath Eliza's cold, drawn fingers, gently cupping what had become little more than skin-covered bones. "Granny sent Graham to us along with his friend Angus. Graham wanted to meet you. He is your kin." Her voice broke. Lilia swallowed hard and took another deep breath. She didn't dare let the dam break and free her emotions. She had to be strong. Control had to be maintained or she would never regain it.

Eliza finally managed to open her watery eyes and focus on Graham. Her thin lips twitched at the corners as she wheezed in a shallow breath. "'Tis about time ye got here." Her whisper was weak and broken but at least finally audible.

Graham shifted closer. A sad smile lifted a corner of his mustache. His voice fell to the hushed, consoling tone usually heard in the presence of the dying or out of respect for the already dead. "Aye, my kinsman. I did tarry. But I am here now and that is all that matters."

"Aye," Eliza whispered, her eyes slowly closing. "See that ye do well." Without lifting her hand from the pillow cradling her bruised arm or reopening her eyes, she pointed a shaking finger at him. "I will haunt yer arse the rest of yer days if ye hurt my wee lass."

Graham solemnly bowed his head in acceptance of Eliza's verdict. "I swear to ye that our fine lassie here will never again face this world alone, m'lady." Graham eased his hand to the small of Lilia's back and gently pulled her closer. "I give ye my oath, Mistress Eliza, I shall protect this fine woman well and guard her true."

Eliza didn't respond but the quiet beeping of the heart monitor changed in rhythm, increasing in speed for an extended string of rapid erratic beats. The wavering green line bounced faster, additional spikes jumping across the screen. It carried on for several minutes then gently smoothed back to the weary beep with the neon line barely rippling. Eliza's fingers twitched in Lilia's hand, curling a bit tighter in a weak squeeze, then relaxed and went still. The old woman's sunken chest shifted with a slow deep inhale then her body settled back in place as she released the breath.

Lilia held her breath, afraid to move as she stared down at Eliza's face. The palest flush of color now washed across Eliza's cheeks and she seemed almost serene. "What pact did you two just make?" she whispered, blinking fast and hard against the tears stinging in her eyes.

Graham pressed a warm, soft kiss against her temple. "That I will always be with ye." His voice dropped to a lower whisper—a deep, lilting caress that lifted her up and held her. His soothing tone reassured her at a very basic level that all would somehow be well. "I grant ye, lass, she will rest easier now as she prepares for her final journey."

Settling Lilia's hand firmly in the crook of his arm, he gently pulled her away from the bed and turned them toward the door. "Come. Ye ken she wishes ye to go. Leave her to her rest now that she knows ye to be safe and protected."

CHAPTER 10

He jerked awake, body tensed, all senses alert. A cold sweat peppered across his brow. Graham sucked in a deep, shuddering breath, floundering to remember where the hell he was and how the hell he had gotten here.

"We're here." The clear, sweet voice soothed him immediately.

Lilia turned to him with a smile as she twisted the wee bit of metal shoved into the odd black post that seemed to control the beast of the machine and its deadly racket stilled. What in blazes had they called this thing? Au . . . to . . . mo—what-the-hell?

He scrubbed the heels of his hands against his eyes. He couldn't remember a sorry thing. Son of a bitch, his mind felt wrapped in wool.

Bumping the door open with her shoulder, Lilia fixed him with an apologetic look. "Sorry. I was afraid those pills might knock you on your ass. Your body isn't used to stuff like that." She yanked open the second door on her side of the beast and retrieved a great black bag out from behind her seat. "But at least you didn't puke."

"I will have ye know that not a damn thing knocked me on my arse. I chose to sit in this accursed bit of sorcery because ye said that *center* place was too far to reach on foot from the hospital." Damned if his mouth didn't feel dry as dust and as crusty as week-old horse dung. He yanked up on the silver handle and shoved open the door. The sooner he was shed of this wickedness, the better. He unfolded his way out of the cramped belly of the beast, turned, then kicked the door shut. 'Twas a damn bit of sorriness when folk set aside the plea-sure of owning a good horse to trek around in such twisted bits of metal that would be better put to use in the making of shields and swords.

"This way—come on." Lilia waited at the grassy edge of the gravel lot beside a fence that looked like endless lengths of chain mail stretched between evenly spaced, headless spears. Her inviting smile curled a bit higher with just enough wickedness to make his mouth water. He was truly damned and he had already come to love every aspect of it. He'd never be able to resist this woman nor—he had firmly decided—would he ever wish to try.

"Come on. We'll see if Alberti has any workout clothes in the shop that'll fit you. Then you can play too." Lilia pulled open one side of the double glass doors leading into a great, gray metal building that was damn nigh big enough to hold not only the grand twenty-horse stable back at MacKenna Keep but the paddock and bailey as well.

Graham stopped just before entering the building, craning his neck to examine its massive height and width. "What is this place?" He took a step back, still staring up at the building and determined not to enter it until he learned more. "And I dinna *play*. I am not a bairn." He'd follow her to hell and back. That he already knew. But she best be clear and know him for the man that he was.

"Bairn?" Lilia repeated, frowning as she bounced her fine round butt back against the glass door and held it open even wider. Her brows arched with recognition. "Oh, don't get all huffy. I call it *play* for lack of a better word." She rolled her eyes and jerked her thumb toward the darker interior of the building. "I'm betting once you see what I'm talking about, you'll want to join in. Come on." Her wicked smile returned. "Trust me."

Something about the way she looked when she said those words made the hair on the back of his neck stand straight on end. But he had to admit, she also made his heart pound harder. He would trust her, all right . . . and that would more than likely be his undoing. He waved her forward. "Lead on, dear lass. Lead on."

Lilia hitched the wide black strap of her bag higher on her shoulder and spun into the room. "Alberti—over here!" She waved across the great tomb of the place at a brightly lit patch of the room farther down the way. Her call echoed up through the heights of the massive beams arched across the ceiling.

Saint's bones. Graham stared at the size of the wide beams marching down the sides of the building then curving overhead like the skeleton of a great ship turned upside down. What the kind of forge had produced such monstrous pieces of metal? 'Twould take all the smithies in Scotland to hammer out such lengths. His steps pinged and echoed as they walked across the gleaming floor—yellow and looking to be made of wood much akin to the floors in Alberti's home—but how had they achieved such a shining finish?

"'Tis about time ye got here, man." Angus came up behind him, clapping him on the shoulder as he lunged forward with what looked to be a small sword that had never been sharpened. "They want us to help them practice for their wee competition." Angus stepped back, waggled a bushy brow, then took *battle ready* stance. "Mistress Vivienne wishes to learn some of our *moooves.*"

"What the hell is wrong with ye?" Graham glared at Angus. The man acted the fool. "And ye sound like a Highland cow." He took a step back and frowned up and down at Angus's odd-looking, skintight apparel. "And what the devil are ye wearing?" He'd left the man to himself but a few hours and he looked as though he'd stuffed his body into a wee lass's stockings; and he was talking as daft as old Herschel whenever he came down from his mountain after sampling the wild herbs.

"These should fit you, my fine man." Alberti held out a thin pile of neatly folded clothing. "Luckily, one of my taller clients changed his mind after ordering them and I graciously agreed to add them back into my shop's inventory." He waited, nudging the stack of black, silky-looking material a bit higher and closer to Graham.

Graham stared down at the clothes then glanced over at Angus, who immediately grinned and smoothed his hand across his barrel chest, proudly patting his own bright blue shirt that damn near hurt Graham's eyes to look at it.

"I thank ye." At least the clothing Alberti offered him was not colored as though woven for a whore. He dropped the silky pile to the floor, peeled off his shirt, then started to unzip his jeans.

Alarm filled Alberti's face. "No, no, no!" He scooped the clothes up, shoved them against Graham's chest, and turned him toward a stone block wall inset with two shining steel doors. One door had a bright white glyph of a figure in a kilt. The other door had a similar white representation of a figure with no kilt. Alberti pointed to the door with the kiltless glyph. "Through that door is the men's shower room. You can change in there."

Men's shower room. What the hell was a men's shower room? Graham shrugged. Must be yet another strange facet of this time. As Graham headed that way, the door bearing the simple picture of the kilted figure swung open and Lilia stepped out.

He halted, swallowing hard as every nerve ending flashed hot and ready. Lore a'mighty, what the devil was the woman wearing? It was more revealing than her clothing on the night they met.

Thick-soled black boots encased her feet and she held one of the dull-edged swords in each hand. Her plump, generous breasts shimmered and strained against the bit of silk binding them, accentuating the bare, *come to me* curve of her waist. Saint's bones. Her fine arse, round and full, perfect for filling a man's hands as he buried himself in her heat, swayed and bounced with a mouth-watering wiggle with every step she took. Her blonde hair was swept up into a high golden braid that swung back and forth like a gleaming pendulum marking time.

Graham struggled to generate the least bit of wetness back into his suddenly parched mouth. The woman nary needed a sword to stop an enemy. The mere sight of her in that shining black cloth encasing her curves like a second skin was enough to bring any man to his knees and have him begging for mercy—and more.

Lilia pointed one of her swords at the steel doors. "Hurry and get changed. We're going to practice in the ring for a bit and then we'll go out back and work with the horses." A relaxed smile lit her face as she slid her swords into the sheaths hanging from a bit of strapping hugging low around her fine hips.

Lore a'mighty. He would give anything to be that bit o' cloth.

She clapped her hands. "Hurry and get changed. When we're finished working out, I've got another surprise for you. I really think you're going to like it."

"Aye." Graham nodded with a tensed jerk. He dare say no more lest he shock the lass with talk of what he truly wished she would give him. The word *like* wouldn't begin to cover it. He forced his gaze away from her delectable curves and walked stiffly to the shower room.

He pushed through the door. The darkened room immediately flooded with bright light. "Sons a bitches!" What strange magic lit the flameless torches without even touching the wee switch embedded in the wall? The more he discovered the ways of this time, the less comfortable he felt in this worrisome place.

"Mistress Vivienne said ye might need a bit a help with the clothes." Angus shoved through the door after him, grinning as he folded his arms across his chest and looked around the room. "Can ye imagine the stonemasons it must ha' took to chip out all these wee squares?"

Graham dumped the clothes on the long wooden bench balanced on steel poles embedded in the floor. "I dinna give a rat's arse about the building of this strange place." He shucked his jeans into a pile at his feet then picked up the silky black trews and the strange tunic fitted with narrow straps at the shoulders rather than respectable sleeves. His biggest concern at this particular moment was stuffing his rock-hard cock into the thin bit of silk and putting it on display.

He was not ashamed of his man parts by any means but didn't wish to parade around like a stag rutting for a mate. That would not do at all when it came to making the proper impression on the fine Mistress Lilia and wooing her into becoming his wife.

"Think of Mother Sinclair." Angus leaned back against one of the many gleaming white basins jutting out from one wall. "That should take the bone out of yer willy."

The mere mention of Mother Sinclair was as effective as a heavy dousing of icy loch water. "Aye . . . now the problem is *keeping* the bone out of my willy." Graham yanked on the skintight trews, huffing as he strained to pull them up his muscular legs. "Hell's balls . . . these damn things are so swiving tight, my cock willna have room to raise its head."

Angus yanked down at his own crotch as he squatted up and down. "Nay. The things give. Ye best keep the old woman in yer mind. When Mistress Vivienne took to bouncing around in her wee lovely tights, my cock had no problem at all lifting his head to pay her proper respect." His eyes widened a bit, then he twisted around and picked something up from the steel shelf mounted above the ceramic basins. "I nearly forgot. Here." He held out a milky white object with black edging that covered the palm of his hand.

"What the devil is that?" Graham took the strange oblong bowl and studied it.

"Yer codpiece." Angus thumped on his own crotch. "The man Alberti said to wear the wee bowl to help protect yer parts lest a sword goes astray."

Graham squeezed the cushioned rim of the odd apparatus, then ran his fingertips around the slitted openings running the length of the cup. "A codpiece?"

"Aye." Angus winked as one corner of his mouth lifted in a wry grin. "Or do ye need a much smaller one?"

Sliding the cup down the front of his pants, Graham rolled his eyes as he shifted the piece firmly into place. He would not lower himself to such a discussion with the irritating numpty. He smoothed the tight shirt down across his chest, then sat on the bench and put on his boots. "See to it that ye control yer swordplay so ye dinna hurt the women." He stamped his feet down harder in his heavy boots as he stood and flexed to settle the strange clothing more comfortably in place. "If ye make the mistake of getting too rough with my Lilia— ye'll not be needing a codpiece at all after I'm done with ye."

CHAPTER 11

"Holy shit," Vivienne said in a voice filled with such awe, there was no doubt the term was meant as the highest possible compliment.

Lilia turned and immediately forgot to breathe. *Holy shit* didn't begin to cover it.

The formfitting workout gear accentuated every lickable ripple of Graham's muscular body that his silk T-shirt and jeans had failed to properly display. The bright floodlights lighting the practice arena reflected off the material stretched tight across his wide chest. The electric glow shimmied down his laddered abs, gleaming across his bulging thighs and all the delicious bumps and grooves in between. Every move Graham made flexed in a sensual *come and get some of this* kind of way.

"This place has never seen a man like that." Vivienne gently nudged her. "Close yer mouth, lovie. Ye've got a wee bit of drool running down yer chin."

Lilia slammed her jaws shut and swallowed hard. *Dammit.* She squirmed in place, painfully aware that her hardened nipples were dangerously close to slicing through her sports bra. She folded her arms across her chest and lifted her chin as Graham and Angus came to a stop in front of them. "Are you ready?"

"More than ready, lass." The twinkle in Graham's deep gray eyes left no doubt that he was in no way referring to swordplay. The tilt of his head, the way he leaned forward with a knowing smile—Graham was ready all right.

"Uhm . . . yeah." Lilia backed up a step and motioned toward a roped-off area without taking her folded arms away from her chest. "Vivienne and I have already stretched and warmed up. Why don't you and Angus demonstrate some of your techniques and then we'll pair up and try them out."

Graham gallantly bowed then swaggered over to the dueling arena and stepped over the ropes. He tossed one of the practice swords to the side and motioned Angus forward with the other one. "I prefer one sword. A fine shield would pair well with it but I can make do without one."

Awesome. She had been struggling with wielding a shield for ages. Maybe Graham could show her what she was doing wrong. Lilia held up a finger. "Hang on a minute." Her pinging nipples would just have to get over themselves. She trotted over to the long, broad storage chest along the far wall and hefted up the heavy lid. She'd never quite been able to get down good moves with a sword and a shield. Maybe concentrating on what Graham could teach her would keep her mind off the other *moves* she felt certain he would be more than happy to share.

She tucked four practice shields under her arm, let the lid to the storage chest drop, then hurried back to the roped-off mat. "These are a lot lighter than the ones used in competition but if you could show me what to do, I know I can adapt to the heavier model."

"Aye, lass, come to me." Graham smiled, waving her forward while at the same time pointing for Angus to leave the ring. "I'll have ye handling a shield with ease in no time at all."

Lilia stopped just outside the ropes, glancing first at retreating Angus then back at Graham. A disturbingly delicious mixture of *hell yes* and *oh shit* shifted her heart rate to pounding level as Graham held out his hand again and repeated, "Come to me, lass."

"I meant you and Angus could show me." Dammit. If her voice squeaked any higher, she'd sound just like that billion-dollar cartoon mouse. Lilia cleared her throat. This was ridiculous. She was the self-ordained queen of playing with fire and not getting burned. Emotions and trust stayed on lockdown—especially after making the mistake of trusting David to the point where he'd nearly financially destroyed her. Only Alberti and Vivienne could be trusted. She never made the same mistake twice. "Why don't you and Angus demonstrate?" There. That sounded much better.

"Och no, lass." Graham's smile showed no mercy. He slowly moved forward as though stalking her. "Ye'll learn much better firsthand."

She flexed both hands and rolled her shoulders. Fine. She could do this. Time to engage cold, calculating ice princess and shut out the dangers of the emotional world. Besides—once she immersed herself into the physical strains of learning the battle, she'd be fine. Working out until she collapsed had saved her empathetic ass on more than one occasion.

Turning to Vivienne, she held up her right hand. "Sword."

Vivienne lobbed the weapon across the broad expanse of floor as she'd done a thousand times during Highland competitions and medieval reenactments.

Lilia easily caught it, then slid between the ropes into the matted arena in one fluid movement. Straightening, she settled her footing, faced Graham, and nearly burst out laughing.

A mixed look of shock, disbelief, and open admiration filled the man's face. For some inexplicable reason, his expression filled her with the warmest sense of *happy* she'd felt in quite some time. He admired her. Excitement released a wave of pleasant fluttering through her middle. She'd bet money if someone pressed their ear to her side, they'd swear she was purring. She looped her hand through the two leather straps in the back of the shield and raised her sword. "I'm ready."

Graham blinked as though struggling to awaken from a trance. "Nay. Ye are not ready." He scrubbed his fingers through the dark reddish-gold mat of neatly cropped beard outlining his jaw as he approached her. He pulled the shield to one side, lifted her arm, and frowned down at the hand she'd latched through the straps. He tapped a finger against the inside of her forearm between the two loops of the shield. "Ye'll not be able to properly shield yer body with a hold such as this and ye could verra well break the small of yer arm with the first good strike from the enemy." He wobbled the shield back and forth, twisting her arm in the process. "When ye dinna have the one handle properly balanced in the center of the disc and covered by a weighted boss, it takes a great deal of strength to control the heft of the shield. Ye'll find yerself fighting the weapon rather than fighting yer foe."

In one brief explanation, Graham had nailed down exactly why she hated using a shield. Lilia slid her arm out of the loops and tossed the practice disc to the hard arena floor outside the ring. She pointed at it, then nodded to Alberti. "I know we can't have new shields before next weekend but maybe you could find some like Graham described and he can teach us all how to use them in time for the big meet later this fall."

"Absolutely." Alberti gathered up the practice shields and stacked them against the bleachers. "We'll donate these to the Beaver Scouts. I'm sure those innovative young lads will derive a good use for them." He bent and retrieved an additional sword, then tossed it into the ring. "Now, let's see a bit of swordplay. We've a reputation to keep and you've got a title to defend."

Lilia scooped up the second sword, rotating the weight of both weapons in her hands at a slow, familiar turn. Now, this was more like it. She turned and faced Graham. "Do you want another sword or are you okay with your one to my two?"

One of Graham's brows arched a bit higher, directly parallel with the lifted side of his mustache hiked above his patronizing grin. "Whatever ye think, lassie." His grin blossomed into a full-blown smirk. "Whatever ye think."

Good. He was underestimating her. Fatal mistake, handsome. She settled easily into sparring mode. More than one male competitor had lost to her with just such thinking. Ever so slowly, she circled to the left each time he inched to the right. Clockwise. Good. She liked clockwise.

Keeping her knees bent and ready to spring at a moment's notice, she kept her gaze locked with his. Most opponents telepathed their moves with their eyes and Graham seemed to be no different.

He lunged forward, sword raised, a smug look on his face.

She easily spun under his reach, then swatted his ass with the flat of her sword as she circled behind him and danced to the opposite side of the ring. Graham was holding back. If she wanted a good workout, she was going to have to get his ego engaged.

"Saint's teeth, Graham. I canna believe ye let a wee slip of a lass smack yer arse for ye." Angus clapped and crowed, then hopped to a higher level of seats in the bleachers. "The MacKenna shall hear of this, I grant ye that."

Graham rolled his shoulders and resettled the sword in his right hand as he paced around the opposite corner of the ring. Ignoring Angus's catcalls, he started circling her again. This time the placating smile was gone—replaced by a steely, slightly perturbed look of determination.

Good. Now that she had gotten his attention—time to play. She charged forward, swords raised, a screeching battle cry ripping free of her throat as she bent her knees and lunged.

Graham's eyes flared wider. At the last possible minute, he lifted his sword and muscled down to deflect her attack.

Blades crossed around his, she locked both arms and shifted her weight. With a hard, well-practiced turn of her wrists, she sent his sword flying out of the ring, then tucked and rolled, twisted around, and whacked him across the ass again. "Come on, Graham. You're not even trying."

"Ye are as worrisome as a biting midge. I gi' ye that." Nostrils flaring, Graham bared his teeth and dove across the mat after her.

She scampered up the taut, rubbery ropes surrounding the ring and launched herself into an arc passing over his crouched form just as he reached her. Landing with a rolling handspring on the other side of the ring, she spun around with swords lifted and ready, waiting for him to turn. This was pathetically too easy.

"Bad form, Lilia." Alberti brought his hands together with a sharp clap. "There'll be no ropes in the sword competition next week. You will refrain from using them to your advantage. That is not the behavior of a grand champion."

Angus thumped excitedly up and down the bleachers, his piercing whistle splitting the air. "Let the lass be, lad. She's besting the man good and proper."

Vivienne snuggled up against the ropes behind her, leaning in close so only Lilia could hear. "Give the poor man a wee break, ducks. Ye ken he canna help but hold himself in check against a woman. 'Tis the time he's from." Vivienne winked and added, "And he's met yer grandmother. I'm sure she's scairt the living shit out of him."

Well, there was that. Lilia barely turned, peeping back at Graham, currently glowering in the far corner. He was passing his sword between his hands in an agitated swinging move. She really should show him a little bit of mercy. The memory of one of Granny's many lectures played across her mind. *A wise woman always knows when to allow her man to at least think he's won.* A warm knowing lightened her heart and bubbled through her soul. For the first time in her life, She understood exactly what Granny meant. Time for a little male ego damage control.

Lilia stepped back to the center of the ring and settled her footing. "Alberti's right. I shouldn't have cheated and used the ropes." She tossed her second sword out of the ring, crouched low, and lowered her chin in a solemn nod. "I'm sorry and it won't happen again."

"And now ye think to treat me like a spoilt bairn who's greeting about how the other lads bested him?" Graham flung his own sword out of the ring and strode two broad steps forward. Eyes narrowed and jaw set, his hands flexed open and closed as his approach slowed to an ominous, purposeful stalking.

"Well . . . " She resettled her grip on her sword. She couldn't make this look too easy. He already suspected what she was up to. "You *are* pouting like a sore loser." She risked circling a bit closer. "Show me what you've got. I'm not afraid."

He didn't speak, didn't breathe, didn't even blink.

Lilia launched herself upward a half second too late.

Graham spun low, one long muscular leg extended. He effectively swept her legs out from under her then bore down with his teeth clenched in a fierce snarl. She tried to roll but moved too late, hitting the mat flat on her back with a stinging thud.

"Dammit!" She flailed to the left but a calloused hand latched hold of her right wrist and jerked her back. She needed to keep her sword. She rolled toward Graham, straining to keep him from prying her weapon free of her right hand. If she could just pass it to her left, she could retaliate with a few well-placed whacks and win her freedom. So much for letting him *think* he was winning. He was about to.

Graham squeezed her wrist tighter and brought his face close to hers. "Nay, lass. Ye'll not be using this poor excuse for a blade across my arse again." He plucked it free of her fingers and flipped it out of the ring. "And now I believe I owe ye a taste of yer own tonic." Kneeling down, he firmly planted one foot forward, then yanked her up from the mat and pulled her over his bent knee.

"Oh, hell no!" Lilia squirmed from side to side, kicking and flailing to escape. Dangling facedown, her ass hiked up in the air and an easy target, panic mounted as she strained to wrench her wrists free of his iron grip. "You are not going to whip my ass in the middle of this ring."

"The hell I'm not." Graham brought the flat of his hand down hard across the meatiest curve of her buttocks with a resounding smack.

"You son of a bitch!" Dammit, that stung. She curled forward, still trying to yank her hands free. If she could just bend sideways far enough, she could bite his leg. Another echoing smack stung across her backside. An enraged roar ripped free of her lungs.

He rolled her off onto the floor and stood. "Let that be a lesson to ye. Ye should always be prepared to endure whatever ye've meted out." He brushed his hands together as though they were soiled, then turned and stomped away.

Lilia rolled across the mat, wiggled under the ropes, and retrieved her sword. Grabbing the pointed tip of the dull blade, she drew it back, took deadly aim, then powered the throw with every iota of rage pounding through her. Nobody whipped her ass. Nobody. The sword flew across the room; end over end, then the weighted pommel connected with the back of Graham's head. Hard.

The man crumpled, dropping to the floor as though he'd been shot.

"Lilia!" Vivienne and Alberti scolded her in unison as they hurried to Graham's downed form.

"Well . . . shit." Lilia flinched with a delayed sense of guilt, heavily riddled with a *maybe I shouldn't have done that* feeling.

Angus rushed to her side. "Dinna fash yerself, lassie. The numpty's thick-skulled. Just ask yer kin." He winked, then swept forward in a gallant bow. "And I am honored to ken such a fine warrior."

"Not now, Angus." Lilia scurried around him. She couldn't see past Alberti and Vivienne to make out if Graham was moving. *Please don't let him be dead,* she silently prayed.

"Dammit to hell and back." A strained growl rumbled up from where Alberti and Vivienne crouched with their backs toward her.

She couldn't see Graham yet, but from the sounds of it, he wasn't dead—just thoroughly pissed. A sense of relief washed over her, allowing her to breathe again.

She hurried over, rounded her friends, and crouched down beside him where he sat rubbing the back of his head. "Uhm . . . I'm . . . sorry. Are you all right?"

"What the hell did ye do that for?" He kept his eyes squinted shut as he turned toward her. His grimace was colored a ruddy shade—whether from pain or anger, she didn't know . . . more than likely, a whole lot of both.

"She rarely thinks her actions through when she's suitably irritated." Alberti pulled Graham's hands away from the back of his head and pressed a towel-covered gel pack in place. "This will help. Hold it tight."

"Really. I am sorry." And she was. Lilia moved closer and gently replaced Graham's hands with her own, cradling the icy pack against the back of his head. "And Alberti's right. When I'm pissed . . . I don't always think things through before I act on whatever pops into my head. Gets me in trouble sometimes. Well . . . not just sometimes. A lot." She knelt closer, still holding the ice pack snugly against his skull. Bending forward, she peered up into his face. "I really am sorry. Forgive me?"

Graham's narrow-eyed gaze locked with hers. His mustache barely twitched to one side as an unreadable look settled across his face. "A kiss," he growled.

"What?" The ice pack slipped. Lilia caught it, palming it higher and harder against his head. The herd of butterflies residing in her stomach spread their wings and readied for takeoff.

Graham flinched, closing one eye as he leaned forward, pulled her hand away, and held the wad of towel and coldness himself. He wet his mouth and lowered his voice, easing a finger under her chin as he repeated, "Yer penance shall be a kiss."

Somehow, and she wasn't quite certain how, she and Graham were suddenly very much alone. Part of her panicked. But another part of her, the side of her warming to the opportunity and about to thoroughly embrace the idea of the seductive penance, thrilled at the prospect.

"A kiss?" she whispered.

"Aye." Graham slid his fingertips up along her jawline, cupping her face as he leaned in closer. His gaze lowered to her mouth. The heat of him drew her in, caressed her, promised to make her whole. The ice pack hit the floor with a plop as Graham curled his other arm around her waist and dragged her astraddle his lap. He never blinked, just pulled her against his chest. "A thorough kiss. A claiming and a proper apology, ye might say."

She framed his face between her hands. The soft springy curls of his closely cropped beard caressed her palms with an addictive tickling sensation that made her ache to hug him closer. A nervous giggle escaped her.

One burly brow arched a bit higher. "Ye laugh about yer punishment?"

"Your beard makes you cuddly—like a teddy bear." She caught her bottom lip between her teeth and held her breath to keep from groaning. Damn, she needed better filters on her mouth. She just called the man a freaking teddy bear. Lovely. At least she didn't add that she could just imagine how orgasmically wonderful that beard would feel tickling the insides of her thighs.

A deep chuckle rumbled him against her as his arm tightened around her and settled her more firmly in his embrace. "I'll be yer cuddle bear anytime ye wish." His fingers slid deeper into her upswept hair, gently steadying her as his mouth closed over hers.

Urgency. Need. Longing. Were those Graham's emotions she sensed or her own? She found herself melting into him, sliding her hands across his shoulders and holding him tighter as she closed her eyes and spun away into the heat of the kiss. He gently sucked at her lower lip then groaned as he opened her mouth wider, exploring, tasting, claiming until her body hummed with the need for more. She squirmed, still straddling his lap, arching against him as his hands slid down her back, cupped her ass, and pulled her tighter against an exquisite hardness that couldn't possibly be just a sports cup. She could take him right here in the middle of the arena. Alberti's dance class could just be damned.

Finally, she pulled back; struggling to catch her breath. "Uhm . . . penance. Paid up. Right?" They had to stop this before one of the dance class mamas showed up and either called the police or threatened Alberti—or both.

"Nay, lass." The emotions flashing in his eyes left no doubt that her penance had just begun.

CHAPTER 12

Thank the gods, Lilia had suggested changing back into their regular clothes before they went to the stable. A rock-hard cock and that damnable codpiece did not make for comfort. The wicked cup had nearly beheaded his aching member. Graham rolled his shoulders and yanked at the snug crotch of his jeans. These damn trews were nearly as bad. What the hell had happened to a man and the freedom found in soft leather trews and a freely flowing plaid? His poor bollocks couldn't breathe and his cock wasn't faring much better either.

"I'm a thinking ye best be striking whilst the iron is hot, I do." Angus fell into step beside him and elbowed him in the ribs. "And I owe ye greatly for the heat of that kiss back yonder."

"What the hell are ye talking around?" Graham shoved through a swinging gate opening into the largest covered paddock he had ever seen in his life. A great dirt plot was fitted with its own metal roof and walls—larger than the entire walled-in grounds surrounding MacKenna Keep. Who would have thought to build such a thing?

"Mistress Vivienne has grown quite friendly since watching ye fill yer hands with Mistress Lilia's fine bit a round arse." Angus's face fairly glowed as he threw out his chest and rolled up on the balls of his feet with each hopping step.

Graham spun, grabbed Angus by the throat, and shoved him back against the railing. "I'll rip yer disrespectful tongue out of yer head if ye ever speak in such a way again." No one talked about his Lilia in such a way. No one. Graham rattled him again, jerking Angus so hard that the man's head bounced back against the wall behind the railing. "Never again. D'ye understand?"

Angus squirmed to be free, hands flailing in the air as he sputtered and spit. "Forgive! I spoke ill without thinking." He coughed and wheezed in a strained gulp of air as Graham's grip tightened around his throat. "Meant no harm, man . . . I swear it! Willna happen . . . ever again."

Graham slammed him hard against the fence one last time then pushed him away. "See that it doesn't."

"Angus, are you all right?" Lilia rounded the corner, arms overflowing with folded padding and a leather saddle.

Angus bobbed his head up and down, stealing a quick glance at Graham as he coughed and thumped his fist against his chest. "Aye. Just fine, m'lady. I must have sucked a midge down my throat." He hurried away, trotting to catch up with Vivienne and Alberti, where they had disappeared into a separate wing of stalls.

Lilia hiked the saddle higher against her chest as she watched Angus scurry away. "I hope he's all right. His face is awfully red. That *midge* must've been the size of a horsefly."

"The man is fine." Graham hefted the saddle out of her arms, cutting off what he knew would be a protest with a stern shake of his head. "Not a word or I'll bend ye over my knee again."

She cocked a brow and totally failed at assuming a reprimanding scowl. The corners of her mouth twitched with a barely held-back grin as she spoke. "You and I need to have a long talk about your predilection for spankings."

Aye. That's it, lass. Allow yer heart to warm to me. Graham wasn't entirely sure what *predilection* meant but he did admire the wicked gleam in her eyes when she said it. "Aye, sweetling. I would love to have such a long discussion with ye anytime ye like." He swallowed a grunt as the inseam of his jeans cut even deeper into his crotch. Damn and for certain. A hard cock was a hindrance in these trews.

A delightfully rosy flush spread across her cheeks as she hurried around him. She cleared her throat and waved him toward a nearby line of stalls. "Uhm . . . this way. Odin's over here."

Graham chuckled to himself. Lore, he loved when the color rode high on her cheeks. They came up even with the stall just as a long black nose pushed open the top half of the wooden double door. Ignoring Graham and Lilia, the great black horse mouthed at the metal latch on the outside of the door until he managed to rattle free the mechanism and unlatch it. Then he nosed open the lower half of the door and walked out of the stall.

"Odin." Lilia's tone reminded Graham of a mother's affectionate scolding of a favorite child caught stealing a treat from the kitchens. "You know you're not supposed to do that."

The monstrous black horse whickered in reply and bumped his nose against her with an affectionate rub. She hugged his muscular neck, smiling as she stretched on tiptoe to scratch behind the tall horse's ears. Odin obligingly leaned her way, rumbling with a happy grumble as he guided her hand to the perfect spot with a turning of his head. "You knew it was time to ride. Didn't you?"

Odin replied by grumbling some more.

Graham settled the saddle across the low wooden railing beside Odin's stall without taking his gaze from the horse. Fine animal. Strong. Big. The perfect warhorse. The symmetry of the horse's lines gave testament to his pure blood—until Odin turned to fully face him. One side of the horse's face was badly scarred and his right eye was missing.

For the first time since they had arrived, Odin noticed Graham. The eerie-looking beast flattened his ears, bared his teeth, and stomped a pace toward Graham, clearly daring him to come closer.

"What happened to him?" Graham held both hands open, palms up, and didn't attempt to approach the horse. Before he had been cursed to live as a dragon by day and a man by night, he had spent his days training Ronan's father's horses. Respect from the animals had to be earned.

"Abuse." Lilia bit out the word as though spitting out poison. She pressed a cheek against the horse's neck and hugged him close again. "But Odin is *my* friend now and the one who hurt him will never deal out such suffering again. Ever." Her tone was cold, the look in her eyes even colder as she turned and leveled an emotionless gaze on Graham. "I do not tolerate the abuse of innocents."

Graham understood completely and admired her for it. "I hope ye killed the bastard slowly."

"Oh no," Lilia replied softly. "I didn't kill him—at least not physically. In this day and age, the destruction of a person's image . . . his public persona . . . is much more satisfying than their death." A chilling look of satisfaction settled across her as she affectionately combed her fingers through Odin's long black mane. "They suffer longer when you take them down financially and ruin their careers."

A yapping black ball of fur exploded out of the stall, charged between the great horse's feet, then came to a stop right in front of Graham. Tiny teeth bared, bouncing forward then back with every growling bark, the viciously vocal fury made it clear in no uncertain terms that Graham was not to take a step closer to the horse.

Lilia's hardened expression softened and she smiled down at the little dog. "And this is Buzz, protector and best friend to Odin, the fearless black Percheron."

Graham slowly squatted then extended the knuckles of his right hand toward Buzz. "Courageous beastie, ye are. Will ye find me friend or foe?"

"I wouldn't do that. Buzz hates every . . ." Her words faded away as Buzz eased forward, still rumbling but with his tiny, black nose twitching as he cautiously circled Graham's hand. The small dog paused, his short, pointed ears perked at Graham, then charged ahead with an excited wiggle and a high-pitched yipping bark. He bounced around, yapping and licking Graham's fingers as though they were reunited best friends.

"I've never seen him react like that with anyone except me."

Hands fisted atop her hips; Lilia studied the little dog as though he were some alien creature. "How did you do that?"

"Animals know." Graham scooped up the little dog and cradled him in one arm. Odin ambled forward with a grumbling nicker then shoved his velvety black nose between Buzz and Graham's chest. "Poor beast. Never fear." Graham understood Odin's uneasiness. "I would never hurt yer wee friend. Ye can be sure of that, I grant ye."

Odin jutted his nose up under Graham's chin and gently shoved as though testing to see if the man could be trusted. Cautiously, Graham lowered Buzz to the ground, then slowly straightened. He lifted his right arm out to his side, palm up. Best let the lad see his hand preparing to touch him. Let the beast know him to be safe.

Odin stepped forward, tilting his head so he might better see Graham, then tossed his head toward Graham's hand.

"Aye, lad." Graham gently rubbed the horse's muscular neck. "Ken me as a friend. I will never bring ye pain, I swear it."

Odin responded with a more relaxed whicker as he leaned into Graham's touch.

A sharp, hiccuping intake of breath pulled his attention away from the horse. Graham turned toward the sound. "Lilia?"

She turned away, ducking her head while furiously raking the back of her hand across her eyes.

Graham closed the short distance between them and turned her around to face him. "Do ye cry?" The lass had never given way to tears. What the hell had he done?

Lilia's pale brows arched higher and her eyes widened. The dark green of her irises shimmered brighter than fresh spring grass beneath the sheen of her unshed tears. She sniffed and blinked hard and fast, refusing to meet his gaze. "I'm not crying. I never cry. Not ever." The quiver in her voice betrayed her. "I was merely touched because Odin and Buzz trust you."

"Aye, and now ye ken ye should be able to trust me too. Why do ye find that so difficult to accept?" Graham gently cupped her chin and forced her to look up at him. "I only wish to keep ye safe." He didn't add that he would be making her his—not just yet. He must move cautiously even though he had little time. Instead, he brushed his mouth across the warm velvety seam of her lips, breathing in her irresistible sweetness as he whispered, "There is no shame in sharing yer tears. I have strength enough for the both of us."

His gut wrenched as she pushed away. Son of a bitch. That was the wrong thing to say. He pulled her back into his arms, holding her so tight, her head tilted back of its own volition. "Ye are a strong woman, Lilia Sinclair. Tears take nothing from that strength." Easing his hold, he cradled her head in one hand while softly stroking her face with the other. "Me mam, right afore she died, when I was but a wee lad . . . " Graham paused, struggling to sort through the myriad of emotions he saw playing in her eyes.

Help me find the words, he prayed. His mother had been so wise— surely her words would bring Lilia peace. *Help me,* he silently pleaded, then thanked the gods and his mother's memory when he felt Lilia gradually relax in his embrace. Certainty filled him as the rest of his mother's words came to him. " Me mam said tears are not a sign of weakness. Not ever. They are but the soul's way of growing and healing."

Lilia eased back but didn't pull completely out of his hold and he was sorely glad for it. But her unshed tears had disappeared. His lovely lass had quickly restored her calm mask of control.

"Why are you here?" Her chin lifted as she stirred in his embrace. "And I want to know the truth this time. Why did Granny really send you here?"

"Come, come," Alberti interrupted from the end of the line of stalls. "We're losing the day and still need to practice your running jump with Odin."

Lilia spun out of Graham's arms, then paused and turned back to face him. "This conversation is not over. I expect an answer later." She hefted the saddle off the low railing and clumped up a three-stepped stile leaning against the fence. "Come on, Odin. Playtime."

Odin flicked an ear then ambled over alongside the fence and patiently waited for Lilia to put the padding and saddle across his back. Buzz yapped around the base of the steps, bouncing and leaping around like a spring-loaded ball of fur. "I'll put you in your pouch in a minute. You know you have to wait until I get all the straps tightened down." Lilia gently pushed the little dog back as she descended the steps and deftly adjusted and tightened the saddle's straps.

Graham was impressed. Lilia's sisters might not have known anything about a horse other than which end ate and which end shit but it was obvious, Lilia was as comfortable with the beasts as he was. Perhaps there was hope of returning to the past and taking Lilia with him after all. Graham shoved the thought away. He needed to bide his time and not rush her. And he suddenly realized, as long as he was with Lilia, he didn't truly care what year it was.

"What horse shall I ride?" He'd be damned if he'd stand by and watch Lilia and the others enjoy a good ride without him.

"Alberti should have Freya ready for you." Lilia bent, scooped up Buzz, then fitted him in the custom-made leather pouch strapped across the broad slope of Odin's right shoulder. The little dog crossed his front paws atop the rolled lip of the thick leather bag, his little face split wide open in an excited doggy grin.

Graham rubbed Buzz's tiny head as he examined the odd-looking pouch that snugly held the wee dog against the horse's side. "Why do ye not allow the lad to just run along beside ye?"

Lilia pulled herself up into the saddle and settled comfortably in place. "He's too little and doesn't pay attention. I'm afraid he'll get stepped on." She reached down and hooked two short straps to the back of Buzz's harness. "I have to attach these straps to his harness because the little turd sometimes tries to jump out." Lilia shook her head and double-checked the silver clips. "Odin is an eighteen-hand horse. If Buzz jumps, it's a long way to the ground but Sir Yaps-a-Lot is fearless."

"Freya is ready for you." Alberti waved Graham forward.

A gray, slightly smaller horse, but definitely the same large breed as Odin, tossed its head in Graham's direction.

Odin stepped sideways, danced a few paces forward then retreated back. His nervous whickering echoed through the paddock.

"Odin's too restless today to practice the jump." Lilia smoothed the reins between her hands and nodded at the far end of the building where a set of double doors opened out onto a pasture. "We might have practiced too long the day before. I think he just needs a good stretch of his legs today."

Alberti studied the great black horse. "Agreed. Perhaps we did push a little hard." He motioned across the building to Vivienne and Angus. "We'll head back to the center and double-check the gear for the competition while you take Odin out for a bit of exercise. We can all meet at the paintball arena afterwards. Agreed?" He glanced up at Graham already comfortably settled in the saddle atop Freya. "I assume you'll be going with her?"

"Aye." Graham sat a bit taller in the saddle. "That I will." And if he had his way about it, it would be a long slow ride of discovery for both Lilia and himself. The ride held infinite possibilities.

CHAPTER 13

The slow steady thump of hooves against hard-packed earth broke the peaceful stillness of the afternoon ride. The well-oiled leather of the saddles softly squeaked, echoing the horses' meandering gait and the rhythmic motion of their powerful bodies.

Lilia pulled in a deep breath as they left the noise of the bustling city behind. She rolled her shoulders, relaxing as they steadily climbed higher, closer to the highest peak overlooking Edinburgh, known as Arthur's Seat. From a distance, the hillside looked as though it was coated in green and brown velvety moss. The closer they drew to the sharp definitions of the craggy hill, the more pronounced and varied the colorful tapestry of the flora became.

"Yer spirit finds peace here." Graham gifted her with a soft smile, nearly hidden by his mustache but clearly sparkling in his eyes.

She found it mildly disturbing that he could read her so easily but with Eliza's sharply declining health, it had been a rough few weeks. Maybe it wouldn't be so bad to relax her shields a bit and just *be*. She was weary—damn tired of running ninety to nothing until she collapsed in bed at night just to keep from feeling. She barely nodded. "Yes. Rides like this restore me." She turned toward

Graham and allowed a genuine smile, an expression totally free of carefully masked emotions. "What about you? How are you handling your discovery of the ways and whys of the twenty-first century?"

One of his burly brows arched a bit higher as his head tilted to the side. "'Tis . . . different."

A snort escaped her. "I bet." There was no possible way Granny and Trulie could've prepared Graham for all the mysteries of the future.

"But different is not necessarily bad." He shrugged and affirmed his words with a subtle nod. "'Tis what I seek after being trapped within sameness for well over three hundred years." Graham shifted in the saddle, encouraging Freya to slow her pace even more.

"Wait—what did you just say?" Lilia gently pulled Odin to a stop. Surely, she had misunderstood. Three hundred freaking years?

He shrugged again, squinting wistfully up at the bright blue sky combed with wispy strands of faded white clouds. "Did yer grandmother not tell ye about me when yer sister, Mairi, married Ronan Sutherland?"

Recollection rolled across her, triggering goose bumps across her flesh. The witch's curse. The Fates' evil priestess's fit of jealousy and the wicked spell she had cast, trapping Ronan's mother into the form of a wolf when the poor woman had been pregnant with Ronan. Then he'd been born a wolf too, living like one of the wild animals until he'd reached the age of puberty and learned he could shift into human form. Both Ronan and his mother had also been protected by a dragon.

She frowned, struggling to remember all the details. *No.* Not just some magically conjured dragon but another cursed soul who changed back to a man by night and was trapped in the form of a dragon by day. Another victim who'd unknowingly angered the sorceress while she was being drowned for practicing witchery. It had taken Ronan over three hundred years to find the woman capable of breaking the curse to make him mortal again. Her twin sister, Mairi, had been that woman.

Lilia pointed the loop of her reins at Graham. "So . . . you're the dragon?"

Graham shook his head and leaned toward her just a bit. "*Was* the dragon." He thumped a fist against his chest and smiled. "As ye can see, I am the dragon no more." His smile widened and he winked. "And now that the curse is broken, like yer good brother Ronan, I am no longer cursed with immortality." He sat a bit taller in the saddle and his carefree expression faded, growing thoughtful and almost sad. "Living forever can be a terrible thing—a sad lonely thing that I am glad to be done with."

Lilia shook her head and urged Odin to resume their ride. There was something about the look in Graham's eyes that unsettled her—something he wasn't saying . . . for fear of . . . what? What was he not sharing and why?

She twisted in the saddle and looked back at him again. "Just how old are you and what did you mean when you said you'd been trapped in sameness? If you lived over three hundred years, you had to witness everything changing around you."

Graham scowled back up at the sky, his eyes narrowing as he scrubbed his fingertips just under his bearded jawline. "I dinna ken exactly how old I am for certain. I was but a young man when the witch cursed me—barely past my twenty-third summer. And even though the spell allowed my human form to age a wee bit over the years, the length of the curse did not send me to the decaying weakness of the grave as it did Ronan's mother."

"What? Wait." Lilia motioned toward an inviting swell in the hillside just a few feet off the path. "Let's go over there and sit down. Buzz can stretch his short little legs and the horses can enjoy the breeze coming down the hillside while you explain yourself—in better detail."

Mairi and Granny had barely mentioned any particulars about Graham in his dragon form and neither had wished to dwell on all that had happened at the exact moment the curse had been broken. Lilia hadn't pushed them. They didn't need to describe it to her. She'd felt the exhilarating highs and the painful lows of that day through them—as though she'd been there and witnessed the event herself. Whatever had happened that day had created emotions strong enough that the feelings had easily crossed through the fire portal and hit her like a tidal wave.

Lilia pointed a warning finger at Graham. "And don't leave anything out."

"Aye, lass. As ye wish." He easily dismounted, then held up his hands to her. "Come to me. Ye've no wee steps to help ye down from the mighty Odin's back."

There were those three words again. *Come to me.* How could three innocent words trigger such a deliciously hot shiver and amp her up to *hell yeah* mode in the blink of an eye? Lilia clasped her hands atop the saddle horn and shifted the slightest bit. The warm leather between her legs suddenly seemed a bit damp.

Graham's mustache barely twitched and a knowing look glinted in his eyes as he held up his hands, fingers spread wide, waiting for her to lean down into his arms.

"I know what you're doing." She dove into his grasp then quickly slid to the ground and scooted free before he could pull her close.

"Do ye now?" His slow wink shifted her heart rate another notch higher.

Lilia brushed past him and led Odin to the rolling curve of softly waving grasses just behind the moss-covered swell of earth facing the panoramic view of the city below. She settled Buzz down on the grass beside the horse then plopped down on the knob of land and patted the ground beside her. "Have a seat and finish explaining your history."

An infuriating smile brightened Graham's face as he led Freya over to join Odin. "There is not that much to explain. I was dragon by day, man by night. Ronan's mentor and guardian. I dinna ken for sure but I'm fairly certain he and I didna age as severely as his mother because we wished to live past the curse—regain the lives that we had been promised if the wicked spell was ever broken. Ye might say our stubbornness added to our longevity."

All humor left his expression as he continued, "Ronan's mother,

Iona, her deepest wish was to join the only man she had ever loved—
and that man, Ronan's father, died by the witch's prophecy a year
after the black-hearted wench spoke the words that cursed us all."

He settled down on the hillside beside her. A sad smile curved his
mouth as he stared down at the long blade of grass he'd plucked from
a tangled clump and slowly wound between his fingers. "Never let
anyone tell ye immortality is a blessing. Outliving all ye have ever
loved or known is a cursed, lonely existence—and being tethered to a
mist-covered stretch of land or the sea makes that loneliness all the
sharper." His gaze gradually lifted from his hands and he stared out
across the land while pulling in a slow deep breath. "All feared the
dragon in me and kept their distance over the centuries. All but
Ronan and his mother. 'Tis a terrible thing passing yer days with not
a companion or heartmate to care if ye live or die."

She hugged herself against his words. Whether it was his sadness
or hers, or an aching combination of both of their emotions eating
away at her, she didn't know. All she knew for certain was, the twisted
knot of feelings made the center of her chest hurt. She understood
completely how he felt. She'd always felt . . . alone . . . even when
living with Granny and her sisters. She supposed it was because she'd
always had to keep herself centered and walled off against the
emotions of the world. Granny had taught her that was the only way
to survive life as a highly tuned empath. And now with Eliza, the only
person in this century who really understood her about to die, she
would be completely alone.

Alberti and Vivienne had tried their best to convince her they'd
fill the void after Eliza's passing but Lilia knew better. Everyone had
their own lives to lead, including her caring friends. Someday, they
would move on. The Fates had painfully made her see it, shown her
each of her friends' promising futures in a vision. The paths of her
life and those of her friends would eventually split off in their respec-
tive directions.

She reached over and barely ran a fingertip down his forearm that
rested on his muscular thigh. His light dusting of silver through the
dark hair shadowing the hard cut ridges and veins of his bulging

muscles made him shimmer in the sunlight. Such strength pulsed beneath that subtle sheen of pale silver and gold. His confession of solitude's painfulness drew her to him like the moon eternally draws the tide. He understood the gist of her feelings. Completely.

"I know what loneliness is," she said. "I've had to keep everyone away to survive." A bitter laugh escaped her then she quickly shrugged away the uncomfortably private confession. "Once Eliza moves on and Alberti and Vivienne embrace their fates, I could *go softly into the night* and not a soul on this side of the time portal would even notice my light was gone."

Graham turned toward her, slid a finger beneath her chin, and gently lifted, forcing her to meet his gaze. "I will not listen to such," he said.

He moved in closer, pulling her near and preventing her from turning away. "Yer precious light burns bright and strong against the darkness of this world. I grant ye, if that light was extinguished, it would be sorely missed."

He leaned in then, until his warm lips brushed her mouth, the softness of his mustache feather-light across her skin. She breathed in the heat of him, a heart-pounding shiver racing through her as his deep voice lowered to a rasping whisper, "I shall see to the tending of yer light, lass." He took her hand and pressed her palm to the center of his chest and held it there. "I'll thank ye to see to the tending of my heart."

"Why . . ." She wet her mouth as she watched the hypnotic motion of the tip of his tongue sliding back and forth across his bottom lip. "Why are you here?" She curled her fingers into the neck of his T-shirt, pulling him closer even though she knew the risk. She should push him away. So much safer if she just pushed him away. She blinked away the annoying voice of reason and rubbed the back of her fingers against the tempting heat of his skin. "Why are you here," she repeated, unable to resist leaning in to steal a nipping taste of his wetted and primed lips.

"To love ye." His arm circled around her, then easily pulled her into his lap. He held her close, his need . . . and so much more reaching out to her from the depths of his gaze. He silenced any further questions with a deeper, hotter kiss—one that set off a chain reaction of ripples across every nerve ending from her tingling nipples to the aching wet juncture of her thighs.

She pulled him down with her as he lowered her back across the softness of the hillside. The raw, urgent hunger of his mouth—kissing, tasting, ever so gently biting in all the best places. His teasing hands played lightly across her body, strumming her flesh as though he were a sensual musician and she his beloved instrument. A weak bit of common sense wallowed through the carnal inferno threatening to consume her and rage out of control. "We can't do this here," she panted out in a strained whisper. "Someone might see us."

An impatient, high-pitched yapping sounded somewhere behind her then a sharp tugging yanked at her braid. Even Buzz knew they couldn't do this in broad daylight on the hillside overlooking Edinburgh. The well-traveled path winding around Arthur's Seat was a favorite among locals and tourists alike. Odin whickered nearby and thudded a hoof against the ground, adding his opinion regarding their very public display of affection.

Graham rumbled with what sounded like a cross between a growling string of swearwords and an impatient groan as he lifted himself above her the barest bit. "I dinna give a sweet damn if the King himself sees us." He blew out a ragged breath. "But I would cause ye no dishonor nor bring ye any shame. Pray tell me, *mo nighean bhan,* I must have ye, where can we go?"

She forced herself not to pull him back down on top of her, fighting against her own sexual meltdown as she snuggled deeper into the crook of his arm. Dammit. Where could they go—fast?

Common sense overruled her libido again. They couldn't go anywhere and dive in *quickly* because she didn't have any protection with her. She flicked her fingers across the ridge of his ear, currently tipped a deep shade of red with his frustration. At least he was struggling with this just as much as she was. "You don't happen to have any protection with you, do you? Maybe in your back pocket? I rent an extra stall at the stables—with a couch—and privacy. I sort of lived there when I first adopted Odin." She leaned up and nuzzled her cheek against the soft springy curls of his beard. Again, the thought of that nicely trimmed beard providing a delicious tickle inside her thighs came to mind. She shuddered at the exquisite possibilities.

Graham pulled back and traced his thumb across her bottom lip. His gaze raked down her body, followed by a hurried caress. He huffed out another impatient groan then stole a quick glance around the hillside. "Protection, ye say? My finest dagger is in my boot. I'm never without it. What danger is there here? Do ye sense something amiss?" His frustrated gaze settled back on her. "And I'd never carry my dagger in my back pocket. Ye ken weapons. Why would ye ask such a thing?" He searched the area again, frowning at the two horses and the little dog behind them.

Lilia arched her back and looked back, giggling at the sight of all three animals watching them with ears perked forward in interest.

"Tell me what ye fear?" His arms tightened around her. "Ye ken I would never allow a thing to harm ye—even though, I must admit, the verra wanting of ye is sure to do me in quicker than a weapon any rogue of this time might wield."

She pressed her lips tightly together. The more sexually frustrated Graham became, the thicker and heavier his lilting brogue rolled across his tongue. It would be so wrong to laugh at him right now . . . especially since he had her buzzing in all the right places. "I'm not talking around your dagger or weapons. I was referring to condoms—uhm . . . sheaths?" Graham's confused stare threatened to release more giggles. "French envelopes?" What the devil did they call condoms in his time?

"The only sheath I own holds my dagger and I dinna ken what the hell a French envelope be." His eyes narrowed as a snorting giggle finally escaped her. "Why do ye laugh?"

"I am not laughing at you."

"The hell ye are not."

Lilia coughed away another giggle and stroked his face with both hands. "No. I'm not laughing at you. I'm laughing at our situation. I never dreamed I'd find myself so wound up in broad daylight on a hill overlooking the city. I'm not exactly a teenager without any options."

One of his brows ratcheted a bit higher and his eyes narrowed as he settled himself more comfortably on top of her, then wedged himself tightly between her thighs and propped his elbows on either side of her shoulders. A wicked grin tickled the corners of his mouth as he none too subtly ground his denim-splitting hardness against her aching mound.

She gasped, instinctively arching as she tightened her legs around him. "We . . . can't . . . do this here. We'll get arrested."

"Then the question begs asking again. Where shall we go?" Graham rocked his hips back and forth, successfully grinding home each and every word. "Quickly," he added with a teasing flick of his tongue against the tender flesh behind her ear.

Lilia clenched her thighs tighter, bucked once more, then rolled him to one side. "Back to the stable. Last one there has to get on top," she said as she scooped up Buzz and bolted for the horses.

CHAPTER 14

He would give anything to be that damn horse. Graham forced a hand down the front of the irritatingly tight jeans and adjusted his aching cock to one side—again. May the gods help him. The way that woman moved as she rode. He swallowed hard and urged Freya to a faster gallop to close the distance between Lilia and her mount.

Damnation. He nearly groaned aloud as Lilia hiked her fine round arse a bit higher in the air and crouched low over mighty Odin's back. Her tempting rear hovered mere inches above the saddle, waving back at him with just enough up-and-down swing to make him nearly spill himself in his trews.

The teasing glance she tossed back at him was like pouring fresh pitch on an already blazing torch. He stretched tall in the saddle, grinding his teeth as she laughed then turned back, urging Odin to thunder even faster toward the stable.

Last one there gets on top, she said. Gladly. He would take her any way she liked just as long as she allowed him to take her—and soon.

The horses pounded through the gaping archway of the wide sliding doors, prancing and tossing their heads as they playfully high-stepped around the barred-off perimeter of the dirt arena. Lilia allowed Odin to dance around the ring twice then gentled him to a stop beside the gate leading to the rows of stalls. In a fluid motion that made Graham's mouth water, she slid her legs to one side of the horse, rolled to her stomach in the saddle, then gracefully dropped to the ground.

Lore a'mighty. Thank ye, Mother Sinclair, for matching me with this fine woman. He would drop to the ground and kiss the hem of the old woman's cloak when next he saw her. Graham dismounted, then set to the task of removing Freya's saddle and draping it across the wooden stand waiting outside the stalls. He knew his woman well. She would not stand for the horses to be neglected. The quicker he saw to the needs of the beasts. the quicker she would see to his.

Released from his pouch strapped to Odin's shoulder, Buzz sped in circles around Lilia's feet as she hurriedly unbuckled the horse's gear. Mouth split wide in a doggy smile and his little red tongue a bouncing curl as he panted, Buzz strutted back and forth between Graham and Lilia as they stripped both horses down to nothing but their hackamores.

"Freya's stall is over there. Across the aisle from Odin's." Lilia pointed at an opened half door farther down the way. She wet her lips and her voice took on an almost sultry purr as she nodded to a closed door nearest them. "And this is the one I was telling you about. Earlier."

"Come, gentle Freya and mighty Odin. I will see to yer oats afore I see to yer mistress." Graham glanced pointedly at the closed door that surely promised to be the gateway to heaven. "Wait for me whilst I see to these fine animals." He shifted his gaze to her and winked. "I swear to ye, I willna be overly long."

His groin ached as she hungrily licked her lips, then nodded while backing toward the private stall. "While you do that, I'll call the others and let them know we won't be paintballing with them this afternoon."

He had no idea what the devil *paintballing* was and didn't truly care. He had much more enjoyable plans for this afternoon and if he had his way, those plans would extend well into the evening.

Both horses obediently plodded into their stalls—Buzz followed Odin into his and settled into his own corner that was obviously well-fitted for the needs of a tiny dog. Both horses hungrily shoved their noses into the feed buckets attached to the wall. Graham latched Odin's door, then paused as the horse lifted his head from his feed and angled around to fix a one-eyed glare on the latch.

"None of that, mind ye. Behave yerself and see to yer rest." Graham softly patted his fingers on the gate, then leaned forward and lowered his voice. "If ye grant me an uninterrupted afternoon with yer mistress, there will be a fine treat in yer wee bucket by morning, ye ken?"

Odin flicked an ear, agreed with a nickering grumble, then turned back to his feed.

Graham noted the emptiness of the stable as he made his way back to the private stall that Lilia had promised was more like a sitting room than a straw-covered pen. Good. Not a soul seemed to be around. There would be no more interruptions. He filled his lungs with a deep breath then pushed open the door.

"Hot damn! Viv left behind an entire box."

Graham didn't know what the blazes Lilia meant. In fact, he didn't know for certain what the devil she had just said. The sight before him effectively shut down his ability to reason.

Her back was to him. She had freed her long blonde hair from its braids and it cascaded down her bare back like a silken river of gold. Her fair skin shimmered a warm welcome in the flickering light of the thick pillar candles she had lit and placed around the room.

He pulled in another deep breath, grazing his knuckles against the roughness of his jeans as he appreciated the rest of her. His palms itched to cup the dimpled mounds of her ass and squeeze her to him. He tilted his head to one side as he eased another step closer. What was the woman wearing?

His erection nearly burst free of the damnable trews as she bent away from him to rummage deeper in an open drawer. She cast a wicked glance back at him and smiled. The gods had surely blessed him beyond words. He stripped off his shirt, never once looking away from the mouthwatering curves of her fine round bottom divided by that teasing bit of black satin and lace. "I've never seen a woman wear such . . . " Had he said the words aloud?

She smiled as she turned, clutching several odd-looking items, purple squares decorated with strange glyphs against the temptation of her bare breasts. "You've never seen a thong before?"

"A what?" He ripped open the metal contraption fastening his trews, shoved them to the floor then impatiently kicked them away. Those dusky nipples peeping through her golden curls. That black triangle of silk and lace covering her mound. What had she just said?

She seemed to float across the room. The color deepened on her cheeks as she examined him with a slow up-and-down sweeping gaze. "A thong," she repeated as she drew close enough to envelop him in her scent, barely brushing the bit of silk at the vee of her thighs against the tip of his aching member. Her grin widened as she leaned in, gyrating harder against him as she propped both hands filled with the strange purple packets on each of his shoulders and barely brushed her hardened nipples against his chest. "And I found Vivienne's stash of condoms and . . . uhm . . . toys."

"Toys?" What the hell did they need with toys? Surely the woman knew he would not be acting the bairn? Especially with nothing but a wee scrap of silk and lace betwixt their naked bodies.

She slid her arms around his neck, stretched on tiptoe, and pulled him forward. With a soft laugh, she tickled the tip of her tongue across his Adam's apple then nibbled kisses up his neck. "We'll help ourselves to Viv's lovely little purple packets but her personal toys are not for sharing. I just didn't want you to think they were mine . . . and available."

He had no idea what sort of toys she spoke of and didn't care. "Enough talk." He slid his hands down her back and filled them with the fine fullness he'd admired every time she had walked away from him. He hiked her up his torso, grunting with satisfaction when she wrapped her legs around his waist and held on with her thighs.

"Ye are a fine woman," he whispered into her hair as he turned and sat, lowering them both onto the plush cushions of the worn couch. He looped his thumbs in the strips of lace running across her hips then yanked hard, ripping the last barrier between them free and tossing it across the room.

"Those were my favorite pair of panties."

"Ye need no panties whenever ye are with me." He moved to pull her closer, but she planted a hand in the center of his chest.

With a gentle push, she smiled wickedly around one of the square packets she held between her teeth as she tossed the rest to the table beside the couch. She ripped the shining square open and drew out a strange-looking circle. "We'll discuss panties later." Leaning in, she barely grazed his chest with her nipples and rubbed against his rock-hard length. "Right now, I'm not interested in talking."

Aye. Neither was he. Sliding his hands under the cheeks of her ass, he raked his fingertips across her slippery wetness and pulled her higher up his chest while hungrily sucking her nipple deep into his mouth. Matching the teasing slide of his fingers across her slit with the gentle nipping and sucking of her delicious breast, he inhaled the sweet hot scent of her as she wriggled atop him.

She hugged him harder into the heaven of her bosoms, softly moaning as she gyrated and arched against him. So close. So ready for a wee bit more. As he nibbled his way to the other breast, he slid a hand down her outer thigh, then ever so slowly trailed his fingers around and up the smoothness of her inner thigh.

Her breathing came faster. Soft, endearing yips escaped her as he slid a finger deep inside her, diving into her burning wetness and cupping her in his hand. He pulled her nipple deep into his mouth as he ground his thumb around and around the knot of pleasure throbbing at her center. He slid another finger in alongside the first, then ground his thumb faster and harder against her pulsing button as the wetness filling his hand begged him to give her more.

She rocked against his hand, gyrating her hips as she arched and raked her fingers across his shoulders. Her slippery heat clutched and shuddered around his fingers as she trembled atop him. "Son of a bitch," she cried out, clutching his shoulders and grinding hard into his hand.

She finally collapsed atop him, pecking gasping kisses to his throat as he curled her tight against his chest. "You are . . . " She gasped and shuddered again while nuzzling her face into the crook of his neck.

"I am?" Graham encouraged as he cupped her breast and gently rolled her nipple between his fingers.

"Talented," she said as she slid to the floor and knelt between his legs. "And blessed," she added as she tickled a finger down the length of his hardened shaft then lovingly palmed his bollocks. She slowly rose higher on her knees, lifted her full breasts to his crotch, and nested his cock firmly between them. Without taking her eyes from his, she slowly slid her silky mounds of flesh up and down either side of his aching shaft.

"I am—" A groan escaped him and he clutched his thighs tight around her as she dipped her chin and ran her tongue around the engorged head of his shaft. "Indeed blessed," he hissed out as she took him in her mouth, ran her tongue up and down his cock, then squeezed him with a deep humming swallow.

Lore a'mighty. He didn't wish to spill himself too fast. He lifted her by the shoulders, nearly losing control as the suction broke and popped his cock out of her mouth. "I must have ye . . . now."

"Wait . . . " She pressed a hand to his chest, smiling as she held the circular oddity out to him. "We don't need any surprises."

"Ye held on to that wee bit of silk whilst I pleasured ye?" Perhaps he had not served her well enough. He would have to improve upon that in the future.

"It's important." She smiled as she pushed the circle around the head of his cock and unrolled it down the length of his hardness. Then she palmed his coated erection, rubbing the tip up and down through the hot slipperiness of her slit as she leaned up and raked her tongue across his nipple.

"Dammit to hell—I can take no more." He brushed her hand aside, rolled her to her back, then shoved in as deep as his cock would go. "I've ached to claim ye." He settled into her beloved heat, groaning in the bliss of the moment as he nuzzled his face into the silkiness of her hair.

She arched up against him, entwining her legs with his as she ground into him and gripped him with her thighs. "I don't want to feel anything but you," she whispered against his cheek as she raked her fingers down his back. "Make everything else go away. I just want to feel you."

"Aye, *mo nighean bhan.*" He braced himself above her, slowly slid out then shoved in deep again.

She dug her nails into his arse as she bucked beneath him. "Just you," she whispered as she met him thrust for thrust. "Don't want to feel anything but you."

"Ye are mine, *mo nighean bhan,* forevermore." He forced himself to withdraw until just the head of his cock throbbed inside her. "I shall guard ye heart and soul, I swear it." He buried himself with a slow deep thrust then pulled out again. Leaning down, he brushed his lips across hers, his heart soaring as her panting gasps brushed across him and her hands clutched at him. "Ye swear it, as well?"

"I swear." She bucked beneath him, then dug her nails into the flesh of his buttocks. The erotic sting nearly made him lose control. "Now seal this oath with fire and pound it home."

A groan escaped him as he slid back out then steadied himself for the task at hand. "As ye wish, *mo nighean bhan,* as ye wish." Then he hammered into the age-old rhythm with enough fire to incinerate both their souls.

CHAPTER 15

She hitched sideways with a jaw-cracking yawn then rolled and propped her head in her hand while glancing around the once neat and tidy room custom-made for comfortable lounging. Lilia huffed out a snorting giggle. They had lounged all right. In one afternoon, well—actually, one afternoon and one night —they had drastically altered the décor with used condoms and scattered clothing. It looked like someone had set off a condom bomb and the shredded purple packets had rained down like confetti.

She smiled down at Graham's peaceful countenance as a soft, whistling snore escaped his barely parted lips. The man had done himself proud. And—damnation, that beard and mustache of his were better than any battery-operated tickler she had ever owned. She flashed hot and wet all over again at the memory of Graham's expert use of what he had affectionately termed his lady pleaser.

She eased up from the pallet of sofa cushions and pillows they had piled on the floor, snatched the extra throw off the back of a chair, and wrapped it around herself like a sarong. Pulling a small bin out from under a table, she tiptoed around the room, retrieving and disposing of all the little balloons of love and their wrappers. Sheesh. They had gone through a bunch of the little buggers.

Her stomach growled just as she eased past Graham's head. Lilia froze and glared down at her middle. That had been loud enough to wake the dead. She held her breath and watched the steady rise and fall of Graham's chest. Good. She hadn't wakened him. The poor man had earned some rest.

"I am not asleep."

She shoved the trash bin back under the table, making a mental note to empty it herself before they left the stable. After all, there really wasn't any need for anyone else to see just how many condoms they had gone through. "I'm sorry. I didn't mean to wake you."

Without opening his eyes, he held out his hand. "I am not asleep. Come ta' me, love." His grin widened. "Keep me warm."

"You *were* asleep because you were snoring." She fished her jeans out of the corner behind the sofa and wiggled into them. She really didn't enjoy going commando but she hadn't brought any extra panties with her and he had totally destroyed her thong. "And you should be plenty warm. It's August. Remember?"

He rolled to his stomach, propped his chin atop his fists and smiled. "Take off those trews, dear one. They only get the way."

She picked up the empty condom box and shook it. "We're out of condoms. Sorry, but playtime is over. Time to go back to the real world." A gnawing sense of disappointment filled her.

He winked and rolled his upper lip, wiggling his mustache from side to side. "We can still enjoy a wee tasting this fine morning. We'll not need yer wee skin socks for that."

"You are insatiable." She shook her head as she turned back to her bag on top of the desk and rummaged through it for a hairbrush. Before she realized he had even risen from the pile of pillows, he sprung across the room and embraced her from behind. His morning wood prodded her in the rear as he pulled her back against his chest and filled his hands with her bare breasts.

"Aye, my woman. My hunger for ye never wanes." He rolled her nipples between his fingers and flicked his tongue along her nape and down across her shoulders.

She couldn't resist pressing back against the heat of his chest, lifting her arms to pull his head closer and arch her breasts more firmly into his teasing hands. He already had her aching to ride him and the crotch of her jeans was now soaked. "Maybe there are some condoms in the back of the drawer," she wished aloud as she ground her ass against his hardness.

He reached around her, yanked open the drawer to the desk, and rummaged through it with one hand. While doing so, he slid his other hand down the front of her jeans and worked two fingers inside her as he held her back against his chest. She arched into his expert touch, grinding her aching clit into the heel of his hand. Eyes closed, head thrown back against his shoulder, she squirmed and groaned as he deftly fueled her fire.

"What the hell?"

Gasping through a pre-orgasmic shudder, she forced her eyes open and stilled. "What's wrong?"

His wonderful fingers stilled inside her as he pulled a sealed clamshell package with a bright red-and-blue battery-operated cock ring and a matching star-spangled condom out of the drawer.

Lilia nearly choked on another snorting giggle. "Vivian must have kept her Fourth of July party favors here and missed that one." She glanced up at him, amusement building at the perplexed look on his face. "They were quite the hit at the party. I told her about the celebrations back in the States but apparently, when I mentioned sparklers, she got a little confused." Lilia cleared her throat and failed miserably at assuming a calm, matter-of-fact expression. "Quite the patriotic party favor, don't you think?"

Turning the package in his hand, he frowned down at it. His other hand remained anchored down the front of her jeans. "I ken what the wee speckled sock is but what the devil is that beebaw bit of gaudy jewelry beside it? 'Tis far too large for a finger but too small for a wrist."

She held her breath and counted to ten. Now was not the time to explode with uncontrollable laughter—not when the morning had suddenly gifted her with such a pleasant opportunity to introduce Graham to a fine example of twenty-first-century engineering. She took the package, eased his hand out of her jeans, then turned to face him. With an innocent smile, she tapped on the knobby-fingered knot at the top of the ring. "Would you like to see where you wear this?" She glanced pointedly down at his erection, smiling as the head of his cock slightly bobbed as though agreeing of its own accord.

Understanding dawned across his face like the rising of the sun. "Aye," he rumbled out as he quickly undid her jeans and yanked them to the floor. "Teach me."

The heat of the room increased exponentially. She squirmed in place, considerable dampness wetting her thighs. What on earth was up with her? They had been at it like rabbits all night with just a few naps in between. How could she still want him so badly—as if she'd never had him at all? She pointed to a heavy, ladder-backed chair sitting beside the pallet of cushions. "You go sit over there while I open our toy."

He obediently walked to the chair, flexing his sculpted ass and thighs with every slow step. The grand tease knew what he was doing and did it well. She shook herself free of the mesmerizing play of muscle beneath burnished flesh, grabbed a pair of scissors out of the desk drawer, and hacked at the plastic clamshell packaging until she managed to work the precious playthings free.

Sitting with his legs spread, his cock at attention, and his hands folded behind his head, he slowly licked his lips as Lilia walked toward him. "Ye've got me aching as though I've never felt the wonder of yer heat before."

"Good." His feelings mirrored hers. She knelt between his knees, then leaned forward and ran her tongue from the base of his shaft slowly up to the tip. His sharp intake of breath made her smile. Wait 'til he felt the vibrating cock ring while he was buried inside her. She squirmed in place, her clit throbbing at the very thought of it. In one sliding motion, she smoothed the star-studded condom down his swollen shaft. "Ready?"

"Oh . . . aye, love. That I am."

Heart pounding with anticipation, she worked the cock ring

down over the condom and settled it against the base of his impressive erection. "Not uncomfortable?" She watched him closely. The man was well hung. She didn't want anything to damage his fine piece of artillery.

He shifted a bit in the chair. "Nay. Not too tight—just different."

She rose, straddled his body, then leaned forward and gave him a reassuring, blood-heating kiss. Then she leaned back with a smile. Rubbing her body up and down his torso, she pushed her breasts together and guided her nipples to his mouth.

He slid his hands up and down her back as he sucked and nipped at her. The head of his cock bounced against her, teasing up and down across her slit until he groaned, grabbed her just below the cheeks of her ass, and slid her down into place.

With his hands still kneading her breasts, she slowly rocked backward then forward on his long hard shaft, then stretched forward and claimed his mouth, tonguing and suckling him with the same erotic rhythm of her body. His hips matched her rocking movement, bucking and arching into her as she rode faster.

She lifted her mouth from his, smiling as she slid her hand down between them. She wanted to see his face when she flipped the switch. Oh so carefully, she found the knobby bead snugged up against her clit and squeezed. A moan escaped her as the cock ring and its promising little knot of *hell yes!* vibrated to life.

Graham's eyes flew wide open and his hands clutched at her ass. "Saint's teeth!" He peered down between them.

"Do you like it?" How could he not? She rocked and ground into him harder and faster. At the rate she was careening toward orgasm central, this might not even be an eight-second ride.

"Son of a bitch!" He clutched her harder, bucking his hips to drive himself deeper.

Orgasmic bliss overtook reason. Lilia grabbed hold of the spindled tops of the chair, crying out and hanging on for dear life as she shuddered and shook atop his buzzing shaft.

He roared and rolled them to the floor, lifted her ankles to his shoulders, and pounded furiously into her. Veins bulging, muscles tensed, he hammered harder and harder until another wave of shuddering orgasms rocked through her. He suddenly stiffened, clutching hard against her with a strained groan. Lilia fell limp back into the pillows, her legs still draped over his shoulders as he pumped and spasmed inside her. Not bothering to open her eyes, she slid her hand down to the magical ring and squeezed the wondrous little clit-pleasing knob until the vibrations stopped.

He collapsed atop her, still gasping for breath. "Never in my life. . ."

"I know." Lilia snuggled against him with a contented, purring groan. "Aren't batteries awesome?"

"Aye." Graham pecked a weary kiss to her damp temple. "The wee bastards are a gift from the gods themselves."

CHAPTER 16

Graham bent, hanging onto the door of the strange metal box as he sorted through the items in the bright frigid interior. Not a bit of meat to be found. What he wouldn't give for a bit of venison. A hard clear box filled with what looked to be a block of yellow cheese caught his attention. That would have to do. He tucked it into the crook of his arm and closed the door to the magical tomb of coldness.

"I had begun to think ye'd gone back to the past without me." Angus pushed through the swinging kitchen doors, yanked a chair out from the table, and plopped into the seat. "Where the hell were ye last night?" He drummed his fingers on the table. The drumming gradually faded then stopped. "Never ye mind. I ken by the look on yer face."

Graham ignored him and retrieved a crusty loaf of bread from the tin at the back of the counter. When he turned back toward Angus sitting at the table, he froze in place. "What the hell happened to ye?"

Glowing yellow-green splotches of color stained Angus's arms, hair, and the lower half of his face. The only part of him completely free of the strange splashes of color was the area around his eyes.

Angus shook his head and lifted his hands in despair. "I didna ken this thing they called a paintball gun and I didna wield the weapon well. They said I shouldha wore the full face mask and overclothes they offered but I dinna think it wouldha helped my aim a damn bit."

Graham plopped the bread and cheese on the table, returned to the cold box, and retrieved a glass pitcher filled with the orange-colored liquid Lilia had called juice. "Yer bit of paintball war was late yesterday, was it not? Do ye not think ye should be washing this morn?"

Angus stared at Graham as though he thought he had lost his mind. "I washed yesterday morn. Ye ken 'tis not healthy to wet yer body overly much—even in the heat of summer."

"Ye smell worse than a Highland goat most of the time. I ken that well enough. I grant ye would find ye survive just fine if ye found yer way to the water a bit more often than ye do." Graham wrinkled his nose as the oddity of the small, bladed machine whirling on the kitchen counter blew a gust of air past Angus and wafted it over to him. Angus might have washed as recently as yesterday but ye would never know it by the smell of him. The man reeked.

"Never ye mind about me washing. Where be yer lady?" Angus stretched across the table and helped himself to a chunk of the cheese.

"My fine woman took a . . . " Graham paused, glared at Angus, then drew out the word slowly, *"shower."* Angus was oblivious to the subtle hint. There was no changing the stinking bastard. Graham huffed out a disgruntled breath while nodding toward the door leading to the garage. "And now she's gone for her morning visit with Mistress Eliza."

"Ye ken 'tis not going to be pleasant when the old woman decides the time has come to move on?" Angus wrapped his hand in his shirt-tail, then scrubbed at a particularly large splotch of green paint staining his arm.

Graham tore off a hunk of bread, wrapped it around a bit of cheese, then shoved it in his mouth. He washed it down with a deep draw of the orange liquid. Strange, stringy stuff, that juice. Lilia had called it *pulp*. He swished another swallow of the tangy liquid around his mouth and slowly lowered the glass to the table. Angus was right. Lilia would not handle her guardian's passing well. "That unpleasantness is one of the verra reasons we are here." He refilled his glass then clamped the lid back on the jug and pushed the juice to the center of the table. "Do ye not recall Mother Sinclair telling us so?"

Angus spit on the length of shirt wrapped around his hand then scrubbed harder across a bright yellow splat covering his forearm. "Even spit doesna work. What the hell is this dye made of?" He wrestled his hand free and yanked his shirt back in place with a shrug. "Mother Sinclair told us too much. She had me poor head aching with all her nattering."

The man had a point. Graham wouldn't argue the truth of that statement but he wasn't fool enough to say so aloud. The old she-devil could damn well be listening somehow. He cut off another chunk of cheese, bit into the waxy, pungent bite, and pondered as he chewed. There was not a doubt in his mind where Lilia got her fire.

Lilia. His soul exhaled a relieved sigh at the thought of her. Never in his life had he ever hoped to meet such a woman as Lilia. Now here he was, blessed by the Fates and Mother Sinclair herself with a match to the incomparable lass. They had to take the oath. Soon. His soul wouldn't rest until he was properly tied to his lady love for all eternity.

Vivienne burst through the swinging kitchen door, one hand holding aloft one of the strange metal squares—one of the *phone* things. "I just got a text from Lilia." She came up short behind Angus, a grimace of distaste puckering her face as she quickly sidestepped away from him. "*Phew,* love! Ye stink like shit."

A look of shock widened Angus's eyes. He jumped up from the chair and hurriedly edged toward the back staircase. "Forgive me, lass. I was too weary to wash last night. I was just about to shower when Graham begged me to sit with him a bit and advise him."

"Ye are a lying bastard." Graham folded his arms across his chest, leaned back in the chair, and nodded to Vivienne. "What were ye saying about my Lilia?"

Vivienne's brightly stained red lips tightened into a flat worried line as she glanced back down at the square of black and silver in her hand. "She says I'm to bring ye to hospital. She says she needs ye." Tears glistened in Vivienne's eyes as she worried her fingers through her spiked red hair. "Mistress Eliza must be worse." She hurriedly clicked across the room in her spike heels, pinched free a paper napkin from the stack, and pressed it to the inside corners of her eyes. Waving Graham forward, she hurried to the door leading to the garage. "Come on, ducks. Time's a'wasting."

A sense of dread and urgency launched Graham out of the chair and across the room. His poor dear lass. He had to get to her. Fast. "Get me there. Now."

Angus started toward Vivienne then tucked his face close to his armpit and hitched in a loud sniff. He wiggled his nose and ducked his head. "I best stay here and have a wee scrub."

"Ye think?" Vivienne rolled her eyes then waved for Graham to hurry. "Come on, love." She hurried them both down the steps, through the garage, and out the rear door leading to the street. She paused once they reached the sidewalk and glanced back at Graham with a worried glance. "I'm not sure how we'll be fitting ye in my wee Audi. But we've got to find a way."

"I'll ride on top of the damn thing if I must." Graham hurried to the passenger side of the bright red bit of curiosity that looked like it was made for a child rather than a full-grown man. He bent down, yanked open the door, and peered inside.

Vivienne pushed past him, bending down to grab hold of a black handle. She lifted it up and shoved the tiny seat as far back as it would go. "There. Now ye'll have a wee bit more room." She scurried around to her side of the car and hopped inside. "Come on, ducks. I've not got a good feeling about that message."

Graham backed his arse into the tiny vehicle, whacked the back of his head on the doorframe, then shoved himself into the seat. He curled forward, scrubbing the back of his skull as he folded in his long legs. Knees nearly up to his chin, he sat hunched forward, one arm wrapped around his bent legs. A grunt squeezed free as he stretched sideways, hooked the door handle with a finger and pulled it shut.

"I don't think it's closed properly." Vivienne tapped on a glowing glyph on the panel in front of the tiny leather steering wheel. She gave an apologetic shrug. "Sorry, lovie. See the little door that's lit up a bright red? That means ye've got to give it another go."

"Surely ye jest." Graham grunted and huffed as he squirmed around to better fit in the tiny space.

"Sorry." Vivienne tilted her head and tapped on the glowing board again.

"Never in all my days did I ever dream I would be trapped inside a metal box by choice." He wormed his hand down beside his right leg, found the handle, opened the door then yanked it shut again. Hard.

"That's it, lovie! Light's out now."

The vehicle roared to life. Graham squinted his eyes shut and sucked in a deep breath. He refused to get ill. This was no time for weakness. His precious Lilia needed him.

They picked up speed and careened around what seemed like an endless stretch of sharp turns and curves, his body swaying from side to side with every turn. His stomach gurgled and lurched. He tightened his gut and swallowed hard. Lore a'mighty. This woman would surely kill them both. Vomiting became the least of his worries.

"I'll have ye there in no time flat."

"Just have me there in one piece," he said through clenched teeth without opening his eyes.

The humming beast squealed and growled as they swerved and bounced through another set of turns, then came to a screeching halt with a hard jolt.

"Open yer eyes, my brave beastie. We have arrived."

Graham risked cracking open an eye and looked around. Aye—he know this place. 'Twas the cave Lilia had called the parking garage attached to the building where Mistress Eliza waited for death.

"Thank the gods." He shoved open the door, whacked his forehead against the frame, then rolled out to the ground beside the infernal contraption. "Sons a bitches!"

"Lore a'mighty, lovie. Now the front of yer nogging has a knot to match the one in the back." Vivienne grabbed his arm and helped him stand. She frowned as she shoved a hand into the pocket of her jeans. "I just got another text. Pray we're not too late."

Graham didn't wait to hear what the wee contraption reported. To hell with texts. Lilia needed him. Now. Ignoring Vivienne's shout to wait, he loped through the maze of metallic beasts, found the magical sliding doors, and pushed his way through them before they'd fully opened. The metal doors with the buttons. Where the devil were the double metal doors?

He careened down a vaguely familiar hall of gleaming white tiles and metal plaques bolted into the walls. There. The metal doors. The silver portals with glowing buttons and arrows. Several people stood in front of his target.

"Begging yer pardon." Graham eased through the small group and bounced his fist against the button with the up arrow. 'Twas already lit. He scowled down at the button with the down arrow. The down arrow was lit too. What the hell did that mean? He needed to go up. Aye. Up seven levels. He clearly remembered Lilia saying she would hit the seven button when last they visited Mistress Eliza.

A sharp ding sounded and the metallic doors finally whooshed open. Graham plowed inside, growing more frustrated by the second as more and more people crowded into the wee box with him and jostled him to the back. What the devil did they play at? He would never get to the panel of buttons with this many folk stuffed around him. "I must get to the panel. Begging yer pardon. I have to push the seven button."

"Seventh floor?" A young man that greatly resembled a ruddy-coated Highland cow chewing its cud stood beside the wall of magic buttons, his finger poised as he waited for Graham's response.

"Aye, lad. Please hurry. 'Tis quite urgent." He flexed his hands open and closed against the roughness of his jeans as he waited for the doors to shut and the damnable box to move.

Several of the other people called out different numbers to the shaggy-haired lad beside the wall. He obligingly jabbed a finger against the corresponding buttons until several of the numbered circles glowed with their tiny lights. The doors slid shut and the box jerked with the same stomach-thumping bump as it had the first time Graham visited the strange place.

They didn't travel but a few seconds before the box shuddered to a stop and the doors slid open. Graham shoved his way to the front. He had to get out before the doors closed again.

"Nah, mate." The pimply-faced lad pressed a hand to Graham's shoulder. "Ye said seventh floor, aye? This here's just the second level."

Son of a bitch. Why the hell had he not waited for Vivienne? "I thank ye." Graham stiffly bobbed his head. Damn, if this didn't sorely grate on his pride. "I canna make out the strange glyphs. I thank ye for yer help."

"Forgot yer glasses, eh?" The young man smiled and nodded. "Me da has the same problem. Can't see a fecking thing without his specs." Whatever the boy was chewing popped and crackled with his toothy smile.

"Aye." He didn't have a clue what the lad had just said but apparently, the kind boy was offering a wee bit of balm for his bruised pride.

The box shuddered to a stop again and the doors shushed open. Graham glanced over at the lad and waited.

"This is yer floor," the boy whispered with a wink.

"Thank ye kindly." Graham rushed out, filled his lungs with a deep breath then slowly hissed it out between clenched teeth. Thank the gods. He glanced around. Aye. This was the place. He hurried down the gleaming hallway. An eerie quietness filled the air. The few people standing around softly murmured to one another in low reverent tones. Even the beeping of the strange machines seemed muted. Death walked these halls. He stifled a skin-prickling shudder. This place must surely be the gateway to the other side.

He gently pushed open the door to Mistress Eliza's room and his heart fell at the scene revealed as the door slowly swung aside. The tiny old woman lay curled on her side in a tight knot as though she were still in the womb. Lilia had pulled a chair close to the bed, her face pale and shining with tears as she hugged one of Eliza's mottled, blue-veined hands tight against her cheek.

Lilia's eyes were closed. She rested with her head on the bed, tucking her shoulders up under Eliza's thin arm in a heartbreaking attempt at gleaning one last frail cuddle. Eliza's other hand rested on Lilia's head, the knotted arthritic fingers barely twitching as though struggling to find the strength to stroke the tangle of golden locks flowing across Lilia's shoulders.

"Lass . . . " Graham eased forward. "I am here." It was all he could think to say. Words could not begin to convey how badly he wished he could shield her from this sorrow.

Lilia slowly opened her red-rimmed eyes, her lower lip quivering as she tearfully whispered, "She's leaving me, Graham. Please . . . please make her stay." She hiccupped a soft sob and a new onslaught of tears streamed down her face. "Please," she whispered. "I can't take it if she leaves me now. Don't let her—please, not yet."

Lilia's pain tore into him, cutting him deeper than any length of steel ever could. It grabbed hold and twisted his heart until he was consumed with how terribly she was suffering. Nothing else mattered but getting his Lilia through this darkness.

Graham knelt at Lilia's feet and gently wiped the backs of his fingers across the curve of her wet cheek. Lore a'mighty. He wished he could bear this sorrow for her.

When Lilia finally met his gaze, he nodded at Eliza. The rattle of the dying woman's labored breathing was growing more pronounced. "Mistress Eliza will always watch over ye, my dear sweet love. She will never really be gone from ye—not ever. Ye ken that—aye?"

"But I want her here." Lilia's voice quivered, hitching in and out, weak and trembling as she gave way to more tears. "I need her. I am so afraid of life here . . . without her."

"Ye have nary a thing to fear, my darling one." Graham drew closer, gently combing his fingers through Lilia's tousled hair and smoothing it behind her ear. "I swear to ye, ye will never be alone. I swear it upon every breath I take and with every beat of my heart."

A harsh rattling wheezed free of Eliza. Her thin pale lips twitched. "Bind." One word. Exhaled in a barely heard whisper. Her thin form shuddered, death rattling within her shallow breathing as she struggled to speak louder. "Witness ye bind."

Lilia pressed a kiss to Eliza's cold, bent hand then tucked it gently atop the pillow. She slowly rose from the chair, her hand lightly caressing Eliza's colorless cheek as though branding the feel of those last moments permanently in her memory. She straightened the covers across Eliza's thin sagging shoulders, her fingers trembling as she smoothed back the sparse, cottony bit of hair surrounding the failing woman's drawn face.

Tears streaming down both cheeks, Lilia sadly shrugged. "She keeps saying that and I don't know what she means. *Witness ye bind*?" She turned to Graham, coughing out a choking sob. "How am I supposed to make this easier for her if I don't know what the hell she wants? Why don't I understand?"

Graham ached for Lilia. Lore a'mighty, he had never felt so helpless and he hated that damn feeling worse than anything he had ever encountered before. He took Lilia's hands and gently pulled her closer. He turned her toward Eliza, hugging her back against his chest as he pointed down at the dying woman. "Look at her. See the existence she now has. Would ye wish her trapped in such a prison a minute longer? I have learned ye well by now, my love. I ken ye would never wish Mistress Eliza's suffering prolonged just so ye could keep her by yer side."

Lilia rubbed her cheek against her shoulder, staring sadly down at Eliza. In a small voice, so very soft and low Graham had to bend closer to hear it, she replied, "No." She barely shook her head. "I don't want her to suffer any longer. But I don't understand her request. I don't know what she wants me to bind." Her face crumpled as she pulled aside and stared forlornly up into his face. "I can't live with myself if I can't grant this wonderful woman her last request—not after all she has done for me."

Graham brought Lilia's knuckles to his mouth and pressed a gentle kiss against the coolness of her fingers. Slowly bending, he eased his dagger out of its sheath inside his boot, held out his wrist, and rested the edge of the blade against it. "She wishes us bound. Joined in the old way. Eliza shall be our witness. She will carry our vows with her and record them in eternity's books on the other side."

Lilia looked up at him, her deep green eyes glistening with yet-to-be-shed tears. She trembled, furtively glancing down at his extended arm, then back up to his face. Graham waited to make the cut, fearing she would collapse. He didn't wish to foist anything upon her that she didn't want but this was right—this was how it should be. He felt the pure truth of it deep in his soul with more certainty than he'd ever felt about anything.

"Bound forever?" she finally whispered. "Married?"

"Aye." Graham held his breath, willing her to say yes.

She looked at Eliza, then looked back to him, a maelstrom of emotions and tears shining in her eyes. "Joined," she said with a note of finality.

"Aye, love. Joined for all time." Graham held out his hand. "Ye ken our souls were matched long ago. Ye are mine as I am yours."

Without another word, she placed her wrist in his palm, staring forlornly down at her arm. "Bind us," she whispered without looking up.

With a quick slice, Graham drew his own blood first then swiped the razor-sharp blade across Lilia's pale skin. Slipping the dagger into his belt, he pressed their wrists together, holding them tight with his free hand. A sense of peace filled him—a contented warming like he had never known before. This woman was his other half, the true match he had never dared hope to find.

"Say ye will be my wife. In this life and the next. Say ye will gladly bind yer soul to mine. The words will come to ye—just as they did centuries ago when our souls first met and we pledged our love for the verra first time." A sense of completing his destiny washed across him, strengthening him as he bent and kissed her trembling fingers again. Aye. This was meant to be. The Fates had matched them well. *"Tha gaol agam ort, mo nighean bhan."*

At her quizzical look, he leaned forward, kissed the tip of her nose, and repeated, "I love ye, my fair-haired one."

She caught her bottom lip between her teeth. The corners of her mouth drooped even lower as she blinked hard against the spilling of more tears and stole another glance over at Eliza. She squeezed his hands, closed her eyes, and pulled in a deep hitching breath.

Graham waited, holding his breath, all the while sending up a silent prayer that she would grant him the priceless gift of her love. *Please let it be so.*

"I will be your wife in this life and the next, if you swear to be my loving husband. I will join my soul to yours for all eternity, if you swear to guard me against the darkness that threatens to steal me away." She sniffed, eased forward, and looked sadly up into his eyes. "I already love you more than I ever thought possible and I am trusting you with my heart and soul." She wet her lips, looked back at Eliza, then returned her gaze to him. "Let these words forever bind us. Let our blood seal our souls. As time and fate are our witnesses, let us forever be as one." Tears streamed down her cheeks as she continued, "For the good of all, with harm to none, so mote it be, so let it be done."

"I swear to all those things and more," Graham said. "So mote it be."

A sudden gust of wind whooshed and moaned around the room, billowing out the bed curtains and scattering papers across the floor. The windows rattled in their casings. Tinkling laughter and lilting music—a tune as bawdy and loud as a barroom song filled the air.

"I love ye, my dear sweet child, and I'll be a watching over ye," echoed from somewhere near the ceiling as the howling wind died down. "Dinna fash nor waste another minute with tears. I am free now and ye ken well that I shall always be with ye." The windows rattled one last time as Eliza's laughter softly faded away.

The boxes at the head of the hospital bed beeped and blared out their alarms. Graham scowled at the biggest of the black screens—the one with the bright green line running flat across the center of the screen. "What does the line mean?" he asked as a pair of nurses burst into the room.

"It means she's gone," Lilia whispered.

CHAPTER 17

L ilia smoothed her fingers across the satiny grain of the polished wooden box. So smooth. So cool to the touch. So . . . serene. She embraced the emotions with a sad smile. Even from beyond the grave, Eliza watched over her and sent her bitter-sweet hugs. She felt it as surely as if Eliza stood right beside her.

The box's beveled edges highlighted the wood's golden grain. No bigger than a simple dresser box made to hold bits and baubles of a young girl's jewelry, the small container of oak held all that remained of the most enigmatic woman Lilia had ever known. How odd that such a larger than life, loving person could somehow be reduced to a plastic bag of dust that wouldn't even fill a shoebox.

"Ashes to ashes, lovie. Ye ken well and good that Mistress Eliza isna in that wee chest. 'Tis only the remnants of the shell that once housed her lovely soul." Vivienne pulled a chair up to the table and gently laid her hand on Lilia's. "Just a shell. Nothing more than a temporary vessel for a fiery, awesome-sauce spirit that could never be stopped whenever she made up her mind about what was to be done."

"The house is too quiet. It feels hollow now that I know she's never coming back." Lilia glanced up at the horrendous black-cat clock on the kitchen wall. Its eyes twitched back in forth in time with the pendulum motion of its tail counting off the seconds. And it ticked. Loudly. Echoing through the somber air of the entire house.

Alberti set a steaming cup of coffee in front of her, took her hand off the box, and wrapped it around the cup. "All of us will be staying here with you." He paused as Graham sounded off with a possessive huffing snort. He cleared his throat and settled down at the kitchen table beside Vivienne. "We will *all* stay here until after the services. Did Eliza advise you of her wishes?"

"She didn't want a memorial service—or a funeral." Lilia could hear Eliza's voice right now as though the feisty woman were sitting right beside her. *Fancy funerals and la-tee-da memorial services are not for the sake of the dead, dearie. They're just a way of filching money from those too filled with grief or guilt to have enough sense to see the skinning they're taking from the undertaker.*

Lilia sipped at the scalding hot brew, breathed in the steam, and closed her eyes as Eliza's lecture continued inside her head. *Scatter my ashes to the winds. Toss me out into the sea along the shoreline of my girlhood.* Eliza would always chuckle and wink as she finished the instructions. *And when ye feel the rain on yer cheek or the breeze blowing through yer hair, know that I've come to visit with ye and let ye know I'm always watching over ye.*

"Sweetling?" Graham gently stroked her hair, his light touch soothing as a healing balm. "What would ye have us do to honor Mistress Eliza?"

"She wanted her ashes scattered across the part of Scotland she knew as a girl." Lilia rose, went to the coffeepot, and refilled her cup. "The Highlands she loved—down next to the sea where she used to play when she was a child."

Lilia took another sip of coffee. She'd downed nearly a gallon of the strong black brew in less than a day yet she still felt numb, cold, and exhausted. An aching weariness pushed her down like a two-ton yoke collared around her neck. She leaned back against the counter, cringing as Angus stepped away from the open refrigerator door while greedily guzzling directly from the glass pitcher of juice. She forced herself to look away before she gagged, making a mental note to get Vivienne to work on Angus's manners—again. Totally besotted with the buxom redhead, Vivienne was the only one Angus would listen to and even remotely attempt to impress.

"Angus!" Vivienne hissed.

Angus lowered the juice pitcher, smacking his lips and sucking juice droplets from his mustache as he turned a look of pure innocence on Vivienne. "Eh?"

Vivienne blew out an exasperated exhale, then sagged back against the kitchen counter with a defeated shake of her head.

"We shall take her there together," Graham said, leaning back against the counter beside Lilia and curling a protective arm around her shoulders.

"I was hoping you'd want to go with me." Lilia eased in another sip of coffee, then nodded at Angus. "And you can come too, Angus, since we'll be taking her back to your time. I'm sure you're ready to return, aren't you?" She smiled up at Graham, leaning into his warm comforting embrace. "You're probably ready for a visit back too. Wouldn't you like to see Ronan and compare notes about the twenty-first century?"

"Back to my time?" Graham stiffened and the arm that he had so lovingly draped around her shoulders slowly fell away. "The thirteenth century, ye mean?"

"He canna return to our time." Angus thumped the orange juice pitcher down on the table then backed away with a slow shake of his head. He shook a finger at Graham, but his scowl was fixed on Lilia. "I can go wi' ye but he can't. Not ever." With a jerking swipe of his hand across his mouth, Angus rumbled out a loud belch to underscore the seriousness of the situation.

Fear. Dread. Shame. Lilia increased the distance between herself and Graham as his ever-darkening emotions washed across her. Her stomach twisted with her own dread . . . or was it Graham's? Or a nauseating mixture of the two? Her empathic senses and inner emotions had taken a gruesome beating over the past couple of days. She didn't need . . . couldn't take any more. She backed away a step and faced off, searching Graham's face. "What is Angus talking about?"

Graham tensed, clenching his jaw so hard the muscles flexed beneath the dark auburn sheen of his freshly trimmed beard. He took a step toward Angus, fixing the man with an *I'm going to kill you* glare.

Angus backed toward the kitchen door. "Uhm . . . I am . . . uh, verra sorry. I didna think—"

"Ye never think, ye sniveling bastard. What the hell is wrong with ye?" Graham clenched his fists at his sides, inching forward as though about to vault across the table and throttle Angus.

Angus shook his head and ducked his chin, jerking with a series of short stiff bows as he continued backing toward the hallway, the only hope of escape he had. "I am sorry, Graham. Truly I am. Ye ken I would never cause ye nor yer mistress any hurt or sorrow."

"Perhaps we should step out of the room and give you two a bit of space," Alberti said as he tugged on Vivienne's sleeve and motioned toward Angus, already poised to bolt out of the kitchen.

"I am not leaving." Vivienne yanked free of Alberti's fingertips and clicked her brightly painted nails in his face. "Bugger off and be the coward if ye like. I'll not be leaving until I'm certain there's not an arse kicking due to be meted out." She hopped up and assumed battle stance at Lilia's side. "Go on, lovie. I've got yer back."

Humiliation. Fear. Regret. Shame. Lilia pinched the bridge of her nose and rubbed the corners of her burning eyes. She had cried so much over the past couple of days, her swollen eyes felt as though they were filled with grit. "I appreciate the support, Vivienne, but I'd really rather you and Alberti..." She leaned around and glared at Angus. "And Angus go into the sitting room so Graham and I can work this out privately."

After all, the man was her husband. Well. Sort of. Spiritually, they had taken the ancient vow and, as far as she was concerned, were bound together for eternity. As far as twenty-first-century Scotland was concerned their pagan pledge to each other wasn't exactly legal but it was permanent enough for her.

"Are ye sure?" Vivienne leaned in close, nearly touching her pert upturned nose to Lilia's.

"I'm sure." Lilia pointed at Angus, then motioned toward the door. "And while you're waiting, why don't you explain to Angus the benefits of drinking from a glass rather than straight from the container? Again."

Vivienne turned and glared at guilty-looking Angus. "What have I told ye? We've had that talk a dozen times."

Angus shrugged as he scooted sideways toward the door. "Dammit, woman. Ye are always yapping at me about what I should or shouldna be doin'. How the hell am I supposed to remember every word ye say?"

"I'm going to kick yer arse into the middle of next week." Vivienne rounded the table as Angus shot out of the kitchen.

Alberti held the door open wider until they both fully cleared it. He shook his head, smoothing a hand back across his sleek dark hair while stepping out into the hall. He turned back, still holding the kitchen door ajar. "If she kills him, I shall see to it that she properly cleans up the mess."

"Thank you," Lilia said, blowing out a labored huff as the kitchen door swung shut. Good old Berti. She could always count on him to remain grounded and be their voice of reason. Lilia turned back to Graham with a weary sigh. "Now that they're gone, would you like to explain to me why you're pulsing out waves of humiliation, guilt, and regret like you're some sort of emotionally disturbed satellite sending out a five-bar signal?"

Graham blinked at her like he hadn't understood a single word she said.

"Why can't you go back to the thirteenth century?" she translated.

He closed his eyes and bowed his head, barely shaking it from side to side. Finally, as though he'd won his internal battle, he straightened, stood taller, and clenched his fists at his sides. He looked as though he was ready to be marched in front of a firing squad and shot. "The Buchanan willna tolerate my return to the Highlands . . . of *my* time," he hurried to add.

"Yeah, I already got that part." Good Lord, the man looked as though he wanted her to go ahead and kill him rather than continue asking questions. "Why won't the Buchanan tolerate your return?"

He refused to meet her gaze. Instead, his uneasy focus bounced all over the room, finally settling on some vague point slightly above her head. He cleared his throat, swallowed hard, then replied in a strained voice. "I swived his wife. And his mistress. In his keep." He shuffled in place and stared down at the floor. "Well, it was actually in his stables, not the keep itself." He resettled his boots again, scuffed a toe against the kitchen tiles, then barked out a cough as though choking on the words. "And whilst I was busy with that task—Angus lifted his favorite pair of roans." Graham shrugged. "But I dinna think the Buchanan truly minded the loss of the horses overly much. 'Twas said they werena his. He stole them from the MacClennans."

"Swived?" Lilia repeated, steering the conversation back to Graham's actions. Swived. Hadn't Chaucer used that word? Was Graham saying he'd had sex with the man's wife *and* his mistress?

"Aye." Graham jerked his chin down in a sharp nod. "Swived."

"Both of them? At the same time?" Lilia dumped her lukewarm coffee into the sink, slammed the cup down on the counter, and refilled it with fresh scalding brew from the pot.

"Beg pardon?"

"You fucked the man's wife and his mistress at the same time?" She flinched at the shrewish pitch to her voice, but dammit—"You're telling me you had a threesome?"

Graham's brow knotted into a mixed expression of confusion and dread. "Aye. I had both the women in the stable at the same time." He eased a step forward, holding up both hands as though pleading for mercy. "But the Lady Buchanan seemed to enjoy the pleasuring of her husband's mistress as much as I did. As a matter of fact, the woman fair pushed me out of the way so she could have a taste—"

Lilia held up a hand. "Enough! I don't need a play-by-play of your romp with the Buchanan babes." A pang of unreasonable jealousy elbowed her in the gut, pissing her off even more at the entire situation. Why the hell should she be jealous? She'd known he wasn't some inexperienced, celibate monk and for that matter, she hadn't exactly been a Vestal Virgin when they'd made a drastic dent in Vivienne's supply of condoms at the stable. "So, this Buchanan guy—he's threatened you if you ever set foot on his land again?" She understood the man's jealousy toward Graham but surely if they stayed away from the scene of the crime, Graham wouldn't have any unpleasant confrontations.

Lilia studied him. There was more he wasn't saying. "I need to know all of it. I need all the cards on the table. If you ever lie to me, Graham, I promise you, I will never trust you again." And she wouldn't. She had too good a memory and she'd never be able to erase the feeling of being betrayed.

His shoulders slumped and his gaze fell to the floor. "I canna tell ye how verra much it grieves me to share the foolish mistakes I have made." He slowly moved closer; fists now clasped in a tensed knot in front of his waist. "I dinna wish to cause ye pain . . . or hurt ye. I love ye, *mo nighean bhan,* and I beg yer forgiveness."

"Then tell me. All of it." The pain in his eyes mirrored the emotional suffering rolling off him in thick dark waves. He was hurting. His words were genuine. Her heart swelled, pushing her to rest her hands on his. "It is all in the past, but I need to know what is going on since it's affecting our present."

Graham brought her hands to his lips, closing his eyes as he pressed a kiss to the backs of her fingers, then held them against his cheek as though he feared she would pull them away. Finally, he opened his eyes and clutched her hands to his chest. "The Buchanan, chieftain of his clan lying just to the south of the MacKenna lands, threatened war against Clan MacKenna for the insult I had placed upon his keep." Graham shook his head. "The MacKenna didna wish, and wisely so," he hurried to add. "To risk the lives of MacKenna warriors over the ill-chosen actions of myself."

Lilia squeezed Graham's hands, sensing he had reached the portion of his confession that he really didn't wish to say aloud. "Tell me the rest," she softly encouraged. "I can't help if I don't know it all."

He pecked another quick kiss on her knuckles, as though doing so gave him the strength to go on. "Mother Sinclair, Lady Trulie, and the MacKenna offered to banish me from Scotland. Forever. To atone for all that I had done." He pulled her closer and stared sadly down into her eyes. "The only way the Buchanan would accept such an offer was if the MacKenna swore to turn me over to Clan Buchanan if I was ever to return. The Buchanan accepted. And also promised if that were ever to occur, he would have me publicly drawn and quartered. The bloody bastard allies with too damn many Lowlanders and has adopted their cruel ways."

Graham's face darkened, shadowing his features with shame as he closed his eyes. "But I suppose it is just punishment. The Buchanan wished for all to see what happens to a man's bollocks when they go where they dinna belong."

Lilia studied him, struggling against the wicked voice in the back of her mind whispering the real truth of the matter. *He didn't come to the future for you. He came to the future to escape so he wouldn't have to give up his beloved Scotland.* But she wouldn't accuse him. At least not outright. All Scots, especially those from the distant past, had an unyielding connection to their land—a passionate connection so strong it was as if the soil of their blessed motherland was embedded in their DNA. "So, Granny and Trulie sent you forward in time to save your life while still keeping you in Scotland?"

"Aye." Graham barely nodded. "The Fates sent them a vision. Instructed them that it was the Sinclairs' duty to take me in and protect me—even from myself—as partial penance for their dabbling across the centuries."

Lilia understood the truth of that and it did make her feel somewhat better about the whole situation. The Sinclairs had played fast and loose with time when they visited the past even though they knew the sacred tenet: don't change history. The Fates had looked the other way as long as they could. But finally, all the seemingly minor indiscretions had added up and the bill had to be paid—first with Mairi and her assigned breaking of Ronan's curse. The Fates had decided enough was enough and it was time to charge the Sinclair time runners with the duty of making things right for those whom they deemed worthy of saving. Apparently, it was now her turn to pay a portion of the Sinclair dues.

But she had to ask the question. She had to know the raw unvarnished truth. "Why did they send you to me, Graham? Did they do it just to ensure I'd help you acclimate to the future? Did they just want to make sure you had a chance at surviving the twenty-first century?"

"Acc-li-mate?" he repeated slowly. A confused scowl knotted his bushy brows. "I dinna ken that word but I do ken this—they sent me to ye because they kent we were destined to be together."

She searched his face and set her empathic sensors on wide open, then exhaled with a relieved sigh. No deceit. No treachery. Nothing but pure unadulterated regret well-seasoned with a silent plea for understanding, acceptance, and forgiveness. She pulled one hand out of his desperate grip and gently touched his cheek. "It's all right. I'll just go alone. You and Angus can stay here where it's safe. It'll only take me a few days and then I'll be back and we can settle into our life together—here." The note of finality in those words sent a strange mixture of emotions shivering through her: excitement, anticipation, and a tiny bit of fear.

His face darkened with a thunderous scowl. "Like hell ye will." He brushed her hand away from his face and took hold of both her shoulders. "I may be many things, but I am not a coward and I will be damned if I allow ye to make this journey alone. I'll not have ye fending for yerself in the midst of yer grieving."

"Bullshit." She turned out of his grasp, shaking her head as she circled the kitchen table. "You're not going to risk it." He'd better figure out when it came to stubbornness, she had him beat in spades. She pushed open the kitchen door and shouted down the hallway. "It's safe to come back into the kitchen now. We've got it all settled."

"The hell we do." Graham stormed around the table after her, grabbed hold of her arm, and spun her around to face him. "What kind of man would I be to allow my woman to go through such a thing alone? What kind of fool would send his wife through the Highlands unattended?"

"A live one, dammit." She thumped him hard in the center of his chest. Damn hardheaded Highlander. "If you come back with me, Gray will be forced to turn you over to the Buchanan. He's clan chief. A man of his word. He would have no other choice. I'm not going to put either of you in that situation." She yanked her arm free and squared off in front of him. "You are my husband and if anybody wrings your neck, it is going to be me."

"I distinctly heard you say it was safe to come back into the kitchen." Alberti held back Vivienne and Angus, the three of them craning their heads through the partially opened door. "Shall we give you a bit longer?"

"No," Graham growled like an enraged bear, jutting his chin toward Lilia. "But ye can tell this—"

"You better be careful," she warned.

Graham's face shifted to a deep reddish-purple as he jabbed a finger at her and sputtered, "Tell this *woman* that she best mind the druthers of her husband like a good wife should."

"Oh my." Alberti turned and shooed Vivienne and Angus back down the hallway *away* from the kitchen. "We'll be waiting in the parlor," he called back through the swinging kitchen door.

CHAPTER 18

"You are a stubborn son of a bitch."

Graham chuckled, reveling in the delectable taste of his fiery-tempered wife. He nibbled and kissed a slow trail up her silky belly before settling down beside her. Gently rolling her warm, limber, well-sated body to her side, he pulled her back against his chest and spooned his legs into the backs of hers. "Aye. That I am. But know this . . . " He cupped one of her breasts in his palm and settled his fingers comfortably in the cleft between their fullness. "I am yer verra own stubborn son of a bitch until the end of time."

Lilia giggled and nestled back tighter against him. "It'll be time to leave soon. I've set the alarm on my phone." She patted his arm, then nuzzled a kiss against his shoulder pillowed beneath her cheek. "We really need to get a little rest." She hitched in a yawn, then hugged his arm tighter around her and grew still.

Lore a'mighty. He had never known such bliss. Fear that she'd quickly cast him aside when he told her about his past had filled him. And who could blame her? He'd been no more than a selfish fool back then and allowed his cock to do all his thinking.

But that was then. Before he had met her. The woman he couldn't live without. He pressed a soft lingering kiss on her shoulder. She didn't move, just barely shifted with slow deep breathing. Already asleep. Poor lass. The past few days had taken quite a toll on her. He huffed out a silent chuckle. Aye, but she'd still found the energy to battle him and threaten to kick his arse if he didn't listen and agree to stay in the future whilst she took Eliza back to the past alone. What had he ever done to merit such a fine woman?

They had argued for what seemed like hours. At one point, he'd grown a bit concerned when she'd eyed the block of butcher's knives sitting on the counter. Lore, the woman had a fierce temper. He still sported a fading knot on the back of his head from where she'd beaned him with the pommel of her sword.

Alberti had finally interceded. Thankfully, the man had been listening to their raging from the safety of the hallway. He'd rushed in just in time to suggest that Lilia allow both Graham and Angus to accompany her. Angus could serve as watchman whilst Graham tended to Lilia during her somber task.

Alberti had wisely reasoned that all they need do to keep Graham safe was avoid any contact with Clan MacKenna and stay away from Buchanan lands. The trio could slip back to the thirteenth century unannounced, then slip right back out. The only way anyone would suspect something might be amiss would be if they happened to overhear the telltale boom of the time portal when it spat them out.

Graham relaxed deeper into the pillows. The soothing blue light of the full moon danced through the swaying tree limbs outside the window, painting a mesmerizing play of light and shadow across the bedroom wall. Bless the man, Alberti, for coming up with the simple plan that no one else could seem to find.

And so, they would go. The three of them. They would honor Mistress Eliza's last request and scatter her ashes across the Scotland of her girlhood, upon the very rocks where she'd gazed across the sea.

Bless those three, Graham silently prayed. Whilst he and Lilia stole a bit of rest, Angus, Alberti, and Vivienne worked below, gathering and packing all the trip would require.

Alberti had even promised to conjure the exact point of their entry back into the thirteenth century. Quite impressive since the man was not a time runner nor a seer. He'd promised to use some . . . what had the man called it? Some sort of *app* . . . a small colorful picture trapped within the black mirrored surface of his strange tile of metal that turned into a window to thousands of worlds with a mere tap of his finger.

Lilia swore she could target the jump wherever Alberti directed. She said they would land close to where Mistress Eliza's ashes would be scattered so the entire trip wouldn't take over a day or so. He'd not missed the shadows of sadness in his sweetling's eyes when she'd agreed the MacKennas would never know they'd ever been back in the thirteenth century—unless they happened to hear the time portal boom.

Pulling in a heavy sigh, Graham pressed his cheek against the fragrant softness of Lilia's hair. 'Twas his fault his dear sweet love could not enjoy a wee visit with her family. She'd told him it wouldn't matter. Told him she would see them another time. After all, she hadn't had the time to jump back and visit in several months. She said they would understand.

Aye. They would understand but Graham's heart still ached at the unjustness of it all. Lilia needed her family right now but because of him, she had sworn to avoid them. He closed his eyes and inhaled another deep breath of her sweetness. He'd spend the rest of his life thanking the gods for this woman and ensuring she never regretted her decision to be his wife.

A high-pitched *beep-beep-beep* sounded from her cellphone as it buzzed and bounced across the table beside the bed. Graham forced his eyes open, rubbing the crustiness of weariness from their corners. Lore a'mighty. He had just closed them a moment ago.

Lilia groaned, dragged herself off the edge of the bed, and stumbled across the room toward the adjoining bathroom. A dull thud sounded in the semidarkness just as she reached the door. "Shit!"

Graham lifted his head as the bathroom light flicked on, flinching with sympathy as she hopped through the half-open door, holding her left foot in one hand. "Be ye all right, sweetling?"

"I'm *fine*." The door slammed shut and Lilia's huffing string of curse words accompanied the muffled sound of water running in the sink.

May the gods protect him. He knew that tone. His dear one was anything but fine. She was tired and cross and the safest thing for them all to do to survive this task would be to get some of her blessed coffee down her throat—and quickly.

He rolled out of the bed, forcing his still-weary body into motion by stretching and working free any stiffness. He meandered across the room, jerked open the closet door, and found his clothing from the past. Good. Shield and sword were there as well. He pulled the items free of Lilia's tangle of boots and shoes then quickly donned them while she was still bumping around the bathroom.

"I'll be downstairs, *mo nighean bhan*." He waited for a response, thinking to call out to her again, but then a deeply ingrained sense of survival changed his mind. Best let his dear one work out her preparations alone.

Alberti, Vivienne, and Angus stood around the kitchen table, double-checking the olive-drab cloth bags filled with the trip's necessities and Eliza's oak box. Graham propped his shield against the pile then settled his sword belt lower around his hips.

"Ye ken we'll be on foot." Angus, once again wearing his clothes from the past, scowled at Graham from across the table. He lifted his chin to a jutting angle as though daring Graham to argue the point.

"Aye." Graham kent it well enough but it couldn't be helped. They daren't risk a visit to the MacKenna stables—not even if he and Angus were to remain hidden whilst Lilia went alone. "Lilia says she canna control the great boom the time cloud makes whenever it spits us out. 'Tis why we must target the highest point closest to the sea where Eliza wishes to be freed then make our way down from there. 'Twill be less of a risk, less chance we'll be found out or cause any strife for the MacKenna. Dinna fash yerself. It willna be much of a journey."

"Did ye not wonder about the sound when Graham and I fell from the sky?" Angus turned to Vivienne as she shouldered him over then boosted her behind up onto the kitchen counter. She slid back, then proceeded to swing her bare feet back and forth in front of the cabinet doors.

"Oh no, ducks." Vivienne quickly shook her head and shrugged. "When festival is around, Edinburgh fair explodes with sound. Whatever noise the two of ye made was more than likely thought to be fireworks or such from some of the entertainment."

A slow steady clumping of boots echoed from the stairwell mere moments before Lilia's yawning countenance rounded the corner. She rubbed an eye with the heel of her hand as she ran a bleary-eyed glance across the items piled on the kitchen table.

The woman was wearing that? Back to the thirteenth century? Graham motioned at her clothing. "Are ye certain ye are dressed proper?" A strained groaning sound escaped him. He didn't wish to start their trek with harsh words but the woman needed to see sense. "Women dinna wear such things in my time. Ye should ken that well enough. What if someone should see ye?"

She fixed him with a sleepy-eyed scowl then gave herself a quick once-over. "Jeans. Hiking boots. T-shirt. Lightweight camo jacket with big-ass pockets. This is the perfect gear for trekking across the wilderness. It'll be August there too and if we play our cards right, we won't run across anyone. No human contact. Remember?"

"Still. Ye are quite certain?" A strange foreboding, a sense of uneasiness took hold in Graham's gut and gnawed at him like a starving beast. If anyone saw Lilia dressed in such a way, he shook his head at the disturbing possibilities.

Lilia stifled another yawn as she tightened her leather belt and shoved a knife into the attached sheath. "I'm certain."

She turned to Alberti and Vivienne. "Did you two find the kiddie pool or are we going to have to use the birdbath?"

"Birdbath," Vivienne said with a sad shake of her head. "I've not a clue what Eliza did with the kiddie pool and I'm not brave enough to sort through all the storage bins in the garage."

"The birdbath's fine. All I need is enough water and fire to act as a conduit to open the portal." Lilia hefted one of the bags off the table and strapped it across her back. She lashed a smaller bag around her waist and gently tucked Eliza's box into it then carefully clicked the double set of buckles shut. Pausing with her hands resting on the bag, she stood staring down at it as though trapped within her thoughts.

"Ducks?" Vivienne stepped forward, gently rubbing her hand up and down Lilia's arm. "Ye'll be all right, aye? Be back before we know it . . . yes?"

A troubled expression knotting her brow, Lilia looked at Vivienne for a long moment. Graham tensed even more, feeling as though he were about to wade into battle. His dear one was troubled over a great deal more than just the spreading of Mistress Eliza's ashes. He felt it in his bones.

"Lilia?" Vivienne whispered, reaching out to take both of Lilia's hands in hers. "What is it, lovie?"

"If I don't return . . . " Lilia's voice faded to nothing. She took a deep breath, gave Alberti a quick glance, then looked back at Vivienne. "The papers are in the safe. You and Alberti have copies but my originals are in the safe. Everything goes to both of you . . . because I love you."

Vivienne pulled Lilia into a quick hug, then took her by the shoulders. "Send word if ye decide to stay there, aye? We'll need to know that you're well so we dinna worry." She turned and looked back at Alberti, who agreed with a quick nod. "And if ye come back . . . we'll have ye a stoking hot pot of coffee and a bottle a booze a waitin'."

Lilia's brave smile trembled the barest bit as she gave a single nod, then turned away. She cleared her throat with a nervous cough, resettled the bag on her shoulders, and headed toward the door. "Are you two ready?" She stopped and glanced back at Angus then arched a brow at Graham.

Nay. He would never be ready to ride through that hellish maelstrom again but he would damn well do it for her. "Aye." Graham scooped up his shield and the remaining bag, securing them both firmly and tightening the canvas straps across his chest.

Angus didn't answer, just stepped forward with his white-knuckled fists clenching the straps of the pack lashed to his back.

Lilia pushed through the back door, not looking back. "To the backyard then. Time to light the fires and get the party started."

CHAPTER 19

Lilia tucked and rolled around the boxy bag belted at her waist before she made full contact with the hillside rushing up to meet her. She didn't care if she broke her neck; Eliza's remains weren't going to get busted into a pile of dust and wood chips on her watch.

A deep throaty growl and a string of hissed Gaelic that was more than likely terms Granny would never approve of came from her left. A strangled shout and profanity she completely understood echoed from her right. A hard thud, shaking leaves and snapping branches all around, signaled Angus's and Graham's completed landing. Hopefully, they had survived as well as she had.

"Are you all right?" She hitched forward a few steps, trying to roll the soreness out of one shoulder as she walked. She'd whacked the ground pretty hard on the final roll that had brought her to a stop. The joint didn't seem to be dislocated but from the feel of it, her muscles weren't going to let her forget she'd had a rough landing. "Graham. Angus. Are you both okay?"

Graham barked out a strained "Aye!" The dense shrubbery rattled and snapped as he forced his way through the tangle of branches and crawled free of the brush. "Lore a'mighty. I dinna ken how yer family ever gets used to such madness."

"Practice." Lilia brushed dust and dirt from her jeans as she looked around. "Granny says the more we jump the better we'll get at landing but I don't know." She shook her head, still rubbing and rolling her throbbing shoulder. "The girls and I have never been able to break free of the time cloud with Granny's finesse and grace."

"Sons a bitches, I'll never do that again." Angus staggered out of a ragged growth of saplings and brambles, ripping a thorny vine free of his plaid.

Graham squinted up at the quickly clearing sky, then looked around the craggy jut of land covered with wind-twisted saplings, ragged bushes, and low-growing ground cover hearty enough to withstand the harsh gusts coming in from the sea. "This is a far sight higher than I expected." He walked over to a steep precipice and looked across the land. He studied their location then turned to his left and nodded at a gentler bit of slope shearing downward. "We'll have to travel west a bit. 'Tis too severe a climb to go straight down."

Angus huffed his way over to Graham, still limping and pulling thistles from the rear of his plaid. Gingerly stepping close to the edge, he scowled down at the sheer drop. "Aye. That drop would try the sure-footedness of a wee Highland goat."

Re-buckling the bag holding Eliza's remains, Lilia joined the men standing at the edge of the cliff. "I was afraid to shoot any closer to the sea. I didn't want to land us in the water." A cool breeze blew against her face as the first glimmering rays of the rising sun broke across the waves rippling to the horizon.

The savage land unfolded before her like a jagged tartan of shadowed greens, muted blues, and grays. Swatches of purple and pink winked up through the early morning mist swirling around the base of the mountainside. Heather—next to her pink roses, heather was Eliza's favorite flower. How fitting it should be blooming now.

Lilia inhaled a deep breath of the briny air and a sense of calm settled across her. This place was beautiful but at the same time rugged and strong. The shushing whispers of the wind stroking down the sides of the mountain brought a smile to her. The land here was endless and stubborn and proud of its beauty. Just like Eliza. "We should reach the sea well before sunset—don't you think so?"

Graham shrugged his pack more evenly across his back with a nod. "Aye. 'Tis not verra far and downhill all the way. Come, *mo nighean bhan,* let us be on our way." He motioned Angus forward. "Take the lead, man. Ye are better than most at finding the surest footing."

Falling in step behind Angus on the narrow way down the mountainside, Lilia hooked her thumbs through the straps of the backpack, alternately watching her footing and glancing around the land. It was so untouched here, so pristine, as though humans had yet to discover this magical part of the world.

Then it hit her. Just as she was about to shimmy around a good-sized boulder. Greed. Excitement. Revenge. Bloodlust. Waves of the cold dark emotions rushed across her like the skin-tingling energy of a building storm.

"Graham?" She backed toward him while glancing around. Where was the source of those deadly emotions?

"What is it, sweetling?" He hurried to her, concern knotting his brows. "Ye sound alarmed. What fashes ye, lass?"

"Is there ill afoot?" Angus scrambled back around the curve of the path; sword already drawn.

She covered Graham's hand with hers and concentrated. Unease. Caring. Worry. Love. Those were his emotions—not the ones she had felt just moments ago. Angus pinged out waves of alarm and no small amount of thirst for battle like a high-tech satellite.

She squeezed Graham's hand, struggling not to let her fear quiver into her voice. She swallowed hard and took a deep breath. Got to stay calm. Must focus. "Someone else is here that shouldn't be. I feel it."

Graham drew her close and tucked her back against the mountain. He placed himself in front of her like a human shield. "Where? What did ye see?" He unsheathed his sword, his narrow-eyed gaze searching the area.

"I didn't *see* them." She closed her eyes and concentrated, emotionally scanning the area. Dammit. Where were they? She held her breath, straining to recapture the negativity that only moments ago had slammed into her. A frustrated snort escaped her as she opened her eyes. "I've lost them. The feelings are gone. But someone was here. I'm sure of it."

"I dinna care for this. Not a soul kens we're here." Graham's knuckles whitened as he moved his sword in a slow warning arc while scanning the area.

"I know I didn't imagine it. Someone was here." She shook her head and rested her hand on Graham's rock-hard arm. "They're gone now. I'm positive. If they come close enough, I'll feel them again and warn you." She glanced up at the sky. "It's getting lighter. If we want to reach the outcropping Eliza told me about by this afternoon, we need to get moving."

"Ye are certain we're alone now?" Graham waited, sword still lifted, ready to cut down anyone who threatened them.

Her own tension eased a bit and she relaxed enough to exhale. A part of her on a very primal level warmed at being protected. She had no doubt; he would keep her safe or die in the trying. "I promise they're gone. It's okay. Let's go."

"Hmph." Graham jammed his sword back in the sheath, scowled one last searching glance around, then looked past her to Angus. "Take to the high ground whilst we descend to the sea. Find them. Ye ken what to do."

"Aye." Angus jerked his head down in a single nod. "I ken it well. Take Mistress Eliza to the sea. There will be none threatening ye on my watch, I grant ye that." He sheathed his sword, then carefully worked his way back around them. Before continuing up the hillside, he tossed a smile and a wink back over his shoulder. "I'd rather be hunting a goat-swiving knave than traipsing around with a pair of lovers any day. I leave ye to yer honorable task, Mistress Lilia, and I'll not return until I'm certain ye both are safe, I swear to ye."

"Thank you, Angus." Lilia's heart warmed. He might be a crude and clumsy pain in the ass, but Angus was a true friend. "Be careful. I don't want you hurt either."

He waved away her words. Scratching his ass as he trudged back up the trail.

Lilia and Graham plodded along in companionable silence for what seemed like hours, thankfully, with no recurrence of the upsetting emotions she had sensed earlier. They briefly paused during their descent for Graham to hack off a pair of stray saplings growing alongside the path. He quickly fashioned them into walking sticks for himself and Lilia. At first, she'd argued, thinking she didn't need it, but then she'd grudgingly realized that walking down the steep incline was much easier with the staff to help steady her balance.

"It would not hurt ye to admit when I'm right, ye ken?" Graham swatted her rump with an affectionate smack as they reached a level shelf of rock wide enough to sit upon and take a rest.

"Don't hold your breath." She wagged a finger in his face, then twisted open the straw to the water bottle swinging at her waist. "It is a wise man who knows when to celebrate his victories in silence."

He snorted out a laugh and leaned back against the sheer rock cliff at their backs. His face grew serious as his meandering gaze settled on the squawking terns, following their slow graceful circles across the cloudless sky. The birds dropped, one by one, in targeted dives into the sparkling waves, then burst back up through the surface with their glistening lunch wiggling in their beaks. He reached over and gently squeezed her knee. "Ye never said. Shall we be returning to the future tonight? Or will we be staying here 'til the morrow?"

She shrugged. "I hadn't really thought that far ahead. I guess it doesn't matter. Angus probably wouldn't care either way. He seemed excited to go off exploring on his own. What would you like to do?"

If Graham wanted to stay another day or so, other than the fact they might run a little skimpy on supplies, it really wouldn't be a problem. All she'd been concerned about when they'd finally agreed on this plan was following Eliza's last wishes.

Hunger burned in Graham's gaze as he slowly trailed a finger down her arm. "If ye wouldna be against the thought, I'd rather we stayed on here a wee bit. Just another day or so, mind ye. We'd be alone—and uninterrupted. If Angus fails to find whoever ye sensed, the man will find something else to hunt or fashion a spear for fishing, ye can be sure of that. He'll not be a bother to us."

Then his gaze dropped and his brow knotted into a frustrated scowl. Graham pulled his hand away, his mouth twitching into a deeper frown beneath his mustache. "Forgive me, *mo nighean bhan*. Ye must surely think me a selfish man to hunger for ye whilst yer grieving."

Lilia snuggled beside him on the ledge and leaned her head against the hard muscles of his shoulder. "It's okay."

And it was. Since they'd met, they'd never really been alone—not really. There had always been either friends, phone calls, text messages, or the weight of Eliza's impending passing right there with them. She understood completely what he felt and not just because she was an empath. There was a serene isolation to this place—as though the world had paused in its spinning and told them, *Tarry awhile. Learn of one another. Breathe.*

"I only wish . . . " Graham stopped and blew out a heavy breath. He fisted a hand against his chest. "Ye fill my heart, love. My soul is at last sated and I burn with the wanting of ye." He shook his head. "I canna help myself, *mo nighean bhan.* I was put here to be with ye. I canna imagine life without ye."

A contented smile warmed through her. She looped her arm through his and hugged him closer. "I love you too."

The sun rose high overhead, nearly at its zenith. They were close enough to the glistening sea, to hear the waves alternately crashing, then shushing against the rocks of the shore below. Lilia shifted sideways and stood. "We need to go now. We're almost there."

She felt the pull of Eliza's place calling—the large outcropping of stone Eliza had described so many times that Lilia felt as though she'd sat there with her, staring out across the water. Even with the cancer tormenting her with excruciating pain, when Eliza had spoken of where she had often played as a young girl, her face had lost the deeply etched lines of suffering and illness. She'd smiled as she'd gazed off into space, her weary eyes shining with the memories of her youth.

As they descended the last bit of the incline, Lilia pointed a bit farther down the shoreline. "There. That is Eliza's place."

Graham nodded as he rested his hands on top of his rough staff. He leaned forward and propped his chin on his hands. "Aye. 'Tis a fine place. I feel the peace of it myself."

Climbing carefully across the wet boulders, slippery and treacherous with the wearing of the sea and the leavings of seaweed and foam, Lilia wedged her walking stick between her back and the handles of her backpack then stretched with hands, knees, and feet to scale the stair-step layers and wrinkles of Eliza's rock. When she finally stood upon the dry, sun-bleached summit of the flat-topped boulder, the refreshing wind and salt spray greeted her as though they'd been awaiting her arrival.

Love. Gratitude. Joy. The powerful emotions embraced her, lifted her up, and filled her heart with the certainty that all was as it should be. Eliza was well now—and happy. And Eliza would never really be gone.

"She's here." Tears welled up, then overflowed and streamed down her face. Lilia closed her eyes and allowed the gentle breeze to kiss them away. "She's here," she whispered again as she held her arms open wide, her hands lifted to the warm caress of the sun.

Graham gently pulled her backpack off her shoulders, set it at their feet, and steadied her back against his chest, his arms loosely wrapped around her waist. "Aye, love." He shifted against her with a deep intake of breath then a satisfied sigh. "Her spirit smiles here."

It was time. With trembling fingers, Lilia opened the canvas bag at her waist and carefully worked free the wooden box. The rich honey sheen of the oak grain shimmered like gold in the sunlight. How proper and fitting because Eliza's heart had been pure gold.

Crouching, Lilia slowly opened the lid, carefully emptied the sealed bag of ashes inside the box, then turned it to face the sea. The sound of the waves suddenly seemed livelier as a gusting breeze encircled them, dipped down into the opened box, and drew out the ashes into a dancing ribbon of silvery gray out across the water.

The sea birds' cries and the crashing waves sounded like peals of laughter as the wind whipped around them one last time, blew the tiny vessel clean, then slammed the lid shut. Then all stilled. The sea grew silent and the sound of the birds disappeared.

A faint kiss brushed Lilia's cheek and a feather-light touch rippled across her hair. Eliza's softly chortling whisper tickled her ear. *I love ye as me own, dearie.* The wind picked up along with the rippling waves lapping against the rock. *And I'll be watching over ye—ken it with all yer heart.* Then the sound of Eliza's faint laughter floated out across the sea.

CHAPTER 20

"Where shall we spend the night?" Lilia shielded her eyes against the afternoon sun as she scanned up and down the rocky coastline. "I'm not much on caves. I'd rather sleep under the stars as long as the weather holds."

Aye. He would as well. He'd spent several centuries residing in caves whilst in dragon form and did not wish to return to such a dwelling even for just one night. Graham snorted out a huffing breath at the memory. Caves held a particular stench about them and he'd never cared for the smell of them a whit. He pointed to a dark green crease higher up the mountainside, farther to the east of the slope they'd just traipsed down to reach the shore. "There." He nodded with certainty. "That looks promising. The way the mountain cradles that bit a land, the wind willna trouble us no matter how fierce the gale decides to blow."

"It looks like there might even be trees up there instead of scrub." Lilia picked her way across the rough, rocky ground, steadying herself with her staff as she hopped from stone to stone as nimbly as a wee Highland goat. She looked back at him and smiled. "Maybe there'll even be a freshwater spring. That beats stale bottled water any day."

His heart lightened at her relaxed demeanor. He'd not realized until just now how his dear love had always carried herself with such a poised, tensed stance as though ready to lunge into battle. A chuckle escaped him. Perhaps the old woman Eliza had known what a tonic this place would be for Lilia. "We'd best be about it, then. By the time we reach our spot, it will leave me precious little time to hunt for our supper."

She turned and pointed her walking stick at him as though plotting her aim to thump him on the head with it. "You know better. I brought hard cheese, a tin of biscuits, and some protein bars. There will be no hunting of anything for supper other than fresh spring water."

He grinned. She'd reacted to his subtle gigging just as he'd wished. His love did not eat meat—the entire why of it escaped him but he'd fathom a guess it had something to do with her heritage and the mystical connections she held sacred. He didn't care if they shared a supper or not this evening. All he needed was her. "Aye, lass. I'll find ye the sweetest water ye ever tasted. I promise it, sure as I'm standing here."

Further chatting fell away as they scrambled up the drastic incline of the rocky shelf looking out across the beach below. They zigzagged up, easing even farther to the east of the rugged terrain than they had first planned. The steep, weathered side of the cliff made for deceptive footing.

"Whew. I'm going to need a swim after this little climb." She fisted a hand against the small of her back, then peeled her T-shirt away from her body. "I stayed pretty cool on the way down but going back up is giving me a bad case of swamp ass."

"Swamp ass?" Graham repeated. What sort of ailment was *swamp ass*? He leaned to one side, eyeing her very fine curves. Her arse looked as squeezably fit and biteable as ever to him.

"I'm working up a sweat that's trickling south." She gave him a look that clearly said she couldn't believe he didn't know what she meant as she dug into the small, zippered pouch in the side of her backpack and pulled free a colorful cloth. She folded it lengthwise, then smoothed it across her brow and knotted it at the back of her head. "Viv packed an extra one. Do you want one to keep the sweat out of your eyes?"

He swiped his hand across his forehead. Aye, his head was warm and wet but he would rather not wear such a thing across his brow. A leather strap to hold his hair? Maybe. Something that looked like a colorful rag for a bairn's doll? Never. He shook his head and winked. "I thank ye, but no."

She rolled her eyes. "You won't look like a girl. It's a dark blue one. See?" She pulled free the long bit of cloth that could nearly pass for a length of dark braided leather. Almost.

She'd read him so easily. He relented and took it from her. Some things were not worth the battle. He dried his head with his forearm, snugged the cloth around his brow, and knotted it. Perhaps it wouldn't be so bad. At least there were none around to see him. He tilted his head away from the wind and the shore below and listened.

Aye and for certain. 'Twas the bubbling song of a nearby burn he heard. If the gods smiled upon him, there would be a sheltered pool of water hiding within the bit of wood where they planned to spend their night. His love had mentioned she'd be needing a swim. Such a diversion held infinite possibilities.

"Come." He urged her forward with a nod. "We've not much farther and I do believe I hear the sound of the water ye are seeking."

She gave him a look of disbelief. "All I hear are the waves below. How could you possibly hear a stream up the hillside?"

Uneasiness held his tongue as he shrugged away her words. Lilia's knowing he was once a dragon was one thing. She had accepted his history well enough—more than likely because her own ancestry was filled with things not so easily explained. But sharing the traits that had stayed with him once the curse was broken, he was none too sure she would be so accepting. Keen hearing, a predatory sense of smell, and a set of eyes sharper than a hawk's. The gods had granted him all these gifts when he'd permanently returned to the form of a man. Perhaps it was a bit of an appeasement for all he had endured.

"Graham?" Lilia sidled closer, frowning up at him with concern flashing in her eyes. "Why have you suddenly gone so uncharacteristically silent?"

He pulled free and trudged onward. "I dinna ken yer meaning." Damn her for seeing through him so easily. What the hell was he? As clear as a fresh Highland stream?

She grabbed hold of his arm and pulled him to a stop. "You know about all my oddities and yet you're still here. You haven't run away screaming or threatened to burn me at the stake. Why would you think anything could make me run from you?" She lifted her chin and narrowed her eyes. "You know I'm not a coward."

"Aye. Ye are not a coward, my love." But that didn't matter. Accepting her was easy. He, on the other hand, had made far too many mistakes and foolhardy choices to make her unconditional acceptance of him a matter of no concern.

"Super hearing is not going to scare me away." She snuggled up against him, the inviting scent of her overly warmed body making him ache to strip away her clothes and bend her over the nearest boulder.

He threw down his staff, encircled her in his arms and pulled her close, burying his face in her neck and nuzzling against her salty sweet flesh with a deep, appreciative inhale. "I fear when ye ken the traits I still possess from when I was the beast, ye willna be so inclined to remain my wife."

She sighed as she melted against him, molding her curves into him as though she too wished they stood skin to skin. "You don't still breathe fire, do you?" A soft giggle escaped her as she teased the tip of her tongue along the tensed muscles of his throat.

He filled his hands with the mouth-watering curves of her sweet arse and pulled her harder against him. "I canna breathe fire any longer but I grant ye this, ye've warmed me well and good to the point where I'll not guarantee I willna burst into flame."

"Then let's find this water you're hearing so we can *cool* each other off." She nibbled her way around his neck then sucked his earlobe until he thought he'd surely strip them both down right where they stood and bury himself inside her.

"Patience, my fiery beast." She licked his throat again, then pushed away and scurried ahead a few paces. "Find me a pool and we'll see about putting out that fire."

"Ye ken me too well." He strode after her, then motioned a bit farther to the east. "There. In that bit of wood. That is where we need to go."

She studied where he pointed, her eyes narrowing as she carefully tucked her walking stick snugly between her back and her pack. "Did you happen to bring any of our lovely little purple packets?"

Purple packets? He frowned as he mentally sorted through the items that he had instructed Angus to pack for the both of them. Realization of what she was talking about dawned on him, making him give a frustrated groan. Those damned condoms. He'd not thought to bring any of those stockings for his cock. "I brought none." How could he have forgotten about the wee socks that guaranteed him access to heaven on earth?

Hope nudged him forward a step. "Did ye happen to mention to Vivienne we might be needing them so she put a few in yer pack?"

Lilia made an apologetic face as she shook her head. "Since Angus was coming with us, condoms weren't really up there on my *things I might need* list—sorry. I didn't realize we'd be able to distract him so easily by sending him off into the Highlands." She closed her eyes and silently tapped her thumb across her fingertips as though tallying up her thoughts. A promising smile lit her face as her eyes popped open. "But by my calculations, we could probably get away with playing a little fast and loose just this one time."

"Fast . . . and . . . loose." He didn't know what she meant for certain but the term sounded as though he would not be disappointed.

Her smile turned into a wicked a grin. "Well. Not *too* fast." She looped her thumbs through the straps at her shoulders, then winked. "Race ya!"

Then she bounded off, scampering over the rough terrain and laughing as she swerved and loped around wildly tufted hillocks and partially overgrown boulders.

The wee minx. Graham charged after her, the sound of her

teasing laughter spurring him on. The ever-thickening tight under-brush and fully leafed-out saplings slowed his progress. Clumps of wild grasses were knotted through tangled branches and roots. The deep green ground cover clutched at his boots, threatening to latch hold of his feet and send him tumbling.

By the time he wrestled his way through the clinging branches and vines, Lilia was nowhere to be seen. "Lilia?" He searched the serene peacefulness of the grove's heart. Thick, velvety moss coated the boulders and fallen trees surrounding the gently sloping banks of a rippling pool. The water danced and bubbled at the narrow end where it tumbled free of the earth, gurgling and frothing down stag-gered slabs of stone vainly attempting to hold it back.

"Lilia! Answer me, love. I dinna care overly much for a game where I canna find ye." He circled the pool, dropping his bag and staff to the ground as he scanned the mountain's hidden bit of heaven sheltered by the walls of the steep ravine and the thick canopy of trees. Then he spotted them. Hastily kicked aside boots, a discarded sock, and jacket, then a bit farther around the circumference of the pool, the remainder of his beloved's clothes.

As he turned, she broke up through the water's surface. Head thrown back, eyes closed, a smile curving her full ruby lips. Her blonde hair streamed down across her shoulders and swirled through the water like liquid gold poured from the heavens. Graham wet his mouth, already tasting the creamy breasts shining just below the surface of the clear water.

"Are you going to stand there staring or are you going to get in here with me?"

Tossing away his clothes, he lunged into the water, completely submerging as he swam toward her. Eyes open, he easily found her, her fair skin shone like a beacon, guiding him home to where he belonged.

He teasingly circled her, her pale legs slowly pumping and her arms gently paddling back and forth to keep her floating upright. He swam up beneath her, sliding his hands up the smoothness of her legs as he pushed his face between her thighs and blew bubbles against her delicious lady parts.

She shuddered, reaching down to pull him up to the surface as she wrapped her legs around his waist and slid her wet breasts against him. As he broke free of the water, she barely gave him time to take in air before covering his mouth with hers.

He slid his hands down across her luscious behind, working his fingers into her cleft as he moved them both toward the shallows. He worked a hand down, then up between the meatiness of her rounded curves, sliding two fingers inside her heat.

She approved with a pleased moan as she leaned back across the mossy bank, arms spread across the velvety green. Her skin glistened, breasts shining in the dappled light of sun and shadows as the leaves above gently swayed in the breeze.

"I have matched my soul to the goddess herself." Graham spread a hand beneath her floating hips, fingers still buried inside her slickness, and lifted her to the surface. He laved her water-cooled flesh with his tongue then sucked her button deep and hard as another finger joined the others. He matched the gyrating motion of his fingers to his tongue as he pulled and sucked her.

Her legs draped over his shoulders, she arched against him, digging her heels into his back and fisting her hands atop the embankment. A gasping cry escaped her. She jerked and cried out louder as the slick, molten walls of her body clutched and grabbed at his fingers—the waves of her spasms arching her higher above the water. He gently slid his fingers free, lifted her higher up the embankment, then spread himself over her.

"I must have ye. I can wait no longer." He pushed inside her, hard and deep, then forced himself to hold fast whilst seated clear to his bollocks. "By the gods, the heat of ye inside whilst I touch the coolness of yer skin . . . " He groaned, pressing his forehead against hers as he slid out, then rammed in again. "I'll not last long."

She bucked against him, raked her nails down his back, then clutched his arse and yanked him forward. "Then I guess we'll have to keep at it until we build up your endurance." She clenched him with her thighs and gyrated against him. "I'll start the timer. Here's to round one."

"Aye." Graham slid out until only the tip of his hardness still rested inside her heat. "To round one." And then he pounded into her until the peacefulness of the wood was shattered with their cries.

CHAPTER 21

The tinny sound of thin metal steadily clattering pattered its way into her consciousness. A muted bubbling hiss softened the rattle. The rich aroma of freshly brewed coffee wafted through the air.

Her eyes popped open. Coffee? Now she was dreaming about coffee? She really needed to cut back. But wait—she wasn't dreaming. Clutching the light blanket more snugly across her breasts, she propped up on an elbow and blinked a bleary-eyed gaze around the dimly lit clearing, misty and cozy with pale beams of early morning light filtering down through the leaves.

Sure enough. Spitting and sputtering at the edge of a small fire, firmly wedged in the glowing bed of hot orange coals, was Vivienne's battered and stained metal coffeepot that always accompanied them on their LARP competition encampments. The precious pot of caffeine was always kept full and waiting on the grate over the ever-present campfire in front of their private tents. And dear Vivienne had been thoughtful enough to stow it in with their gear for this jump. *Bless you, Vivienne.*

Inhaling a deep appreciative breath, Lilia closed her eyes and smiled. And bless Graham, for learning how to make coffee. Of course, she wasn't stupid. While she didn't doubt the man had learned the simple chore because he cared about her, she also knew Graham had learned to make coffee as an integral part of his survival. When not fully loaded with the steaming hot black nectar of the gods, she had to admit she was a royal bitch on wheels in the morning.

Lilia rolled to her feet, tucking the blanket around her body and securing it under her arm. Skipping across the spongy carpet of green moss to the blue-and-white-speckled metal cup waiting beside the gurgling coffeepot, she stole a quick glance around the quiet grove.

Where was he? Graham was nowhere to be seen. She shrugged, turning back to squat beside the fire. He must have gone deeper into the hidden grove to water some trees.

She wrapped a corner of the blanket around one hand, lifted the coffee from the fire, and filled her cup. Rolling back on her heels, she eased in a sip of the scalding black liquid, then heaved a contented sigh. A bit on the strong side but still damn good.

She slowly rose, the hot metal cup balanced gingerly between her hands. Meandering around the gently rippling pool, she sipped the strong, black brew between carefully placed steps. Small stones and twigs embedded in the cushiony moss found the tender soles of her bare feet, threatening to pinch and bruise if she didn't take care.

It was so peaceful here. So soothing. She smiled down at her relaxed reflection dancing across the quickly receding level in the cup. Eliza had known full well how much good this trip to the past would do her. Smart woman, that Eliza.

"I see ye found yer coffee."

Graham's deep seductive voice triggered a delicious shiver. She turned, her mouth, as well as several other parts of her, watering hot and ready at the sight of him, bare-chested and tempting, wearing nothing but his boots and a low-slung plaid.

"I did find my coffee, thank you." She took another long sip, her gaze locked with his. "It's *one* of my favorite ways to start the day." She shimmied the blanket loose and allowed it to fall into a pile at her feet. No sense in letting such a promising opportunity slip away. Still sipping her coffee, she sauntered toward him. "But there is another way that's even finer than bacon and biscuits."

Graham's widening smile lit up his face like the sun breaking over the horizon. "A finer way indeed. That's for sure and for certain." He tossed aside his plaid, leaving no doubt that he would choose morning sex over food any day.

"Yo to the camp!"

"Shit!" Lilia whirled around, scooped up the blanket, and yanked it back around her body. Coffee spilled. Orgasm-over-easy shot to hell. Today was not starting out so great after all.

Angus tromped into the clearing, holding up a pair of limp rabbits by the ears. A proud grin split his grubby face as he waved the dead animals first at Graham, then at Lilia. "I've got us a fine breakfast fit for a chieftain!"

"Damn ye, man!" Graham retrieved his plaid and jerked it around his waist.

Angus's proud expression melted into a confused scowl. "Ye fancy rabbits for breakfast. Always have." He held up the game and gave them a closer look. "And they're fine fat ones. They've fed well this season."

Lilia suppressed a gag. She didn't know whether to cry over the murder of the poor creatures or just knock the hell out of Angus. She stomped over, snatched up her backpack, then leveled a stern look at Graham. "Take him for a walk. I'm getting dressed and then we need to refill all our water and get some extra to carry back to where we arrived. The higher ground will be easier for me to maintain a good visual on the moon for the jump back tonight."

Angus held out the rabbits to her. "What about these? Ye are not going to fix them for us?"

She took in a deep breath and slowly blew it out, reasoning that it wasn't Angus's fault. It was the way of this time. She turned to Graham, his smug grin and knowing demeanor irritating her off even more. He knew she was about to explode and was waiting for the show. "Take him for a walk," she said through gritted teeth.

"But these are fine rabbits." Angus took a step closer. "Fresh as can—"

"Angus—I would advise you to go for a walk." She wrapped the handle of her backpack around her right hand, readying it to use as a weapon.

Graham finally stepped forward, grabbing Angus by the shoulder and steering him back toward the trees. "Ye best do as she says, man. I would hate to see good meat go to waste."

"Go to waste?"

"Aye." Graham glanced back at Lilia with a sly wink. "My dear wife is about to shove those rabbits up yer arse."

He already knew her well. Lilia loosened her hold on the backpack as the men disappeared into the trees. Time to get dressed and pack up the camp. They wouldn't jump back to the future until tonight but with Angus returned, there would be no more privacy.

She hurried into her clothes. How long would it take them to do whatever they needed to do to those poor rabbits before cooking them? Snugging the band tighter around the compactly rolled sleeping bag, she shuddered. The men could eat the rabbits. She'd be happy with more coffee and a protein bar.

Coffee. Definitely more coffee. She retrieved her cup and squatted beside the dying fire. At least there were enough coals to ensure the coffee was still hot. She lifted the pot and started to pour but a heart-stopping surge of hatred and even darker emotions slammed into her senses, knocking the cup and coffeepot out of her hands.

She scrambled backward on all fours, struggling to get to her feet. They were back. So many. So much hate. She had to get to Graham and Angus. Had to warn them.

An enraged roar and an explosive stream of Gaelic cursing shattered the stillness of the quiet glade. Branches snapped and hard thuds shook through the underbrush and saplings just past the large boulder to her right.

Greed. Excitement. Revenge. Hatred. The scourge of toxic emotions vibrated through the clearing even louder than the growled-out words or the sounds of bodies crashing through the timbers.

She dropped to a defensive crouch behind the boulder, then eased up and carefully peeped over the stone's edge. How many and where were they?

"I'll be a killing ye, I will!" Angus shot out of a cluster of saplings, his body airborne, arms and legs pumping. A man twice his size landed on top of him, knocking Angus from side to side with bone-cracking jabs of his meaty fists.

Lilia's heart went out to poor Angus. She was no match for that wooly bastard. She might be grand champion of the Highland war games but without real weapons, she was about as lethal as a kitten.

She took off across the clearing in a crouching run away from the fight. Got to hide. Got to plan. Got to figure out something. She tried not to think about what the men might be doing to Graham. Got to stay calm.

A thick tangle of ivy vines trailing down from the sagging branches of a dying tree caught her eye. Perfect. She worked her way into the small, sheltered space created by the veil of green and hunkered down, holding her breath, and forcing herself to maintain control. She had to hide until she found out what was going on.

"Where the hell is yer witch? We'll beat ye both bloody and make ye beg fer death if ye dinna tell us."

"Ye will find I never beg—not for anything. And ye must be daft or drowning in yer cups. There is no witch." Graham's voice, strained and filled with . . . Anger. Rage. Protectiveness. Lilia knotted a fist between her breasts, pressing hard against the panicked pounding of her heart.

Graham was hurting—not physically—at least not a great deal from physical pain but he was enraged and afraid. He feared for her safety more than his own. She felt it more surely than she felt her fear for him.

She barely fingered aside a few of the waxy green leaves and strained to see. Two men—large, snarling, walking walls of muscle that looked to be more along the lines of unwashed, shaggy beasts rather than humans—stood on either side of Graham, twisting his arms back so hard from his sides that he arched against their hold. If the bastards kept yanking him around and pulling at his arms, they would surely dislocate both his shoulders.

A much shorter man stood in front of Graham, shaking both his meaty fists in Graham's face. Graham's antagonist was nearly as wide as he was tall. He stalked around with his barrel chest thrown out and his grubby, double chins bouncing between his sagging jowls. "Think me a fool, ye goat-swiving bastard? Me chieftain bade me stand guard. Offered me gold, he did. Told me to watch the Highlands for the strange black cloud and the sound of the sky splitting. Said a witch would bring ye back when ye finally felt yer sorry arse might have been forgotten and ye thought it safe to return to yer clan."

The squat man hopped closer, reminding Lilia of an ugly, over-sized toad. "I saw the swirling cloud and heard the sound of which he spoke. And then I laid me eyes on yer evil bitch meself afore I gathered me men and sent word to the chieftain ye had in fact returned. I'll be a rich man because of ye—and I thank ye for that." The brute wagged his head, his face appearing even more grotesque with a rotten-toothed smile. "And I tell ye this: me chief has never forgotten how ye shamed him at the verra heart of his own land."

The repulsive man jiggled his head back and forth from side to side as though keeping time to a silent tune. "Of course, neither his wife nor his mistress helped yer chance at being forgotten—not one sorry whit, I grant ye that. Them women have ensured that the size of yer great cock is well talked about within the halls of Buchanan Keep to this verra day. Hell, man. 'Tis a wonder the Lady Buchanan didna weave its image into her latest tapestry."

A sick feeling shot a burning knot of bile to the back of Lilia's throat. Buchanan. How the blazes had a clan from the lower end of the Highlands so quickly discovered Graham's return this far north?

"Me chieftain filled the Highlands with his spies—even bade them live amongst Clan MacKenna and tend yer witch's family. A cuckolded man's hatred ne'er grows cold, ye understand." The Buchanan toad nodded at Graham's crotch. "And every time his wife moaned about the weight hanging betwixt yer legs, the Buchanan sent more men to find ye. He kent ye couldna stay away from the land forever—no matter what yer chieftain swore."

Graham remained silent, lips curled back and teeth clenched in a sneer.

The short bastard puffed up even more then thumped a stumpy finger against Graham's chest. "Now, where's yer witch?" The scowling man raked the back of one hand across his mouth while he squinted around the clearing. "Surely me chief will reward me double if I drag yer golden-haired whore in alongside ye—after me men and I have sampled her wares, of course."

Graham lunged forward, catching the two brutes lashing his arms behind his back off guard. He butted his head hard against the shorter man's face, bloodying the fiend's nose and knocking him backward before his captors yanked him back in place.

"My goddess returned me to this time." Graham arched against their hold, straining to break free. "And I ken there is only one whore here and that is the one who jumps to do the bidding of a chieftain who has nothing more than a wee stump hanging 'twixt his legs and can think with nothing other than that short stubby head."

The toad-like man floundered to his feet, yanked his dirk from its sheath, and sliced it up across Graham's bared chest. The slash split open a long shallow cut, spilling blood from Graham's lower right rib cage, up across his chest, and to his left shoulder. "Ye best thank the gods me chief ordered ye kept alive if I wanted me gold. If I had me druthers, I'd take ye back to him in pieces."

The man holding tightly to barely conscious Angus shook him like a rag doll. "What of this one here? Can we kill him?" He grinned down at Angus, bloodlust filling his face.

The leader made a disgusted face and shook his head. "Nay. The chieftain will wish to make sport wi' that one afore he kills this one."

Lilia fisted both hands against her mouth, pressing them tight and hard to keep herself from screaming. She had to bide her time. Especially now that Sir Ugly-Ass had just told her that Graham and Angus would be kept alive. At least for a little while. She had to stay calm. She had to plan. She couldn't do anything alone, especially since they'd already trussed up Graham with enough ropes and leather strapping that it looked as though the bonds were about to cut his body into pieces.

She held her breath to keep from sobbing aloud as they shoved and prodded Graham out of the clearing and pushed him through the trees. Angus's captor alternately dragged then propelled the stumbling Angus along behind them.

Taking care to remain well hidden, she angled around, following them through the trees as best she could. She chewed her lip so hard, she soon tasted blood. Oddly enough, the coppery tang calmed her, setting her sense of revenge into place like shuffling a deck of cards and preparing to deal.

She would fire portal Granny. Granny would know what to do. Lilia kept her gaze locked on the path between the trees—the path where they'd just shoved and dragged the men out of view. Tracking them by their sounds, she worked her way through the woods, hiding among the underbrush and behind knotted clusters of saplings until she caught up with the group.

Her heart ached as she watched Graham fight them, thrashing from side to side and doing his damnedest to ram them with his bloodstained head.

Stop fighting them. I'll get help. Just go with them before they kill you. Please—stop fighting them and wait for me. She willed her thoughts and fears into him, praying he would somehow hear her.

He crashed to the ground, his bloodied chest bouncing hard against the rocky terrain. As if he had in fact heard her, he twisted and faced her, his cheek grinding into the earth as he glared at her with a narrow-eyed gaze. His split and bloodied lips barely moved across his clenched teeth but she clearly read the words he mouthed over and over until his captors yanked him back to his feet, looped a leather strap around his throat and forehead, and jerked him toward the horses.

Go, he had mouthed. *Go home.*

Like hell she would. Lilia sank back into the trees and crouched. Time to wait. Time to plan. This wasn't over by a long shot.

CHAPTER 22

Lilia paced another lap around the cold ashes of the spent fire. How had things gone bad so quickly? Just last night, she had been in Graham's arms, drifting off to sleep while watching the dancing flames of their campfire. Contented. Peaceful. Genuinely happy for the first time in her life. And now . . . this.

She squinted up through the gently swaying branches of the trees, noting the position of the sun winking through the foliage. It hadn't been long enough since the group of marauders had ridden past the crest of the hill. If she built another fire now, the Buchanan bastards might spot it and decide to turn back. A column of smoke rising from the woods would be a dead giveaway. But she needed fire —no—she needed red-hot coals—badly. She couldn't reach Granny through the fire portal without them.

Her hands knotted into shaking fists. She hated waiting. Cracking her knuckles, she squeezed her fists tighter as a nauseating combination of rage, fear, and *this can't be happening* churned through her. Maybe it was good she had to wait. She needed to calm down. The longer she paced around what a few hours ago had been a loving nest of sensual contentment, the more her plans to save Graham and Angus solidified into cold, hard tactical certainty.

Let the fire go, dearie. Those Buchanan fools are traveling slow—watching close for any sign of ye. And they've taken pains to leave a few of their own behind. The hateful bastards are hidden on the far side of the cliffs. I heard the goat-swiving curs say so myself.

Lilia whirled around, searching the clearing for the voice she had never thought to hear again—except maybe in her dreams. The shaded glade was empty. Eerily quiet. She eased forward across the carpet of moss, stopping at the edge of the softly rippling water. Her scowling reflection stared up at her. "Stop it. Now is not the time to lose it," she hissed at the rippling image.

Ye are not losing it, silly child. A gentle breeze swirled around Lilia, riffling through her hair as though attempting to console her. *Did I not tell ye I would check in on ye from time to time?*

Eliza's voice disappeared, making Lilia think that maybe she hadn't really heard the feisty old woman after all.

I'll be moving on soon but I wanted to have a wee word wi' ye before I left. Course, I'll pop in every now and then. Ne'er ye fret around that.

Lilia slowly backed away from the pool's edge, swallowing hard and breathing deeply as she looked around the clearing. Keeping her voice low, partly to keep from being found and partly because she felt more than a little odd talking to thin air, she had to argue. "But I can't see you. How do I know I'm not cracking up?"

Did ye not always tell me I would be in yer heart?

Lilia pulled her jacket tighter around her. August or not, she was suddenly quite chilled. Maybe it really was Eliza. "Yes. I did say that —many times," she whispered.

Ye hear me in yer thoughts because ye have me in yer heart—and because ye have the sight. There is that as well. After all, ye are a Sinclair, child.

Emotions churning, the threat of tears burned her eyes. Lilia swallowed hard, then cleared her throat. She didn't need this now. Eliza's loss was still a raw open wound that would have to be tended to later. She had to focus on saving Graham. "Unless you can tell me how to rescue Graham and Angus, I'm really not up to having a chat right now. I'm sorry. I just can't."

Ye ken as well as I what ye need do.

"I need a fire so I can talk to Granny." Lilia paced alongside the pool; hands fisted at her sides. She stopped walking and glared up into the treetops, forcing herself to continue speaking in a soft whisper when she really wanted to shout. "You told me I shouldn't build one because the Buchanans had left some watchmen behind. So, what am I supposed to do now?"

The familiar sound of Eliza's old habit of clearing her throat when she was attempting to steer conversations where she wished them to go echoed through Lilia's mind.

I appreciate ye looking up when ye speak to me—much nicer than looking downward.

Lilia was in no mood for Eliza's sense of humor although it did affirm that maybe it really was her recently passed guardian chattering inside her head. "So what is my plan, Eliza? Sneak up on their camp? Steal their horses? What?"

See? I kent ye'd already thought up a fine ploy. Now . . . get on with it. I've much to do but I wanted to see ye on yer way before I left ye for a bit. I kent ye'd be finer than the King's crown, but I had to be certain. Ye make me proud, lass, and I ken yer fine stubbornness will always see ye through.

Steal their horses and then haul ass to MacKenna Keep for reinforcements. One rider could cover a lot of ground fast. Faster than a group of men dragging two prisoners behind their horses. Prisoners that they dare not kill for fear of their chieftain's wrath.

Buchanan lands were situated quite a bit farther south of the MacKenna stronghold. Graham had told her so when they were planning the jump back. If she could make it to MacKenna Keep in a day's ride, there'd be plenty of time to round up the men she needed to rescue Graham and kick some Buchanan ass.

"I don't suppose you'd be willing to point the way to the Buchanans' spy camp?" Lilia waited, listening hard. The only sound she heard was the gurgling water from the spring and the wind rushing through the trees. "*Now?* You pick now to move on?" Still no response from Eliza.

"Great," Lilia muttered as she yanked her backpack out of the tangled curtain of ivy then carefully draped the vines back in place over Graham's pack and the supplies she couldn't carry. Time to travel light and fast.

She paused before taking up her walking stick. She didn't really need it but she just couldn't leave it behind. Graham had carved two intertwined hearts just above the smoothed handgrip. He had carefully stripped away all the rough bark for the sake of her palms, carved the hearts, then placed it in her hands with a loving kiss. The gnarled walking stick had become a precious gift. Tears threatened again, setting off a prickling burn in her eyes. With a hard shake of her head, she hurried into the woods, stepping carefully with as little commotion as possible. No time for tears. Not now.

Rather than take the easier path back to the cliffs' summit, she stayed to the brush-filled ravines and fissures. She hated the delay of the rougher route but she had to stay hidden—at least until dark. She moved as quietly as she could, constantly straining to hear any sound that might signal she wasn't alone. The only emotional energy her senses detected was her own tormented misery.

Eliza had said the Buchanan men were camped on the far side of the cliffs. She wished her mentor had said how many. As the shadows lengthened, she moved faster, changing her path to the easier footing that was now sheltered by the late afternoon shadows.

By dusk, she'd reached the point where the time portal had spit them out. She paused, crouching between the rough sides of a pair of fallen rocks, and surveyed the area. There didn't appear to be anyone around but the dirt of the clearing was covered with more bootprints than would've been made by Graham and Angus. Deep boot prints. Heavy steps. After a deep drink from her water bottle, she closed her eyes and leaned against one of the cold gray stones. She needed to concentrate. If she was close enough, she would be able to *feel* the Buchanan guards.

Nothing stirred—even the wind had died with the setting sun.

Beyond the cliffs. That was where Eliza had said the watchman were camped. Which cliffs and how far? And how many men were there? Dammit, Eliza.

Frustration. Impatience. Jealousy. Envy. For the first time since Graham's capture, the hint of a smile tickled the corners of her mouth. There they were. "Lead me to you," she whispered. "Keep feeling." Ever so quietly she scanned the area as she moved forward with painstakingly slow careful movements.

Then she heard them. A low humming of deep voices. Farther west. The men couldn't be very far past the ridge where the time portal had opened.

"Never again, says I. Never again." One man who sounded younger with the husky up-and-down pitch of raging hormones.

"Never again what?" A sharp intake of breath and a loud yawn. Another man. Definitely older. And bored.

Lilia crept closer, tightening her hold on her staff just in case. It wasn't the best weapon in the world but it was better than nothing.

"I ain't never again staying back to keep watch. Gonna make'm cast lots to choose the one that has to do it. Ain't fair to me just cause I'm the youngest."

A deep chuckle and then another loud yawn. "Go check the horses, boy."

Peeping through the dense brush, Lilia searched the cleared area the men had scraped out in the middle of an overgrown dip in the mountainside. Their camp was tiny, barely big enough for two. No fire. Apparently, they didn't wish to be found any more than she did.

The heavier man, balding with a scraggly fringe of gray sprouting down around his ears, settled deeper into his plaid, then tucked his chin to his chest. "Ye've got first watch. Wake me after a few hours."

"Why've I got first watch? Ye stayed here drinking all the ale whilst I searched for the witch." A knob-kneed youth, pimply-faced and crowned with carrot-red hair, kicked the boot of the older man lounging against a tree.

The reclining man didn't even open his eyes, just resettled his folded arms across his chest. "Ye kick me boot again and ye'll never wake up the next time ye choose to close yer eyes."

Lilia could see the boy's oversized Adam's apple skitter up, then down his long neck in a hard swallow. Leeriness rolled off the boy in

thick waves. Lilia smiled. Breathing came a bit easier with the knowl-
edge that the odds were in her favor. The kid was unsure of himself.
Inexperienced. Stealing the horses would be easier.

The frustrated lad stood there a moment longer, staring down at
the now snoring man as though struggling to decide if it was worth
the risk to challenge his elder. His insecurities finally won out. With
knotted fists shaking at his sides, he jerked away and stomped out of
the clearing.

Lilia waited a moment longer, closely watching the sleeping man.
Something wasn't right. The emotions he was sending out were too
strong and active. Sleepy drunks didn't ping her senses with the alert-
ness of a predator.

Just as she thought. The old faker. The wily warrior barely lifted
his head, a smug look wrinkling his grubby face as his narrow-eyed
gaze followed the boy. A quiet chuckle shifted him as he settled back
down and closed his eyes.

Lilia waited until she was certain the man slept for real this time.
She preferred not to tangle with a seasoned warrior. She could easily
handle the boy. Carefully skirting the clearing, her steps were
muffled by years of dried pine needles carpeting the ground in thick
layers. She homed in on the boy's fiery emotions and his steady
stream of hushed cursing.

"Lazy old bastard. I'll show 'im what for one of these days." The
boy stumbled and fell against one of the horses. The massive beast
barely shifted, swished his long black tail, and flipped it in the boy's
face. "Leave off!" The boy shoved the horse as he righted himself to
his feet. "Dunno how the hell I'm s'posed to check on the damn
animals. Can't see a thing without fire nor torch!"

The boy was right. The fading light wasn't exactly helping her
observe her prey either. But she had to get the horses before the
moon rose much higher. Lilia crept closer. *Come on, kid. Get somewhere
and steal a snooze. You know you want to.* The more she watched the
sullen youth, the more she realized that wasn't around to happen.
The boy's angst was keeping him wide awake. Her own angst was

keeping her on edge too. Precious time was slipping away. She needed those horses. Now.

Lilia rolled the solid hardwood staff in her hands. Time to help laddie boy take a nap. She'd been penalized in several Highland competitions for knocking out her opponents when her temper got the best of her. She had a reputation for beaning them in the back of the head—much like she'd done to Graham after he'd spanked her. All her competitors had learned never to turn their backs on her when she was mad. But the unsuspecting Buchanan teenager wouldn't know that.

The boy shuffled toward her, glaring down at the ground as he kicked up clumps of pine needles in front of him. He paused within a few feet of her, stopping right in front of a large chunk of limestone. He stared at it for a long moment, stole a quick glance back at the horses, then stood on tiptoe and peered in the direction of the clearing where the old man's guttural snoring was rattling through the trees.

Lilia sank lower and held her breath. *Turn around, kid. Sit on the rock. Make this easier for both of us.* She didn't want to kill the boy—just knock him senseless long enough to get away with both the horses.

The red-haired lad sniffed, wiped his runny nose with the back of one hand, then plopped down in front of the rock and leaned back against it. With one last glance toward the direction of camp, he flopped his long legs wider apart, shoved his plaid to one side, and softly groaned out a loud sigh.

Oh, good heavens. Seriously? The up-and-down motion of the young man's pale right arm shining in the moonlight told her exactly what he was doing.

She silently rose and choked up on the walking stick as if stepping up to bat, then swung hard, making solid contact with the back of the unsuspecting youth's skull. She jumped to one side and drew back again in case she'd missed her mark. Mr. MacSulky might not be a man yet but he was well on his way. But there was no need for another hit. The boy went limp, falling to one side with his dick still in his hand.

She removed the shoulder straps from her backpack and secured the boy's ankles together with one of the straps, pulling the nylon material tight and resealing the hook-and-loop closures. Shoving him over until his hands were behind his back, she tied his wrists together, then pulled that strap down to the one tied around his ankles. She lashed them snug until the unconscious youth was lying bent backward with his hands locked to his heels.

Pulling her cloth headband out of the bag's side pocket, she wrapped it around a small pinecone and knotted it in the center of the strip. She forced the wadded cloth in between the boy's teeth and tied it at the back of his head.

That should slow him. Between her knotwork and the headache he was going to have, even if he did come around in the next hour or so, it would take him a while to sound the alarm. Almost as an afterthought, she discreetly settled the boy's plaid over the prized part that had kept him occupied while she took aim. Poor guy. No sense adding insult to injury.

And now for the horses. Lilia took a deep breath, calming herself as much as possible. She didn't need to transmit her anxiety to the animals. Walking toward them with her hand held palm up, she kept her tone low and soothing. "Hello, my friends. Ready for a bit of a run?"

Both horses studied her, each of them flicking an ear in interest. She untied the smaller of the two from the rope strung between two tall pines and attached the ruddy-coated mare to the back of the much larger stallion's saddle. She made sure there was enough slack in the reins between the two horses before guiding them over to the limestone boulder beside their still unconscious caretaker.

Using the large rock to boost herself up, she launched herself onto the back of the great black brute, settling comfortably in the well-worn saddle. This horse reminded her of Odin. "I hope you've got my friend's stamina and speed," she said softly as she kneed him forward.

The slack went out of the reins between the two horses and Lilia's mount stopped. She looked back, her heart panging at the sight of the chestnut mare nosing the young man while softly grumbling as though telling him to rise. It was obvious the horse cared for the boy but it couldn't be helped. She didn't dare leave a horse behind for the men. Lilia gently but firmly pulled the reins while at the same time urging the black stallion forward.

The reluctant horse finally took a few steps then stopped again, flicked her ears at Lilia, then looked back at the young man lying just behind her. Deathly still, the pale boy looked an eerie blue white by the light of the rising moon.

Before Lilia could pull on the reins again, the mare hiked her tail. An avalanche of steaming turds splatted and bounced across the ground, coming to rest in a well-aimed pile plastered up against the unconscious lad's head. The horse bobbed her nose in an up-and-down wave, swished her tail, then trotted past Lilia and the stallion, taking the lead as far as her reins would allow.

Apparently, the mare didn't like the boy as much as she thought. Lilia hurried the horses quietly away from the camp, keeping them to the silence of the pine-needled woods. With one last glance back, she barely made out the dark outline of the still form against the moonlit backdrop of the limestone boulder. "Sweet dreams, laddie," she whispered.

Clearing the woods and heading to higher ground, Lilia urged the horses to a faster pace. She had a lot of ground to cover in very little time.

CHAPTER 23

Generous splashes of cool spring water helped to wash the grit and weariness from her eyes. Lilia soused her extra T-shirt into the brook, wrung it out, then draped the damp twisted cloth across the back of her neck. She pulled in a deep breath and briefly closed her eyes. Where was Graham now? How was he? What were those bastards doing to him?

Stop it. Panic helped nothing. She reached down and splashed more water on her face. Stretching tall, she rolled her shoulders, working the knots out of her muscles. Hours of riding coupled with mounting tension had wound her tighter than a steel coil.

Downstream a few feet, both horses sloshed in the shallows of the softly gurgling stream, drinking long and deep from the clear crystal flow. She'd hated to stop but she'd pushed the animals hard. If she didn't give them some rest, she'd soon find herself walking.

From the position of the sun, it had to be barely past noon. Maybe. Lilia shaded her eyes, studying the azure sky streaked with wisps of white. She wished she'd listened closer the last time Granny had explained figuring time and direction using only the tools provided by nature.

Lilia felt pretty certain of where she was because she and Odin had explored the Highlands many times. She'd also ridden through them during brief visits back to the past to see Granny and her sisters. The Highlands she knew the best were the mountains and glens of twenty-first-century Scotland. But amazingly—not that much had changed. The biggest difference she noticed was the absence of asphalt roads.

Moving to a better position to see past the sparse hedging of trees growing along each side of the creek, she studied the area. Thankfully she was still very much alone. No sign of any rogue Buchanans hot on her trail nor had she come across the ones holding Graham and Angus prisoner. She'd specifically kept to the higher elevations to avoid catching up with the Buchanans. She intended to rescue Graham and Angus but it was futile to go against a dozen or so men by herself.

A wistful sigh escaped her. *Please let him be okay.* She swallowed hard and scrubbed her knuckles against the center of her chest. She ached to have this over and done. Graham's rescue had to end well. It just had to.

Shaking free of her fears, Lilia made note of the growing harshness of the landscape to her left and the direction of the stream, then turned to her right and squinted up at the sun again. "Good. That was west and from the looks of those cliffs, the keep shouldn't be much farther."

Both horses lifted their heads and looked at her.

"Sorry, guys. Talking to myself." For some strange reason, talking out loud made her feel better. She huffed out a bitter laugh. "Got to keep myself centered somehow."

Pulling in another deep breath and blowing it out hard and fast, she firmly shut down, once and for all, the sickening *what ifs* playing through her mind. She refused to acknowledge anything other than a successful rescue. Period.

Moving back to the shelter of the trees, she took some comfort from the fact that the lay of the land was looking more and more familiar. She was positive she had ridden through here before. This was MacKenna land and she should reach the keep well before nightfall.

A subtle movement in the branches of a nearby tree caught her attention. Lilia moved closer, shading her eyes against the bright sunlight flickering through the shifting foliage.

An owl. A white owl at that, perched high up in the branches and peering down at her with great dark eyes. Around one ankle, barely visible beneath the tufts of pearly white feathers and almost brushing the owl's powerful talons, was a ribbon. A purple ribbon.

Lilia smiled. Purple was her niece Chloe's favorite color. The owl was her guardian, Oren. She must be closer to the keep than she thought.

"It's good to see you, Oren."

The owl spread his wings, silently launched out of the tree, and floated down to a closer branch just above Lilia's shoulder. He primly settled himself more comfortably, turned his head to gaze southwestward for a long moment, then swiveled his attention back to Lilia and slowly blinked.

"I really wish you could talk," she said.

The owl looked southwestward again, then turned and stared back at Lilia.

"What are you looking at?" Lilia shifted, aligning herself with the owl's line of sight and looking in the direction he seemed to find so interesting. The tightness knotting her shoulders eased exponentially.

Two riders, one tall in the saddle with long dark hair in a flowing ponytail and the other rider so tiny as to almost be hidden behind the great horse's head and neck. And what from this distance looked like a half-grown black bear lumbering along in a gamboling run beside the pair of horses. Trulie, Chloe, and Karma.

Lilia vaulted across the shallow stream, waving both arms as she cleared the trees. "Trulie! Chloe! Over here!"

Karma sounded off with a deep baying bark that echoed across the land. He kept up the happy racket as he stretched into the fastest lope his huge body could muster. He plowed into her at full speed, knocking her down with happy yips and well-placed slobbery kisses.

"Oh, Karma, please . . . stop," Lilia giggled, twisting and turning to keep from getting her face thoroughly washed. "I've missed you too."

"Auntie Lil! Auntie Lil!" Chloe's ecstatic squeal made *Auntie Lil* sound like one long Gaelic word that meant pure delight. "Get me down, Mama, 'fore Karma gets all the kisses."

Trulie dismounted, hurried around the horses, and held up her arms. "Jump, kiddo."

Without a moment's hesitation, Chloe jumped, then wiggled free of her mother's protective hold and hit the ground running. She flew across the short distance, dodged Karma's wagging tail, then nudged the big dog out of the way with an impatient bump of her tiny hip. "My turn, Karma. Move."

The huge beast immediately complied, sidestepping out of her way. He plopped down on his haunches, his long red tongue hanging out one side in an open-mouthed doggy smile.

"I've missed you, munchkin!" Lilia grabbed up Chloe, closing her eyes as she hugged the child tight.

Chloe squirmed free, smiling up into Lilia's face. "I told Mama ye were here but she didna believe me." Lightly patting a pudgy hand against Lilia's cheek, Chloe barely nodded, her knowing expression chillingly identical to the look Granny always assumed when one of her plots had come to fruition. "Dinna fash o'er much, Auntie Lil. 'Tis all gonna be just fine. I promise."

Lilia looked up at Trulie, a mix of emotions raking their claws across her already raw nerves. "Just how accurate is she?"

"She hasn't been wrong yet." Trulie gently guided Chloe to one side and helped Lilia up from the ground, pulling her into a hug that nearly cracked her ribs.

Trulie finally released her, stepped back, and held her at arm's length. Lilia could see the moisture misting in her sister's eyes. She understood completely. This visit to the past was different. A lot more was at stake.

Clearing her throat with a light cough, Trulie gently squeezed

Lilia's shoulders, then slowly let her hands fall away. She looked down at Chloe, then gently cupped her daughter's chin in her hand. "Granny says she has never seen the sight so strong in one so young. But she must learn when to speak of what she has seen and when to keep her mouth shut—for her own safety."

"Auntie Lil would never hurt me," Chloe defended with an imperious bob of her dark head. Her wild abandon of springy curls bounced as though affirming her statement. "She's not one of them infernal witch hunting bastards."

"Chloe!" Trulie's eyes flared wide in shock.

Lilia bit her lower lip, holding her breath to keep from laughing.

"You do not talk like that. You know better." Trulie rolled her eyes and blew out a weary groan. With a frustrated shake of her head, she turned back to Lilia. "She spends entirely too much time with her father and Colum."

"Ye said it too." Chloe edged closer and hugged her arm around Lilia's leg, the slyly innocent look on her face a dead giveaway to what she was doing. "So does Granny and Auntie Kenna. That's why I called Rabbie an irritating bastard when he wouldna leave my dolls be."

"When we get back to the keep, you and I are going to have a long chat that you're going to remember this time." Trulie pointed at the stream. "Lead the horses over for a drink. Karma will help you. I'm not happy with you and it would be best if you did as you're told and stayed quiet for a bit before I decide to heat up your tail right here in front of Auntie Lil."

Chloe's shoulders slumped and her lower lip quivered. "Aye, Mama." Without another word, she shuffled back to the horses, scooped up their reins, and headed toward the stream.

Trulie turned back to Lilia but her irritated glare was still fixed on her daughter. "Granny says her curse worked. I have given birth to a child who acts just like I did when I was that age. Beware if you and Graham have children."

"I have to save him first." Lilia's voice broke. She blinked hard and fast against the tears she'd been holding back ever since his capture.

"If I can't get him back from the Buchanans, there won't be any children."

"What?" Mouth ajar, Trulie stared at her, Chloe's indiscretions immediately forgotten.

"The Buchanans found us and captured Graham and Angus."

Trulie caught hold of her hands and squeezed. "Captured? Wait. Go back and start at the beginning. When we talked to you through the fire portal, you said you were coming back to spread Eliza's ashes but we wouldn't get to see you this time because Graham insisted on coming with you. You didn't want to cause any trouble with the clan and risk being discovered. The three of you were just going to pop in, then pop right back out. How did the Buchanans find you? Their lands lie south of here."

Lilia could still hear the squat, disgusting man's words. They were permanently branded into her mind. "Spies." She turned and looked for Chloe. The child had found a stick and was stirring it in the creek. "The ringleader said the Buchanan chieftain had placed spies in MacKenna Keep. They must have discovered my plans. I don't remember for sure but I think I told Granny where we would enter."

"Son of a bitch," Trulie whispered, her brow creasing with a scowl. Eyes narrowed, she stared off in space, one finger thoughtfully tapping her chin.

Lilia took hold of Trulie's arm and squeezed it. "I don't have time to figure out how they found us. I need Gray's help. His men. The whole clan would be even better. We've got to get Graham and Angus back before they reach Buchanan Keep." A sudden sense of time slipping away felt like a red-hot iron burning through her chest. She needed them to weapon-up and ride out to save Graham now.

Trulie looked at her with an expression that chilled her to the bone. A sense of sadness, even hopelessness, emanated from her like a toxic shadow.

Lilia stepped back, forcing her empathic senses back on lockdown—a rare thing for her to have to do when around her family. She couldn't handle anything else right now. She was already in emotional overload. "What?"

"I don't know that Gray will do that." Trulie barely shook her head. "The clan heard his pledge in the hall—that if Graham returned from exile, he would be turned over to the Buchanans. You know what a chieftain's word means to his clan. Gray has no choice."

"I don't give a damn what the clan thinks. You know what they're going to do to Graham." Lilia hitched back a sob. No tears—not now. "They'll torture him, Trulie. Kill him slowly to make sure he suffers. You know that."

"I know," Trulie whispered, turning away.

"What would you do if it was Gray?" Lilia grabbed Trulie by the shoulder and forced her sister to face her. "Tell me, Trulie. What would you do?"

Trulie set her jaw, lifted her head, and locked an unblinking gaze on Lilia. "I would move heaven and earth to get him back. Do whatever it took."

"Then help me." Lilia squeezed Trulie's arm tighter. "Please . . . help me."

Trulie's scowl softened. Her attention shifted to a point past Lilia's shoulder. A faint smile curled the corner of her mouth. "If I can't convince Gray to help, Granny can figure out an angle he won't be able to refuse." Then she looked back at Lilia. "And if Granny fails, there is always my secret weapon."

"Secret weapon?"

Trulie pointed at her daughter. "Chloe."

CHAPTER 24

"I canna believe ye would ask such a thing. I am bound by my word. Ye ken that well enough, aye?" Gray wouldn't face Lilia. He stood beside the hearth, jaw locked and nostrils flared, staring down at the floor.

The air in the usually comfortable chieftain's solar was stifling hot and it had nothing to do with the warmth of the late August day. Gray pounded his fist on the wooden beam running the width of the fireplace. With an agitated rake of his hand through his black shoulder-length hair, he finally turned and glared dead straight at Lilia. Teeth bared in a frustrated scowl; he jabbed a finger first at Trulie then swung his arm and aimed it at Granny. "I spoke Graham's sentence in front of my kin. The scribe took it down in the hall ledger and affixed my seal to it. There is no going back. I canna break an oath."

"There is always a loophole." Granny took Lilia's hand and squeezed it tight. "And besides—Graham is family now. I can't believe you're going to stand there and tell us that you're going to allow your *kin* to be tortured and murdered." Granny's eyes narrowed and she stepped toward Gray, pulling Lilia with her.

Oh, dear. Poor Gray. Granny was going in for the kill. Well . . . so be it. They needed less talk and more action. Time was slipping away. Lilia squeezed Granny's hand, silently urging her on.

"Mother Sinclair makes a valid argument," Colum said from the far corner of the room. He was slowly wrapping the handle of a wooden child-sized sword with a strip of leather. He looped the last of the strand around the haft then pulled it tight with his teeth. He placed the sword on the small table beside him, aligning it with an identical weapon he had already finished. Dull-bladed swords for his twin sons. "Mayhap now the lads will leave Chloe's treasures alone." He rose from the bench and turned to Gray. "Graham is kin now since he's husband to our good sister here."

"That doesna change the man's sentence. I named the terms and they didna hinge on whether he married Mistress Lilia or not. He was not to return here under any circumstances." Gray sadly shook his head, his voice growing softer. "I canna help ye, Lady Lilia. I am verra sorry." He stepped forward and took her hand, ignoring Granny completely. "All I can do is demand that his remains be returned to Clan MacKenna. We will lay him to rest here."

"And *that* is supposed to fucking console me?" Lilia yanked her hand away from Gray, ignoring Granny's sharp intake of breath. Granny hated the f-word but this time Granny was just going to have to get over it. Lilia was well past nice, ladylike requesting level. She'd hit frustrated bitch overload and somebody was damn well going to do something. "If you don't help me, I'll just go by myself and then you can have them box up my remains along with Graham's. A twofer. Will that make you feel better about keeping your precious word?"

Gray backed up as though she had just slapped him. "Lady Lilia—"

"Don't take that placating tone with me." She stomped to the far end of the room and yanked a shield off the wall. "I'm taking this. I need a sword, a bow, and some arrows. Is there anything else in your dumbass edict that says you can't give your sister-in-law any weapons?"

"Lilia, don't." Trulie hurried over and pulled on the shield, frowning when Lilia yanked it back. "Let me have it. We're going to figure something out. We'll get Graham back."

"Not according to your husband, we won't." Lilia tucked the shield under her arm and jerked her chin toward Colum. "You're over the weapons. Where are they kept? I'll just take what I need and then *Gray*"—she inflected his name with all the rage surging through her —"won't be breaking his holier-than-thou word."

"Enough, Lilia." Granny stormed across the room, jerked the shield out of Lilia's hold, and grabbed hold of her arm. Pulling her back to the ring of pillowed seats curled around the hearth, she stood Lilia in front of the small leather-covered chair that everyone knew as *Granny's seat*. "You be quiet now and let me handle this."

Lilia opened her mouth to argue but shut it again when Granny held up a finger and peered over the top of her spectacles with that no-nonsense look all the girls had come to know and fear at an early age. Granny had had enough. Good. So had Lilia. She locked her stance and glared at Gray.

Trulie had joined Gray in front of the fireplace, one arm looped through her husband's and the other hand resting atop his forearm.

If the situation hadn't been so dire, Lilia would've laughed. Gray was too naïve to realize that Trulie was holding him so he couldn't get away from Granny.

Colum's reddish-gold brows shot to his hairline. In one swoop, he scooped up the pair of play swords and strode to the door. Kenna had told her how Colum had tangled with Granny before—and lost. Wise man. He knew what was about to happen to Gray.

Pulling open the door, he paused and waved the swords at Lilia. "I'll be taking these to my lads and giving Kenna a break from the wee beasties. With another bairn on the way, she tires easy. Whenever the lot of ye decide what is to be done, come and find me."

"Thank you, Colum," Lilia said. Twin two-year-olds and pregnant again. No wonder Kenna had dark circles under her eyes. A heartsick pang ached through Lilia's core. She had to save Graham. She needed the happiness her sisters had found and she needed it with a vengeance.

Granny paced slowly up and down the length of the woven rug stretched in front of the hearth. Head bowed. A thoughtful scowl in place. She walked with hands clasped against the small of her back. She reminded Lilia of all those movies she'd seen where trial lawyers went in for the kill during their summation.

"You swore that if Graham ever returned that you'd turn him over to the Buchanans. No matter what. Right?" Granny ceased her pacing. She turned and glared at Gray.

Gray shifted to one side, casting a quick frowning look at Trulie when she yanked on his arm and kept him in place. He turned back to Granny and stubbornly lifted his chin. "Ye ken verra well that I did. Ye were there."

Granny's narrow-eyed gaze shifted back to the floor and she resumed her pacing. She reached the far end of the carpet, slowly turned, then stopped again. A victorious smile blossomed, brightening her expression like the rising of the sun. "But your edict said nothing of Angus. A true MacKenna—by blood. No ultimatum was made should he decide to return. True?"

A percolating silence filled the room as though everyone held their breath. Lilia's heart hammered, its excited pounding echoing in her ears. She watched Gray closely, praying he would take Granny's tempting cue and run with it.

The man's demeanor visibly relaxed. Without looking at his wife, he gave the hand Trulie still clenched around his arm an affectionate pat. "'Tis true. And all know I willna tolerate an innocent kinsman to be taken prisoner and tortured by a neighboring clan." He grinned at Lilia. "Angus is without sin against the Buchanans. Horse thievery is more of a pastime in the Highlands—not a crime."

"So, you're coming with me then? To rescue Graham?" Lilia scrubbed her palms, damp with nervous moisture, up and down her jean-covered thighs. Finally. Some action.

Gray shook his head. "Nay, lass. Ye'll be staying here with yer family whilst I take a few chosen men to fetch Angus. And I promise ye, if Graham happens to leap onto one of our horses, we'll not have the time to stop and take him back to the Buchanans. 'Tis harvest season. I've much to do and should be visiting my tenants—not returning prisoners to the Buchanans when they've not been skilled enough to keep them from escaping."

"I'm going with you. I'm good with a sword and even better with a bow." Lilia hurried to the door, yanked it open, and stepped out into the hall. She had to find Colum. Tell him exactly what she needed. Hand still holding the heavy latch of the oak door, she ignored Gray's reddening face and nodded toward Trulie. "I don't have time to argue with him. You and Granny fill him in. It's time to lock and load."

Then she pulled the door to and jogged down the hallway. *I'm coming for you, Graham. Coming as fast as I can.*

CHAPTER 25

"Here. Take it."

Graham barely heard the hoarse whisper through the muddled fog of his half-conscious state. Something rough scratched the back of his shackled right hand. He forced his eyes open, blinking hard to beat back the bone-aching weariness.

Pinpricks of light floating in a blue-black darkness winked down at him from the cloudless sky. The light of the moon cast eerie shadows across the ground. Where the hell were they now? The land seemed familiar but he couldn't tell for certain. Did he truly know these hills or was it wishful thinking brought on by the pain?

Stifling a groan, he repositioned his throbbing legs. And how many days had his arse been dragged behind a horse? Graham shifted against the crumbling wall of stone, flinching against the nauseating burn the movement caused. A cold sweat covered his body, stinging his wounds even more. His back was a raw field of torn flesh courtesy of his captor's whips.

Angus nudged the grimy remnants of a dried oatcake against his hand again. "Eat it, man. They spared ye little food today. If we're to be rid of these bastards, ye must eat."

Graham pushed the food aside. "Leave off." He didn't need Angus fretting over him like some mother hen. The man had done quite enough by getting them captured. If anything happened to Lilia, he would skin Angus alive and make him wish his father had never met his mother.

"Eat it," Angus whispered again. "For her."

At least the bloody fool had stopped apologizing. Graham snatched the oatcake out of Angus's fingers and shoved it into his mouth. He chewed the tasteless chunk of baked oats as best he could, nearly choking when he forcibly swallowed. Lore a'mighty. He didn't have enough spittle to wash the mess down. He'd do just as well eating the dried mud from the sides of the road.

"Here." Angus held out a deflated waterskin. "There's not much but ye are welcome to it." Grimacing as he scooted closer, Angus held his grimy left arm tucked to his chest. The Buchanans had broken it between the wrist and elbow. "I have news for ye. I heard that arse of a leader send some of his men away."

"Send them away?" That was promising news indeed. They had started this journey with six captors. Fewer Buchanans improved the odds for escaping. "Where did he send them? How many?"

Angus stole a surreptitious glance around the camp before answering. "On ahead to Buchanan Keep to tell their chief we would arrive in less than a day's time."

Less than a day's time. Graham drained the remnants from the water bag, holding the stale warm water in his mouth for a long while, savoring it for the wetness if not for the taste. Beatings paired with little food and water were wearing him down. Thank the gods he had his stubbornness and rage to fuel his strength. He'd be damned straight to hell and back before he'd give in without a good fight. "If we be less than a day away, that means we are well across MacKenna borders. This is MacKenna land."

"Aye." Angus dipped his chin in agreement. "And on our land and this close to the keep, we've a better chance of escaping and making our way to safety."

"And how many did ye say remain?" Graham leaned forward,

hissing out a strained breath as the wind brushed across his tormented back.

"No more than four. Maybe less. I havena seen the one called Scrunge since just before nightfall." Angus leaned back against the wall next to Graham. "We'll ken our odds better come morning when they go to tie us back to the horses."

Graham rolled his hands, grabbing up the length of chain between his shackled wrists. For what seemed like the hundredth time, he jerked the chain taut, searching for weakness. "If there is naught but three of them . . . "

"Aye," Angus hurried to agree. "Ye can strangle one of them with the chains whilst I take out the other two." He held up his good arm, shaking his fist in the air.

Graham lowered both hands to his lap, taking care to rattle the chains as little as possible. Clinking metal stirred his captors to mete out more beatings. "Ye are a fool, Angus. Ye've but one arm. How the hell do ye mean to take down two men?"

"There's not a damn thing wrong with me sword arm. All I need is a weapon." Angus pounded his fist atop his thigh. "I ken that ye think little of me and I dinna blame ye for that. What with all the grief I've caused ye. But ye canna say I'm not good with a sword."

Graham eased himself back, gingerly searching for the least painful spot to lean against the wall. Angus spoke the truth. The man was damn good with a blade. Graham pulled in a deep breath and closed his eyes. "To the morning then and the promise a new day holds. At first opportunity, I will draw the Buchanans away whilst ye get to a sword. Aye?"

"Aye," Angus whispered. "To the morning and the spilling of Buchanan blood. Here's hoping the gods be with us."

Aye. But may they watch over his dearest love first and keep her safe above all else. Graham opened his eyes and stared up into the night. Where was Lilia? Was she well? He'd told her to return to the future but doubted very much that his stubborn lady love had done as she'd been instructed. Graham swallowed hard. The gnawing ache in his chest, the burning worry in his heart, pained him worse than any of his wounds. He had to get free. He had to find Lilia and make certain she was safe.

"Angus," he whispered with a nudge of his boot against Angus's leg.

"Aye?"

"Ye feel certain ye can wield a sword? Ye are wounded and weak, man—no insult to yer talents intended."

"None taken," Angus replied with a weary sigh. "And aye, I can swing a sword long enough to slit a few throats. Damn and for certain I will make it so."

"Aye, Angus." Graham closed his eyes again. "Together we will make it so."

CHAPTER 26

"Kismet is more lethal than she looks and she's been hankering for a good fight. Things have been entirely too quiet around here lately." Granny sat the disgruntled-looking black cat on the custom-made padded board attached to the front of Lilia's saddle.

"If you ask me, she looks pissed about having her nap disturbed." Lilia smoothed a hand down Kismet's back and was rewarded with a soft growl. "See?"

Granny waved her words away and patted Lilia's leg. "She'll take care of you, gal, as best she can even if she is in a foul mood. She loves you as much as I do. Just doesn't always show it."

"If you say so." Granny sending her guardian along touched Lilia's heart more than she could say. Only the eldest time runner of each line was blessed with a guardian to help them navigate through life from cradle to grave. A guardian was a kindred soul—a lifelong friend and protector.

"I promise I'll watch out for her." Lilia looked past Granny. Trulie and Chloe were patiently waiting at the edge of the bailey, holding their torches high to beat back the darkness while the men readied the horses. Lilia had insisted they leave as soon as possible. She didn't care that it was well past midnight by the time they got the supplies readied. A frantic urgency gnawed at her heart. Daybreak would be soon but waiting for the full rising of the sun to begin their journey wasted too much precious time.

Lilia sat taller in the saddle, forcing a smile to Trulie. "I'll watch out for Karma too, Sis. I promise."

"Watch out for yourself," Trulie advised. "Karma and Kismet will be fine. They're wicked sly when they need to be."

"I wish I could send Oren wi' ye but Mama said no." Chloe scurried up, stretched on her tiptoes, and held out a length of purple ribbon. "Tie this 'round yer braid. 'Twill bring ye luck in getting Uncle Graham back."

"Thank you, Chloe." Lilia took the ribbon and tied it tightly around her hair. "I feel safer already and I'll have Uncle Graham back in no time." *I hope,* she silently added.

Chloe blew a kiss then scampered back to her mother. Oren perched on the wooden hitching post beside her. The great white owl spread his wings their full glorious span then fluttered them a bit before resettling them back against his body. It was almost as though the bird, in his own way, was blessing the journey and wishing them luck too.

"Are ye ready then?" Gray brought his horse up beside her. His dark scowl almost made her laugh out loud. All the men were more than just a little perturbed that she was coming along. But once she'd shown them how good she was with a sword and bow, they had acquiesced—grudgingly.

Granny, Trulie, and Chloe waved their torches one last time then hurried back inside the keep. Lilia clenched the reins tighter, hoping the family superstition held true. Granny had taught them all at an early age that you should never watch your loved ones leave. If you did, you risked them never returning. Always part face to face with kind words and a smile. That guaranteed your loved one would have a safe journey and make it back home safe as well.

Gray cast a frowning glance at Colum and the three other MacKenna warriors selected for the task. With an almost imperceptible nod, he turned his horse and led them all through the bailey, under the ancient stone arch carved with the clan crest, then across the bridge connecting the impenetrable stronghold of MacKenna Keep to the mainland.

Once safely across the bridge, Karma took the lead. He looked like a silent shadow skimming across the ground, his trotting lope set at an impressive land-eating pace. Lilia urged her horse to catch up with the great black dog and stay close to him. Odds were that Karma would find the Buchanans faster than the several runners Gray had sent out ahead of them to home in on the rival clan and discover their location. Karma's instincts and sense of smell missed nothing.

Lilia fought the desire to push her mount into full gallop. Got to be patient. Levelheaded. Save berserker mode for the Buchanans.

Gray and Colum caught up with her, aligning their horses on either side of her.

"Stay between us. Aye?" Gray said. The half-light of approaching dawn made his dark look even more stern. There would be no arguing with her brother-in-law on this point.

"If anything happens to ye, there'll be hell to pay with Mother Sinclair and yer sisters," Colum added, his reddish-blonde brows knotted with a stern look of his own.

Lilia didn't bother answering. Just rolled her eyes and shook her head. Protective alpha males. Delightfully delicious but hardheaded. She hitched back the urge to give in to tears. What she wouldn't give to have her own hardheaded alpha back in her arms right now.

Glancing to her right, Lilia looked past Colum's wild red hair whipping in the wind. A pale morning mist, soft as a lover's touch, already stroked the rugged unforgiving landscape. This close to the sea, the land was wild and rocky but even in the gentle light of the new day, velvety patches of green and stunning purples of blooming heather hinted at the breathtaking beauty the full rising of the sun would soon reveal.

Cresting the sea, the horizon was just beginning to lighten. The warm yellow-pink glow slowly crept ever higher brushing away the winking lights of the stars. The sun's fiery rim barely peeped above the glistening waves as though shy about bringing the dawn.

New day. New hope. They had to get to Graham today. Lilia worried with the leather reins, willing Graham to hold on.

Karma's deep baying bark interrupted her thoughts and the rhythmic pounding of her horse's hooves against the packed earth.

"He's found something." She spurred her mount faster, rushing to cross the narrow glen and catch up with the dog somewhere beyond the next hill.

"Dammit, woman!" Gray thundered past her; his sword already drawn. "Stay back until we see what the beast has found."

"Like hell I will." Lilia crouched lower, urging her horse into full gallop. Gaelic cursing filled the air around her, triggering a wicked smile as she clenched the reins tighter and leaned forward like a seasoned jockey. Her brothers-in-law might as well learn now; she did as she wished, not as she was told.

Lilia crested the next hill, then pulled her mount to a full stop.

Gray had stopped his horse, his form seeming quite relaxed. He sat with hands folded atop the front of his saddle and head tilted slightly to one side. As Lilia pulled up beside him, he nodded toward the base of the hill at a lone tree growing beside the glistening path of a creek. "It appears Karma has something for us—and though the light be dim—I do believe that be a Buchanan plaid in the beast's mouth."

Lilia was first down the hillside. She eased her horse closer, peering up into the leafy branches of the great sprawling oak that had more than likely thrived for centuries in the sheltered glen beside the stream.

Gray, Colum, and the other three MacKenna warriors followed behind her with their weapons readied.

Karma stood at the base of the tree, hackles up, fangs bared, and the remains of a shredded plaid snagged in his bottom teeth. Gnashing and popping his jaws, he lunged upward against the broad gray trunk of the tree. His deep booming bark nearly shook the ground.

Kismet perked up, sitting taller on her padded seat. Ears pitched forward and the tip of her tail twitching, the black cat vibrated with a high-pitched growl. Her tail slowly grew in diameter, puffing up from the very tip and lifting a stiffened ridge of hair all the way up her back to between her ears.

"Who's your friend, Karma?" Lilia slowly circled the tree without dismounting. She finally spotted a pale hairy leg wrapped around the trunk. A helpful breeze shifted the leaves and smaller branches, revealing the hairy ass attached to the leg. Whoever it was had climbed as high he could go to perch among the safety of the tree limbs that would still support his weight.

"A Buchanan bastard." Gray pointed to the plaid. "Those are definitely their colors."

"Call off yer beast!" The branches shook and the bare ass disappeared, replaced by one bare foot and one foot in a half-eaten boot trembling on the limb. A grubby hand shoved the leaves aside, revealing an equally filthy face. The man squatted low, balancing an elbow on one knobby knee, his sagging man parts swinging down from his nasty matted crotch. "Call off yer beast and release me or the chieftain shall hear of this."

"I am the chieftain," Gray replied.

"Ye are not *my* chieftain," the man sneered down at them. "My fealty lies wi' the Buchanan and he will make ye rue the day ye ever stepped on Buchanan land."

"This is MacKenna land, fool," Colum said.

"Not for much longer—not when the Buchanan finishes wi' ye."

"You talk amazingly brave for a man who's bare-assed and trapped in a tree." Lilia paced the horse back and forth, taking care to stay out of spitting distance. She knew this guy's type without a scan of his feelings. "The Buchanans took two men as prisoners. Ambushed them farther north of here. Where are they now?"

"Ye are the witch!" The Buchanan weasel jabbed a bent finger at Lilia, his delighted cackle raking across her already raw nerves. "Old Borden said MacTavish's witch would come a looking for him. Damned if ye didna do just as he said."

The man licked his lips and reached down between his legs. With a look that made Lilia want to vomit, he grabbed his limp cock and shook it at her. "I ain't telling ye nothing, whore. Not unless ye wish to barter."

Colum whipped out his bow and nocked an arrow. "Tell Lady Lilia what she wishes to know afore I nail yer cods to that tree."

The squatting man quickly stood, scampering along the limb to a thicker shield of leaves. "I can stay up here as long as it takes."

"I've had enough of this shit. Kismet—you're on." Lilia drew closer to the tree and the softly growling black cat gracefully launched herself up into the branches. Lilia returned to her designated position between Colum and Gray.

Colum slowly lowered the arrow and bow and turned to Lilia with a gleam in his eye. "Ye are a great deal like yer grandmother, are ye not?"

"I hope so," Lilia said. "Kismet will get him down without maiming him so badly that he can't give us any information."

The outer limbs of the tree shook and rattled. Leaves exploded free of branches as Kismet convinced the man it was time to climb down. The Buchanan's shouts and curses played a perfect duet with the feline's yowls and hisses.

"Off me, black demon. Leave off, ye bastard!" Limbs cracked and popped. The man bellowed, bouncing down through the branches with Kismet firmly clamped around his face. He hit the ground flat of his back with a hard thud. Wheezing and gasping for air, he flailed both arms, clawing at the cat still attached to his face.

"Good job, Kismet," Lilia called. "It's Karma's turn now."

The black cat immediately disengaged, leapt back to her perch on Lilia's saddle, and started licking her paws, furiously grooming away the filth she had just encountered.

In one great lunge, Karma straddled the man's body, bringing his snarling muzzle within inches of the man's face.

"Now." Lilia eased her horse closer. "I'm going to ask you again. Where are the two prisoners? And if you lie to me, I will make you wish Colum's arrow pinning your nuts to the tree was the only pain you had to worry around."

The man lay perfectly still, terror in his face as he kept his unblinking gaze locked on Karma's dripping fangs. "Not far. Go north. Keep to the glens. Ye should meet them well before midday."

"How many?" Gray asked.

"Four." The man blinked rapidly as Karma lunged closer, his clicking growl sounding hungrier. "But more come. The Buchanan himself. And his son. Maybe more."

"When?" Colum asked. "And how many more?"

The man didn't answer, just locked his jaws and flinched his face away from Karma's teeth.

"Why are more coming?" Lilia asked. "Why are more men needed?"

The man remained silent, his mouth clamped shut in a stubborn scowl.

Karma settled his jaws around the man's throat and rumbled a deeper warning growl.

The man's eyes popped open, his expression a strange mix of defiance, rage, and fear. "The Buchanan means to regain the honor stolen from him. He'll not stand being cuckolded by MacTavish nor made the fool by the MacKenna. He means to make ye both pay for the way ye've soiled his name. MacTavish will pay with his life. The MacKenna will pay with his clan's land."

Karma crunched down and twisted with a hard jerk. The man hissed out a gurgling wheeze; his legs jerked and kicked. Then he went still. Karma shook the limp Buchanan clansman one last time then stepped away. The great dog sneezed and raked a paw down his muzzle. With one last glance down at the man, Karma sneezed again, then calmly trotted over to the nearby creek. He splashed in and drank deep, blowing and sloshing water in and out of his mouth as though rinsing out the taste of the filthy Buchanan.

"Well . . . " Lilia chewed the corner of her bottom lip, then looked over at Gray. "I guess that settles that. Now what do we do with him?"

Enemy or not, they couldn't leave the man's body exposed to whatever might wish to pick his bones clean.

"When our business is finished, word will be sent to his clan." Gray scowled down at the man, obviously pissed at the inconvenience. His cold, matter-of-fact gaze lifted and settled on her. "I will allow them safe passage to retrieve their kinsman and take him home. Nothing more. We've no time to tarry."

Lilia suppressed a shudder. This was the first time in all her visits back to the past that she'd keenly felt the rawness of the era. She forced her gaze away from the dead man and looked to the MacKenna warriors, their mounts fidgeting in place, waiting for orders from their chieftain.

"I ... uhm ... understand." Lilia cleared her throat and sat taller in the saddle. Gray was right. Graham's life, and now the well-being of the MacKenna clan, depended on them. There was no time to tarry. "The plan then? Send for reinforcements or take a chance on our timing and kick some Buchanan ass by ourselves?"

"Both." Gray nodded to the largest of the three guards. "Duncan —back to the keep. Double the guard then send the rest to join us. Alert everyone to what ye've just witnessed. Ye ken what must be done."

The brawny man thumped a clenched fist to his chest while turning his horse back in the direction from which they'd just come. "Aye, my chieftain. It will be so."

Gray looked at Colum and the remaining men. "Now let us be on our way to show the Buchanans the error of their thinking."

CHAPTER 27

Dammit to hell. Four bastards after all. Graham kept his gaze lowered, feigning sleep, as the four remaining Buchanans shuffled around the makeshift camp, making ready to carry on with the journey. And sure enough, one of the bastards was not only the ugliest but the biggest of them all: Scrunge. Aptly named because he stunk worse than an overcrowded castle's cesspit.

But the other remaining Buchanans triggered a bit of hope for a successful escape. The short squat toad-like leader could easily be overcome. Graham would knock him flat of his back. The round bastard couldn't regain his footing without a sturdy handhold.

And then the other two. Older. Slight of form but more than likely quite a bit cannier than the leader and Scrunge. Those two never stopped glancing around the hillside and if they'd checked their weapons once they'd checked them a thousand times over.

Graham slowly rose to his feet. Sizing the four Buchanans up, it was plain what course he should take. He looked to Angus then pointedly shifted his gaze to Scrunge.

Angus lowered his chin in subtle acknowledgment, tucked his

injured arm tighter to his torso, and flexed the fingers of his good hand.

Angling sideways to a taller portion of the crumbling wall behind him, Graham double-wrapped the shackle chain around his fists and pulled the metal links taut.

Scrunge shuffled out of range, wadding up an extra plaid and knotting the corners before securing it behind one of the saddles.

Come over here, ye stinking bastard, Graham silently willed. He propped his arse against the stones behind him and braced his feet.

Slowly but surely, Angus inched closer to one of the horses tied to a nearby tree. Each time one of the Buchanans glanced his way, he quickly assumed a stoop-shouldered stance and cradled his broken arm.

Graham spotted Angus's target: an axe hanging in the loop of the saddle. Well done. May the gods guide his aim.

Scrunge finally lumbered closer and Graham lunged. He kicked the back of Scrunge's right leg, knocking the giant to one knee. Throwing the chain over the man's head, Graham straddled the man's broad back, twisted the length of metal around the guard's throat and yanked backward.

Scrunge gasped and sputtered, fighting wilder than an untamed stallion to knock Graham free. The sound of his own blood pumping rushed and roared in Graham's ears. Just a bit longer. Die, stubborn bastard. Graham strained to hold fast, twisting the chain ever tighter to cut off Scrunge's air.

Alerted by the furious scuffle, the other men sprang into action.

A wet thunk sounded and the leader of the marauders stopped in his tracks then teetered forward, the axe buried deep in the back of his skull. He hit the ground and didn't move.

The slighter of the remaining two men beat Angus to the other horse bearing a weapon. He unsheathed a sword and tossed it to his partner. "Cut the hands off that goat-swiving cur that's choking Scrunge!" Then he snatched up a deadly pike propped against a boulder on his side of the camp. He turned toward Angus, hefting the spear in one hand. "I'll skewer ye like the vermin ye are, MacKenna rat."

Angus took cover behind a gnarled tree broad enough to shield him. "Come after me like a man," he taunted with a glance around the trunk. "Only a coward wields a spear against a one-armed man."

Doing his damnedest to watch both deadly Buchanans, Graham pulled the chain higher, hooking it behind Scrunge's heavy jaws and yanking it tighter. He arched backward; his raw back scraped the wall, triggering a searing burn across his shoulders. The pain would just have to be damned. If he didn't shield himself with the wall to his back and Scrunge to his front, he'd never get out of this alive.

Scrunge finally went limp. Graham nearly lost his footing when the mountain of flesh sagged forward. He struggled to keep Scrunge up in place between himself and the advancing Buchanan with the sword.

"Aye, ye are done for now. Ye've lost yer shield." The henchman grinned as he slowly advanced. "I'll keep ye alive. I grant ye that. But the chieftain didna say ye had to have all yer parts." He gripped the haft of the sword with both hands, hefting the long heavy blade high over his head. "I sharpened me sword to a fine edge last night. I wager I can lop off both yer arms along with Scrunge's head with one good swing. What say ye? Will ye take that wager?"

Whizzing sounds ripped through the trees followed by a series of solid *thunk-thunk-thunks*.

A shocked look registered on the face of the Buchanan with the raised sword. Slowly, the weapon teetered out of his grasp and hit the ground in front of him with a clatter. The man sagged forward, knees hitting the ground first, then his body flopped across the sword, two arrows protruding from his back.

The Buchanan with the spear was dead as well: another pair of arrows from seemingly nowhere embedded deep in his chest.

Graham untangled himself from Scrunge and stumbled to one side, staring at the dead men in amazement. He wilted back against the wall, the realization of being free made his knees weak. Safe. Finally safe. Now he could find Lilia.

Angus exploded with a victorious whoop as he hopped out from behind the tree. Then all triumph left his face as he stared down at the dead Buchanan in front of him. The man's lifeless eyes were still wide open and his fist still clutched the spear.

Angus's scowl darkened with vengeance. He knelt slowly and wrenched the weapon out of the dead man's hand. Then he stood, stretched tall, and jammed the spear deep into the Buchanan's chest just below the breastbone. "That's for breaking me arm, ye bastard." Then he spat on the man and kicked dirt across him.

A rhythmic thundering rumbled beyond the sparse tree line hedging in one side of the camp. The ground trembled as the thudding grew closer. Horses. Several of them.

Pray let it be the MacKennas. Graham straightened, wrapping the chain back around his fists and pulling it tight again. He had to be ready lest it be more Buchanans.

"Graham!"

Lore a'mighty, it was her.

"Lilia!" He nearly choked on her name, so relieved he was to hear the sweet music of her voice.

Her mount was the first to pound into camp. She pulled up hard, leapt from the saddle, and vaulted onto his chest.

Arms pinned by the chains of his shackles between them, Graham couldn't hold her but he could damn sure kiss her. The taste of her sent his senses reeling. Now he could die a happy man. He'd held his dear one once again—he was complete with the other half of his soul.

He drank deep of her sweet mouth like a man dying of thirst, then finally pulled back the barest bit and grazed his lips across her forehead.

"I never thought I could love anyone so," he whispered. "By the gods both new and old, I swear I love ye more than life itself." He pressed a soft kiss to her temple. "I canna exist without ye, sweetling. I need ye more than ye'll ever know."

"I know more than you think because I love you just the same." She cupped his face between her hands, her lower lip quivering as she looked deep into his eyes. "I would die without you," she whispered, tears leaving a glistening trail down her cheeks.

Then her eyes widened and a horrified look registered on her face. "Graham. Oh. My. Graham." She repeated the words over and over in a frantic whisper as she stepped back, her gaze scouring his body from head to toe.

"What the hell did they do to you?" Her tears flowed faster and her jaw tightened. Graham knew that look well. His dearest love was enraged.

Lilia ran her hands over the cuts and bruises on his face—not touching them but skimming just above them as though trying to brush them away. She did the same to the wounds on his chest, then down across the shackles, then back to his face again.

She slowly circled him, one hand touching his shoulder, turning him away as she moved behind him.

Graham stood taller, bracing himself. She would be upset. Nay—not upset. She would be more enraged than a berserker filled with bloodlust. He had to make her understand that all that mattered now was that they were back together. Wounds healed. Separated hearts did not. "It is not as bad as it seems, love. I will be mended in no time."

Still standing behind him, she hissed out something under her breath, her words so soft he couldn't make them out. But he knew his sweetling. He had a fair idea of what she'd said even though most women he knew would never use such foul language.

Graham turned to pull her back around in front of him but her look of cold calculating rage stayed his hand. "Lilia," he said softly, reaching out to her. "Leave go of yer rage, lass. 'Tis over. The men are dead. They have paid in full for what they've done."

She didn't take his hand, just clenched her fists and stepped around him. She directed her words at Colum and Gray as they worked in unison to free Graham from the irons around his wrists and ankles. "We should've killed the son of bitches a lot slower."

Karma agreed with a deep growling rumble, leaned against

Graham's leg, then made a softer whining sound with a slow wag of his thick tail.

"Aye, lad. She is a fierce one, is she not?" Graham rubbed the dog's broad head, grateful that the massive beast was on his side.

Colum and Gray looked at each other, then turned in unison to Graham. The three men seemed to communicate without saying a word. Colum pulled the strap of a swollen leather flask from across his chest. He uncorked the skin and held it out. "*Uisge beatha.* Water of life, man. Ye look as though ye could use it."

"Aye to that." Graham gladly accepted the bag and took a long deep drink. Fine MacKenna whisky. A warm streak of renewed vigor warmed down his gullet. Life was good once again.

"Angus?" Graham held out the flask.

"Ye dinna hafto ask me twice." Angus winked, grabbed the bag and upended it, squeezing a steady golden stream into his opened mouth.

"Buchanans a comin'!" The sandy-haired MacKenna guard that had stood watch on higher ground whilst they rescued Graham and Angus thundered into the center of the camp. "Best take cover in the ruins. There be seven of them. Mayhap more."

Protective rage burned through Graham's veins hotter than the whisky. He took hold of Lilia's arm and pulled her toward the fallen-down structure of dry stone walls that had once been an impressive broch. "I want ye to stay down and keep hidden within the walls, ye ken?"

She twisted her arm out of his grasp. "Bullshit!" She jogged over to her horse and retrieved her weapons. "I know how to use these. Remember?" She held her sword in one hand and a bow and quiver of arrows in the other. She motioned back at Kismet, already arched with hackles up, tail fully puffed, and ears flattened against her head. "Come on, Kismet." She turned to the dog. "Karma, you stay with Graham."

"This is not one of yer wee Highland games, woman!" Graham hurried to the Buchanan skewered with the pike and yanked it free of the man's body. He motioned Angus toward their captor's discarded axe and sword, then spun and faced Gray. "Why the hell did ye bring her here? Ye shouldha come for us alone."

"Ye've got a lot to learn about Sinclair women, MacTavish." Colum trotted around the clearing, rounding the horses up. He led them to shelter behind the crumbling stone structure.

Gray jerked a thumb toward Lilia with one hand while pointing at Graham with the other. "Ye will find there is no controlling them once their minds are set. Heaven knows I've tried and now I've got a daughter who's just the same."

"Get behind the broch!" Graham jabbed the spear toward the wall of stone, struggling not to roar aloud when Lilia didn't move. Lore, she would be the death of him. "We dinna have time for this, Lilia. Please do as I say—just this once."

She rolled her eyes, looped the quiver full of arrows and bow over one shoulder, and hurried past the broch. Kismet leapt up the hillside in front of her, scampering around the low-growing ground cover and stones. Lilia nimbly trotted partially up the slight incline, then paused. "I'm going for higher ground. Better vantage point for arrows. You stay safe. I didn't come here to watch you die."

"Come, man. We'll shield her from below." Angus grabbed him by the arm and pulled. "The Buchanan and his son are among the lot. I spied the ugly bastards myself. Ye've no time to fetch her back down now."

If they live through this, he would turn her over his knee again. Graham hunkered down in the center of the toppled-down broch with Angus, Gray, Colum, and the two MacKenna guards. Karma stood at alert behind them, a low warning growl clicking in his throat. The remains of the circular structure would protect them—for a bit. If the MacKenna lad was right, they were evenly numbered against the Buchanans but weaker due to injuries and one surly, hardheaded woman who refused to see sense.

May the gods be with us. Graham shifted the spear to his left hand and took a sword in his right. *Protect her,* he silently prayed. *I beg ye— above all else, protect her.*

CHAPTER 28

L ilia squatted down behind a boulder, propping the sword, bow, and quiver of arrows beside her. Kismet leapt to the top of the rock, pacing back and forth with a nervous twitching of her tail.

She eased up beside the cat, flattened herself along the rough curve of the stone, and peered over the rim, wishing they'd had a chance to work out some sort of battle plan but there'd been no time. Apparently, the plan was to stay alive.

She wasn't as elevated as she would've liked but this vantage point would have to do. She was much closer than arrow range and might be easily spotted. But the approaching clan had been too close to leave her back exposed by climbing any higher.

The Buchanans rode into the camp as though they already ruled the land but pulled their horses to an abrupt stop when they spotted the bodies of their brethren. They drew their weapons and slowly eased their mounts several lengths back from the crumbling broch.

Six. Lilia frowned and counted again. Definitely six in the group. Logan MacKenna had apparently miscounted. Lilia shrugged. Logan was just an oversized kid—barely past his teens from what Trulie had said, anxious to prove himself to his chieftain. He'd probably gotten overexcited when he spotted the approach of the Buchanans and counted wrong. It didn't matter. In fact, it was even better. That meant they had them outnumbered.

The overly round one in the middle had to be the chief. The men looked to him, mirroring their moves according to his. Except one. The man sitting at his left. That one had to be the chieftain's son.

"What a face." Lilia reached down and snagged her bow and an arrow, soundlessly placing them atop the rock in front of her. The Buchanan's son looked like he either smelled a stink or was straining to take a shit. He sat much taller in the saddle than his father and wasn't nearly as round. He kept scanning the area. His oversized beak of a nose twitched while his nostrils flared with every turn of his head.

"Ye made an oath to me, MacKenna." The Buchanan shifted in the saddle, squirming from side to side as though his ass itched.

"Aye, I did at that." Gray kept his back to the wall, taking care to stand to one side of the crude window. "That oath is broken. Ye attacked my kinsman and threatened my clan. I owe ye nothing."

"Give me MacTavish and his witch." The chieftain pointed a pudgy finger up the hillside.

Lilia retreated a bit more behind the boulder, a chill stealing across her when the man's hawk-faced son looked her dead in the eye.

The Buchanan slowly lowered his hand but kept his scowl trained on Lilia. "I came here personally to restore me honor in front of me son. I'll not be leaving this place 'til I've done it. Turn them over now and I will leave yer clan in peace."

Lilia tensed as Graham stood, readied the spear in one hand, and moved closer to the window. *Don't do it, Graham. Stay back.*

"The woman ye call witch is my wife," Graham said, his tone deep and rumbling like the warning growl of a beast. "I will thank ye not to insult her."

"And she is my good sister," Gray added.

"And mine as well," Colum warned.

"She is a witch—just like her kin that have poisoned the blood of yer clan." This time it was the Buchanan's son who spoke. "Our spies told us what goes on at yer keep, MacKenna. Speaking to demons through the hearth fires. Strange healing of those who should not live. 'Tis time to purge this land of yer evil. Reclaim it from Satan and bless it as our own."

Shit. Witch hunters. Lilia nocked an arrow and pulled back, aiming the missile's tip right between the son's beady eyes. Holding her breath, she waited for Graham or one of the MacKennas to make a move. *Give me the sign to part the son of a bitch's hair.* She forced the memory of Granny's horrific recounts of witch hunters and their methods of torture to the back of her mind. This situation had evolved into something much worse than Graham insulting the chieftain. These holier-than-thou fools were threatening her loved ones. They had to be stopped. "Kismet—get down there and help them. I'm safe up here," she whispered.

Kismet leapt from the rock, then melted into the tangled undergrowth and made her way silently down the hillside. Lilia didn't exhale until she saw the cat reappear beside Karma. Good. Now the men had more furry firepower.

A calloused hand closed around her throat and yanked her backward, knocking the weapon from her hands. "Ye'll not be shooting yer bewitched arrows this day, witch!"

Alberti's training kicked in. Lilia went limp, balled up, then shifted while jerking her captor over her shoulder. The man lost grip of her throat but snagged hold of her thick braid and swung her over, bouncing her flat of her back against the ground.

She wheezed in a strangled breath, struggling to regain her footing and the wind the man had knocked out of her.

"Ye be a spiteful bitch, I gi' ye that." The henchman cuffed her hard across the face, knocked her back to the ground, then snatched her up again by her hair.

Lilia pivoted with a sweeping heel kick aimed directly at his crotch. He caught her foot in both hands and twisted hard, nearly ripping her hip from the socket. With a bone-chilling guffaw, he flung her to her back again.

She rolled away, crab-crawling sideways to stay out of his reach. The son of a bitch was too big. Time to get free and run like hell. The man was three times her size and seemed impervious to pain. No way could she win bare-handed.

"Enough play. Time to take ye down to himself." The man lunged, grabbing her by one arm and her braid, then started down the hill-side, dragging her beside him.

She clawed and bit at the brute, doing her damnedest to wrap herself around his legs as he walked. If it worked for Kismet, it just might work for her.

He kicked her free, wrenching her upward until her boot tips barely scraped the ground. Blood roared in her ears. Blinding lights flashed from the bastard's hard knee hitting her temple. She struggled to remain conscious. Graham would kill him. Soon as they were in range. One of the guys would kill him. She twisted and fought with every jerking step. The son of a bitch might win this round but she damn sure wasn't going to make it easy.

As her captor drew closer to the base of the hill, he crushed her across his torso and pressed his dagger to her throat. His arm tightened around her rib cage. She swore she heard her ribs crack and bit her lip to keep from crying out.

The bastard arched his back, lifting her up higher as he shouted to the men taking cover in the ruins. "I'll soak the ground with her blood if ye raise a weapon. Dinna think I won't gut this witch here where I stand."

Blinking against pain and dizziness, she barely made out the mixture of fury and fear on Graham's face. *I'm so sorry.* She willed him to hear her thoughts, praying he would know what she felt right now. *So sorry.* If they got out of this alive, she'd admit that he'd been right and she'd been dead wrong.

As the man sidled the rest of the way into the camp, holding her as a shield, she struggled and clawed with the last of her energy.

Nothing worked. The focused beast was impervious to everything. She finally decided to go limp again. By the Fates, if the bastard wanted to present her to the Buchanans, he could damn well carry her the rest of the way.

Her spirits lifted the barest bit as a deep warning growl rumbled from beyond the stones. Sweet Karma. He was pissed. If and when the men unleashed him, the Buchanans wouldn't know what hit them.

Still holding Lilia between himself and the MacKennas, the wretched Buchanan sidled in front of his kinsmen still astride their horses. The bastard lifted her up by the back of her shirt and turned, presenting her to the Buchanan's son for closer inspection. "Yer witch, Master Andrew."

Two rapid-fire thuds sounded. A gurgling wheeze hissed free of the man. He dropped Lilia, staggered to one side, then collapsed with a pair of arrows protruding out of his rib cage.

Lilia balled up and rolled under Master Andrew's horse, screaming at the top of her lungs while dodging the spooked beast's frantic stomping. Clearing the animal's sharp hooves, she launched herself up with a gimping hop, still yodeling out a high-pitched squeal and clapping her hands. All the horses reared and stomped, the first mount's hysteria quickly spreading to them all.

Karma leapt out of the ruins, barking and gnashing his teeth. A streak of black sped past Lilia with a high-pitched yowl, then a Buchanan shouted and cursed as Kismet reached her target.

Arrows flew overhead as Lilia zigzagged toward safety, the treacherous route hindered by panicked horses and men swinging their swords.

Her heart leapt as Graham cleared the wall. Teeth bared and spear raised, he was headed to save her. A swipe of a Buchanan shield knocked her into a backward roll. She staggered to her feet, nearly back where she'd started.

A horse screamed beside her. She shied away from the lethal hooves pummeling the air.

The chieftain's son lost his seat, cursing as he hit the ground in a controlled roll. With an agile leap, he gained his footing, a deadly mace clutched in one hand. Advancing on Lilia, he didn't blink nor look away as he bent and scooped up his shield, never faltering a step as two arrows and then two more hit and stuck into the disc of metal-covered wood.

Oh shit. Got to get to safety. Now! Lilia turned and screamed, "Graham!"

"Die, witch!"

The roared words echoed in her ears as the hard blow cracked between her shoulder blades and lifted her up from the ground. Her lungs exploded, filled with unbearable fire. Pain crackled through her like a jolt of lightning.

Tumbling through the air, the first thing that registered in her mind was the horrified look on Graham's face as he ran toward her. A dull roaring resembling the hollow growl of a gale force wind drowned all other sound. Lilia tried to reach out to him, clutching the air as she spun into a strangely muted darkness. She hit the ground with a sickening thud. A sharp popping filled her ears as she flopped across the rocky ground and rolled to a stop.

A strangely distorted clash of metal on metal sounded both close and yet far away at the same time. Men were shouting but for the life of her, she couldn't tell what they were saying. Fighting. That's what it was. Definitely, the sound of battle but it seemed so far away—as though she'd been lifted out of the chaos and tucked away into a secluded room. Excruciating pain radiated from the middle of her back and all the way through to her chest, making it hard to focus. The unbearable ache radiated out to her fingertips in throbbing waves.

She couldn't breathe. Or could she? Was she the one making that high-pitched wheezing sound? She kicked—at least she thought she kicked but couldn't tell if anything happened. She knew for certain her legs hadn't moved. She struggled to roll to her side and make it the rest of the way to Graham but her body refused to obey.

The din of the skirmish grew ever softer. Almost hollow and so much harder to discern. Every sound seemed muffled as though wrapped in wool. Why was it suddenly so much darker? It was the middle of the day.

Strong hands gripped her arms, rolling her until she felt the cool wind brush across her face. An embrace held her tight. It was so dark. Her eyes were open. Why couldn't she see? She tried to move her mouth, tried to speak. *Graham?* Why wasn't her voice working? Flinching against the searing burn spreading through her lungs, she struggled to open her unseeing eyes even wider. She had to make it through the darkness. She had to make him hear her.

"Daren't ye die! Can ye hear me, dear one? I love ye, Lilia! Ye must not die and leave me!"

She vaguely felt arms tighten around her, clutching her close. Finally safe. The pain didn't seem so bad now. Maybe she'd just rest for a little while before they went back home. They were finally safe.

"Lilia! Dinna leave me!"

Graham's voice sounded so far away and filled with unspeakable panic. Why? They were safe now.

"I swear by the gods that I love ye and will never let ye go."

Arms tightened around her. Poor Graham. She had to make him feel better. She couldn't bear to hear him so afraid. And then it came to her. Her vision. This was her vision. If she could figure out how, she would smile up at him and tell him to relax. Everything was going to be all right—at least she thought it would be. She recognized the feel of all that was happening but for the life of her, she couldn't remember how the vision had ended. Surely it had turned out all right. Hadn't it? She tried to lift her hand toward the sound of his rasping groan but her arm didn't seem to want to work. Her hand was so . . . heavy.

A hard muscled chest rubbed beneath her cheek. The steady hammering thump of a heartbeat tapped against her face. A shaking hesitant touch brushed across her jawline.

Graham's voice—broken by a heartbreaking mix of a sob and a groan. Clearer now. Closer. "I beg ye, my love. Ye must not die. I canna live without ye."

Die? A distant roaring rushed closer, drowning all other sounds and sensations. Maybe he was right. Maybe she was about to die. A bleak sadness filled her as a sense of free-falling overtook her.

Poor Graham. She was . . . so very . . . sorry.

CHAPTER 29

G raham lifted Lilia up into his arms, clutching her all the tighter. He slowly stood, taking care to jar her as little as possible. She dare not die. He would not allow it. He'd sworn an oath to protect this woman and would be damned if he broke it. He never broke his oaths—not once in his long life.

He looked up, his gaze pinned to the bright patch of blue peeping down through the softly swaying leaves. Raw fury and uncontrollable rage exploded from him in a long throaty roar. He stepped forward, cradling her higher, offering her to any great being that might choose to look kindly upon him. He would beg if he had to—*I will do anything. This is not just and ye ken that as well as I. I beg ye. Give her back to me.*

How could the gods be so cruel? The most precious piece of his heart had finally been found only to be ripped away so quickly.

Wisps of clouds floated overhead. Birdsong tittered through the trees as though all was right with the world. How could it be so? How could all around him keep marking time as his beloved lay dying in his arms? Where the hell were the damn gods now that he truly needed them?

"I will not allow this!" he shouted, striding forward and curling

Lilia to his chest. "Ye will not take her from me—I swear that ye won't —not without the likes of a battle that ye have never seen before and will never see again."

Gray and Colum slowly approached, their somber expressions burning into him like salt in an open wound. Gray rested a hand on Graham's shoulder. "I have sent the boy to fetch her kin. Logan is the clan's fastest rider. Hopefully, he will get them back here before—"

"Daren't ye say it." Graham jerked away, gathering her limp form up to his cheek. He closed his eyes, softly rubbing his face against hers. Lore a'mighty. She was so very cold. He ground his teeth, fighting the urge to roar aloud again.

He opened his eyes and looked down at her, searching, vainly hoping for a sign, or maybe a miracle—nay—he wished for the almighty ones themselves to reach down and make his dear one live and laugh again.

But her skin remained a ghostly white and a sickly blue shadow tinged her barely parted lips. Her chest rose and fell at a more rapid, shallow pace. Graham cringed at the bubbling wheeze escaping with her every gasp for air.

He had easily killed the son of a bitch that had struck the blow but now he stood helpless, clutching her in his arms, the one precious love he had never thought to find, and now—now that he knew life would be senseless without her, he couldn't do a damn thing to save her. "She drowns in her own blood and I canna stop it," he whispered.

A large paw raked at his leg, gently, but digging with an urgency that refused to be ignored. Graham turned and glanced down. Karma, sitting tall and somber, whined and pawed at the air again. Graham easily understood the great beast's silent plea. Slowly, he went to his knees and held Lilia out to the dog.

Karma carefully tucked his nose into the crook of Lilia's neck and softly brushed the top of his muzzle back and forth against her cheek. A faint whine came from the great dog as though he was begging her not to leave.

Graham swallowed hard. The dog's caring gesture nearly shattered his wavering control and sent him keening his unbearable grief to all the Highlands.

Ears drooping and tail sagging, Karma stepped aside, threw back his great dark head and shattered the unholy stillness of the clearing with a mournful howl. As the chilling cry echoed and faded away, the clearing and the woods around them fell reverently silent.

Kismet appeared at Graham's side, purring loudly and rubbing against his side. She tenderly placed her paws atop Lilia's wrist and gently began licking away the bloodstains, cleaning Lilia as though washing a kitten.

"Lore a'mighty," Colum groaned, choking back a strangled sob as he turned away and strode across the clearing to stare out over the land.

Gray bent and squeezed Graham's shoulder. "I go to watch for them." He squeezed Graham's shoulder again, then silently walked away and joined Colum, standing beside him, scowling out at the rolling glen opening before them.

A damp rag appeared in front of Graham's face. He looked up. Angus stood with his broken arm clutched against his body, his expression grim, holding out the bit of cloth. "I thought ye might wish to wipe the dust from her face." He cleared his throat, glanced away, and shuffled in place. "Thought it might give her a bit of peace —make her feel better. Ye ken how clean she always was."

"I thank ye." Graham nodded and took the rag. "I'm sure it will." As he gently wiped the blood and dirt from Lilia's face, Angus quietly moved away.

"Riders approach," Gray called out. "Karma. Greet them. See if they be friend or foe."

The dog rose from his seat beside Graham and loped out of the camp.

Friend or foe. A bitter snort escaped him but Graham didn't take his gaze from Lilia's ragged breathing. How the hell could it be anyone other than more Buchanans? The boy had nary had the time to reach MacKenna Keep, much less fetch the Sinclair women. He settled Lilia more comfortably in his arms. He hoped it was more

Buchanans. Surely he could goad them into sending him on his way to join his dear sweet love on the other side.

An excited happy bark traveled back to them from the stretch of open ground at the base of the glen.

Graham looked up. Colum and Gray both shielded their eyes with their hands, squinting at the approaching riders. Whoever it was —Karma liked them.

"It canna be." Gray hurried back to Graham. "'Tis Mother Sinclair, Trulie, Lady Mairi, and Lady Kenna."

"Ye've gone daft." Graham gently lowered Lilia to the pallet of blankets Angus had spread beside him. He slowly rose, took up his sword, and positioned himself at Lilia's feet. "They've not had time to receive word."

"See for yerself," Colum shouted, waving to guide the women's horses into the clearing.

Granny rode in first, her twisted staff held high in one hand. Trulie followed, with Mairi and Kenna close behind. Granny dismounted with the ease of a woman a third of her years, not bothering to wait for the girls before rushing to Lilia's side.

"'Tis as I feared," Granny said in a broken whisper. She knelt and traced a bent trembling finger along the curve of Lilia's ashen cheek. She closed her eyes and shook her head, pressing her other hand tight across her mouth.

Graham eased back a step as Trulie, Mairi, and Kenna rushed to their sister's side. He had grown numb, hollow, and cold within his grief but the sight of Lilia's kin weeping for her was nearly more than he could bear. "Heal her," he rasped out. "Give her back to me —now."

Granny looked up at him, the uncertainty on her face squeezing his heart with suffocating dread. "I don't know that we can," she said. "We always sense when one of our own is about to leave us." She reached down and lifted Lilia's limp hand into hers, staring sadly down into her granddaughter's face. "That is how we knew to come so quickly. All of us saw what was about to be before it even happened. We'd hoped to get here in time to stop it. But then we knew . . . " Granny closed her eyes, shaking her head against her sorrow. Her face crumpled with pain as she opened her eyes, her tears overflowing. Ever so gently, she lifted Lilia's hand and pressed a kiss to it. "We met the messenger you sent when we were already over halfway here," she whispered. She turned back to Graham, tucking her fist to the center of her chest as she struggled to speak. "It may be her destiny to cross over now. I don't know if we can heal her or not."

Graham dove to his knees beside Granny and stole Lilia's hand out of her grasp. They *would* heal his dear one. By the gods, he would make it so. "I dinna give a damn about destiny or fate. I choose to make my own. Heal her. Ye gave this woman to me—to love and protect. I'll be damned if I allow ye to let her slip away without even trying to keep her from walking through death's doors."

Granny gazed at him for a long moment, silent tears rolling down her wrinkled cheeks. She hitched in a shuddering sniff, swiped her fingertips against the wetness on her face, then slowly looked at each of her granddaughters. Trulie, Mairi, and Kenna each barely nodded.

"We have to at least try," Trulie said quietly.

Granny nodded with a stiff jerk of her head. Voice quivering, she pointed at Lilia's chest. "We must lift her." She motioned to Trulie and Mairi, kneeling on Lilia's other side. "Raise your sister, gently now. She needs more blankets under her shoulders. She'll breathe easier that way until we either get her healed or . . . "

"She's nearly gone," Kenna said, tears overflowing as she rested her hand on Lilia's shin. "I can barely sense her." Her voice dropped as she moved to Lilia's feet and took hold of her ankles. "We need to hurry."

Help them, Graham silently prayed. *Allow them to lead her back to me, I beg of ye.* Colum and Gray stood on one side of him and Angus on the other. None of them touched him but their strength and support kept him steadied on his feet just the same.

Moving to kneel at Lilia's head, Granny motioned to Trulie and Mairi. "One of you to the right and one to the left." She nodded at Kenna. "Hold tight to her. Keep her soul grounded before it succeeds in breaking free."

Kenna leaned forward, her knuckles whitening with the intensity of her grip on Lilia's ankles.

Granny held out both hands. Without a word, Trulie grasped Granny's right hand and Mairi took her left. All four women bowed their heads, then each of them went so completely still, Graham thought they had stopped breathing.

A building energy filled the air—a tightness that made Graham's flesh sting. He felt as though his skin was two sizes too small and about to burst at the seams.

The women's clasped hands began to glow as though they had trapped rays of sunlight within their grasp.

Graham held his breath as they lifted their glowing hands. The golden light escaped from between their fingers, bursting free and merging into a swirling current of energy flowing from one Sinclair woman to the next, creating a softly humming circle over Lilia's still form.

"As we touch her with the circle of energy, call out to her, Graham. Call loud and strong and let her feel what is in your heart," Granny said, her voice eerily hollow like the tolling of a great bell.

Graham stepped closer. The women slowly lowered their hands and touched Lilia, holding tight as the energy made contact and sparked all across her body.

"Return to me, Lilia! Come to me now!" Graham opened his heart, pouring out all his fear and his pain. "I beg ye, my love, come back to me for I need ye more than I can say." He dropped to his knees, bowed forward, and beat his fists against the ground at her side. "I love ye, my dearest one," he whispered. "Please—I canna live without ye."

He closed his eyes and pressed his forehead atop his fists. She had to come back to him. She could not leave him—not now—not ever.

"Graham?"

He feared to look up and see if the sweetest voice he had ever heard was real or just a cruel dream. What if his sorrow was playing tricks? He couldn't bear it if it wasn't the truth.

A light touch rested on his shoulder. A tender kiss brushed

against his temple. Afraid to take a breath, Graham slowly lifted his head and opened his eyes.

Lilia leaned forward with a shy smile and held out her hands. "I missed you," she whispered.

He gathered her up into his arms, senses reeling at the incredibly *alive* warmth of her and the strong healthy beat of her heart against his. Her soft laugh as he squeezed her tighter assured him that his love truly lived. He buried his face in the crook of her neck, closing his eyes and nuzzling into the fragrant silkiness of her hair. "Lore a'mighty, I never thought to hear yer voice ever again."

"I missed you," Lilia repeated, clutching him tighter as though she feared he would slip away.

Graham drew back and stared deep into her eyes, struggling to give his heart a voice, searching for a way to let his soul speak. "I would have ye know the depths of my love for ye—" The words stalled out. His mind, body, heart, and soul risked exploding with the turmoil of his emotions. "Mere words canna tell ye how I feel at this verra moment—now that I hold ye safe once more." He brushed a reverent kiss across her lips then pressed his forehead to hers. "My love for ye is too great to be measured—or named."

She tilted her head and gifted him with a long slow kiss then eased back, hooked her arms around his neck, and smiled up at him, pure joy shining in her eyes. "And I love you more."

He rose to his feet, never looking away from the most beautiful green eyes he'd feared he would never look into again. He lowered her to her feet, then took her hands in his and held them tight. He'd come to a decision. It was time to make it so. "We must return to the future—as soon as ye've visited with yer family for a bit. We belong there—not here—in this time."

Lilia stole a quick glance over at Granny and the girls, then faced Graham once again, confusion shadowing her face. "I'd already decided we would stay here permanently if you wanted. I thought you'd be happier here." Her voice grew softer and she shook her head. "I don't understand. Why would you want to return to the future and stay?"

"I will not risk losing ye again." Graham cupped her cheek in his hand, his fingertips laced into her hair. "This place . . . this time . . . it is too filled with danger. I've learned my lesson. I canna protect ye here. I canna keep ye safe."

She squeezed his hands, her brow creasing with an apologetic look as though she wished she didn't have to say what she was about to say. "All times have danger, Graham. No century is free of risks. You know that—right?"

"The future doesna have the raw danger of this place." He looked to Mother Sinclair. The matriarch encouraged him with a sad smile and the barest dip of her chin.

He brought Lilia's fingers to his lips and gently kissed them. Tucking her hands to his chest, he rubbed his thumbs back and forth across her knuckles. "Mother Sinclair has warned me of the heartache and pain this time has a comin'. Ye dinna belong here, Lilia. Ye couldna bear it, ye ken that as well as I. We will return to yer Edinburgh. And yer odd friends." He squeezed both her hands and smiled. "Our bairns will fare much better in the future, as well."

"Bairns?" The love sparkling in her eyes made his heart sing. Lore a'mighty, how had he ever lived without this woman?

"Aye." Graham nodded, assuming as serious a tone as he could muster. "Many children. Ye said Eliza's house was entirely too quiet. I'm thinking we could change that."

"I did say that." Lilia grinned, snuggling tighter into his arms. A soft low chortle escaped her as she reached up and pulled his face down to hers. "Somehow I think home will never be quiet again with you around." She brushed his mouth with a tender claiming kiss. Molding her mouthwatering curves against him, she playfully licked the tip of his nose. "And I'm going to love every loud minute of it."

EPILOGUE

A little over two years later . . .
Scotland: Mid-thirteenth century

A warning squawk, irritated and shrill, alerted Lilia to her eight-month-old daughter's impending tantrum. She quickly broke off her conversation with Trulie, glancing around the garden for who currently had her child and what might be displeasing the fiery-tempered little diva.

Eliza Catriona, fondly dubbed Izzy-Cat by Auntie Vivienne back in twenty-first-century Edinburgh, had entered this world with a head full of flaming red curls and a disposition to match. In the child's uncompromising, eight-month-old opinion, there was but one person who could do no wrong and that individual was her father.

"What ails ye, wee one?" Coira asked, balancing the fussy little redhead atop the rounded shelf of her pregnant belly. Coira's husband of six months, Clan MacKenna's new head stable master, Liam, stood beside her, glancing back and forth between red-faced little Catriona and the mound of his unborn child with an *Oh hell no* look on his face. Ever-patient Coira just smiled and bounced the babe back and forth, attempting to calm her with a lilting song and jiggle.

"Nap time maybe?" Trulie asked, holding newborn son, Ian, in the crook of one arm while also keeping a firm hold on four-year-old son Rabbie's hand.

If only it were that simple. Lilia hurried over to Coira, motioning at Graham, who had just pushed through the low swinging gate leading in from the main bailey. Graham grinned from ear to ear, visibly lengthening his stride to double-time it across the garden to his wife.

"She spotted you. I told you to lay low so someone else could hold her for a while." Lilia totally failed at maintaining the scolding tone. How could she chide him? Graham adored his daughter even more than his daughter worshiped him.

Catriona's wail hit a particularly jarring note as Lilia lifted her out of Coira's arms. "I'm so sorry but she's spotted her daddy again. When he's around, she has a fit if anyone else is holding her."

As soon as Graham took hold of squirming Catriona, the wily minx split the air with a delighted squeal, filled both chubby hands with her father's beard and yanked in perfect rhythm with her tiny white-socked feet kicking the lace ruffles of her best dress.

"There's my wee lass. There's my sweetest Catriona-rose." Graham winked at Lilia and Coira, beaming proudly as he took his daughter to sit with seven-year-old Chloe and her owl, Oren.

Kenna walked up with one-year-old Fiona on her hip, her shy blue-eyed daughter chewing on her thumb while she frowned down at her rowdy, four-year-old twin brothers, Caeden and Jamie, who were currently running circles around their mother. Kenna snapped her fingers and pointed the boys over to the bench with Graham, Chloe, and little Catriona. "Take Rabbie and go visit with Catriona. She's going back home in a few hours."

"But she's a girl, Mama—and jus' a wee bairn," Caeden complained. "Aye," Jamie chimed in with a bob of his tousled head.

"Auntie Lil shouldha brought her puppy and left that wee banshee at home. She is too loud."

"Get over there and be civilized before I heat up your backsides." Kenna took a threatening step toward them. All three boys scurried away at survival speed. Kenna rolled her eyes and shook her head at Lilia. "I am so sorry."

Lilia laughed and waved away Kenna's apology as Mairi joined them and sent her three-year-old son, Sawny, over to play with the older children. Ronan, Colum, Gray, and Coira's husband, Liam, joined Graham to help keep the lively herd in line.

A pang of sadness made Lilia's heart ache as she watched the men help entertain the children. What an odd sight. Two clan chieftains, a war chief, Graham, and stable master Liam—entertaining the children rather than calling for the servants to usher the busy bunch up to the nursery.

But that was because it was nearly time. As soon as the sun sank a bit closer to the rippling waves of the sea, it would be time to walk up the hillside to the burial cairn overlooking the water. When the long, trying day finally came to a close, it would be time for the final goodbye.

"Can you hold Janet for me?" Mairi gently nudged Lilia with one-year-old Janet while balancing Janet's twin sister, Jessa, on her other hip.

Lilia blinked away the sting of unshed tears and took the child. "Come here, sweetie. Give Auntie Lil a snuggle." Dark-haired Janet beamed with a rosy-cheeked smile, wrapped her little arms around Lilia's neck, and squeezed.

"She always said she would see us happy and settled before she moved on," Trulie said, watching Chloe hold Oren just out of Catriona's grabbing reach so the owl could properly inspect the newest cousin. Trulie's mouth trembled a bit to one side as she hitched in a shaking breath.

"She did at that," Lilia agreed with a swipe of her fingers against the corners of her eyes. She did her best to hold back the tears as she gazed around the garden. Granny wouldn't want tears. Granny would want a celebration of a life well lived. "We're blessed with men who adore us and a garden full of healthy happy babies," she said, pressing a hand to a heart so full it was about to overflow. "And we've got Granny to thank for it all."

Kenna nodded, her voice quivering as she spoke. "Granny did well." Tears overflowed and slid down her face.

Angus appeared at the gate with the clan piper beside him. Hair slicked back and fully fitted out in his best MacKenna colors, Angus solemnly held up his hand and waited until he had the attention of at least most of the adults in the garden. "'Tis time," he announced quietly.

Yes. It was time. Time to say goodbye. Lilia swallowed and hugged Mairi's daughter closer. Common sense told her this was the natural order of things. You're born. You live. You die. But when it came to Granny—a tear finally escaped and raced down her cheek. How in the world would they all get along without Granny?

"I'm not ready to let her go either," Trulie remarked quietly, walking beside Lilia as they slowly made their way across the garden to follow Angus and the piper. "But it was so peaceful—the way we found them. They all three looked contented. So very happy. It's like they decided it was just time to go."

Lilia could just picture them in her mind's eye. Trulie had said that Granny and Tamhas had insisted on spending Summer Solstice, the longest day of the year, in Tamhas's old croft carved into the side of the mountain. When they failed to return to the keep the next day, Trulie and Gray had gone to check on them and found them.

The old couple had gone to sleep never to awaken in this life again. Tamhas lay on his back with a protective arm curled around Granny, who was snuggled close into the crook of his shoulder, her silvery hair fanned out across the pillow. Ever the guardian tethered to Granny's soul, Kismet was curled in the bend of the old woman's knees, appearing to be fast asleep, but the feline had passed away too, joining her mistress on the other side of the veil.

"I still can't believe she's really gone," Lilia said.

Mairi held out her hands to take back her daughter.

Lilia hugged the little girl tighter. "I'll carry her. Catriona's with Graham and your hands are full with Jessa."

Ronan appeared at Mairi's side, leading Sawny by the hand. He solemnly nodded to Lilia as he took Mairi's hand. "We'll get through this. She would want us to carry on with courage."

A warm welcome weight settled against the small of Lilia's back. Graham leaned in close and brushed a kiss to her temple. "Time to bid Mother Sinclair and Tamhas safe journey. We'll have them give Mistress Eliza a good strong hug from wee Catriona, aye?"

Lilia nodded without a word, walking along beside Graham with tiny Janet on her hip. She looked up ahead. The number of individuals walking to the top of the cliff overlooking the sea triggered a bittersweet knot of love and sadness in her chest. To think this many loved ones had sprouted from one indestructible seed of determination nurtured and tended by a tiny woman with the heart and courage of an invincible warrior.

A husband for each granddaughter and, so far, ten lively great-grandchildren. And probably more on the way. Kenna looked suspiciously pale again and Colum was even more attentive than usual. And Coira might not be blood but she was family and the child she and Liam would bring forth would be called cousin just like the rest of them.

All gathered around a great mound formed of huge squares of white stone. Crystals embedded in the grain of the roughly chiseled blocks reflected the fiery colors of the setting sun. Tamhas, Granny, and Kismet—or the shells that had once housed their dynamic souls—had all been placed in the single cairn to travel through eternity together.

Karma sat in front of the sealed door of the drystone structure, ears drooping and head bowed. Chloe's owl, Oren, soared back and forth overhead as the sun disappeared into the sea.

Chloe, firstborn time runner of the next generation, gently pulled free of her parents and walked over to the cairn. She flattened her right hand on the side of the intricately carved keystone and splayed her small left hand in the center of her chest. Head barely tilted to one side; her ebony curls fluttered in the wind as her expression shifted to one of rapt attention. A slow smile lifted one corner of her mouth, dimpling her little round cheek. She slightly bobbed her head up and down in a quick nod. "Aye, Granny. I'll tell them each what ye said and then ye can be on yer way."

Chloe turned and faced them, primly clasping her hands in front of her. She lifted her chin and stood as tall as she could, calmly surveying all the adults standing before her. "Granny gave me a message for the each of ye—the Sinclair daughters of Granny Nia's heart. She told me to ask ye to step forward and stand together as one a last time afore she goes."

Trulie handed sleeping Ian and wide-eyed Rabbie to Gray, then stepped forward. She turned and motioned for her sisters to join her.

Uneasy about what Granny's message just might be, Lilia lagged behind Kenna and Mairi. She'd *felt* Granny was still close but had hesitated to mention it for fear of upsetting the others. Mairi took her hand and squeezed it tight as she lined up beside her.

"Go ahead, Chloe," Trulie prompted. "Tell us what Granny said."

"Granny says ye are the wise one now, Mama—ye being the eldest of yer generation and all. Said it would be no small task keeping this clan in line but she kens ye can do it and do it well." Chloe smiled at her mother and lifted her chin proudly. "She says that I'm to be a good lass and help ye since one day it will be my turn to watch over my kin."

Trulie acknowledged Chloe's words with a sad smile and an accepting nod.

Chloe shifted her attention to Kenna, her face growing serious. "Granny said a time will come when ye'll have the chance to save many, Auntie Kenna. Ye must be brave and follow yer heart, she said. Never forget that yer instincts will never fail ye."

"Thank you, Chloe," Kenna whispered, her chin quivering as tears slipped down her cheeks.

"And Auntie Mairi—Granny said I'm to remind ye that ye canna heal them all no matter how hard ye try." Chloe shook her head, looking entirely too wise for one so young. "She said to tell ye it doesna mean that ye've failed. It merely means 'twas the path they were destined to follow."

Mairi squeezed Lilia's hand while pressing her other fist to her middle. "I'll do my best to remember that, Chloe."

Lilia held her breath as Chloe turned to her. The child's face now beamed with a delighted smile. "Auntie Lil. Yers was the best message of them all. Granny said to tell ye that she is so verra proud of ye for discovering her greatest secret. She said she kent ye would be the first to sort it out."

Lilia frowned. What the devil was Chloe talking about? "Her greatest secret?"

"Aye." Chloe nodded with a wink. "Did ye not step easily from the time tunnel this time rather than tumble across the ground and nearly break yer wee neck and that of Uncle Graham's and little Catriona's?"

Realization dawned on Lilia, flashing through her with a giddy rush of the biggest *aha* moment she'd ever had. It was true. This trip, the time tunnel, hadn't spit them out like an overchewed wad of gum. Lilia and Graham, with Graham holding Catriona, had all three stepped from the twenty-first century to the thirteenth century as though changing floors on a cosmic elevator. Even Graham had remarked on the grace and ease of the usually painful journey.

There was only one difference in this trip and all the other leaps through time that had beaten her senseless with rough landings: Catriona. Lilia had felt a strength and control she had never known before while maneuvering the time tunnel. That strength had come from her unyielding determination that Catriona wouldn't be harmed.

Chloe clapped and hopped in place, joy twinkling in her eyes. "Now ye ken Granny's secret: a mother's love for her child is the strongest power of all."

A warm gentle wind blew in from the sea, soft as a brushing caress. A chorus of laughter, light, and tinkling as crystal chimes, rose above the sound of the waves shushing against the base of the cliff. A deep rumbling chuckle joined in and if Lilia wasn't mistaken, somewhere off in the distance, she could just make out the contented sound of a purring cat.

Lilia lifted her gaze to the deepening blue-black darkness of early nightfall and smiled. All was as it should be. And she could just see Granny now—laughing and vibrant, convincing Tamhas and Kismet that it was time for the next adventure.

MAEVEGREYSON.COM
Magical Romance Sitting Through Time

If you enjoyed this book, please consider leaving a review on the site where you purchased your copy, or a reader site such as Goodreads, or BookBub.

Sign up here to receive my newsletter:

Author Maeve Greyson Newsletter

Many thanks and may your life always be filled with good books!

Maeve

ALSO BY MAEVE GREYSON

HIGHLAND HEROES SERIES

The Guardian

The Warrior

The Judge

The Dreamer

The Bard

The Ghost

A Yuletide Yearning

Love's Charity

TIME TO LOVE A HIGHLANDER SERIES

Loving Her Highland Thief

Taming Her Highland Legend

Winning Her Highland Warrior

Capturing Her Highland Keeper

Saving Her Highland Traitor

Loving Her Lonely Highlander

Delighting Her Highland Devil

ONCE UPON A SCOT SERIES

A Scot of Her Own

A Scot to Have and to Hold

A Scot to Love and Protect

HIGHLAND PROTECTOR SERIES

Sadie's Highlander

Joanna's Highlander

Katie's Highlander

HIGHLAND HEARTS SERIES

My Highland Lover

My Highland Bride

My Tempting Highlander

My Seductive Highlander

THE MACKAY CLAN

Beyond A Highland Whisper

The Highlander's Fury

A Highlander In Her Past

OTHER BOOKS BY MAEVE GREYSON

Stone Guardian

Eternity's Mark

Guardian of Midnight Manor

ABOUT THE AUTHOR

maevegreyson.com

USA Today Bestselling Author. Two-time RONE Award Winner. Holt Medallion Finalist.

Maeve Greyson's mantra is this: No one has the power to shatter your dreams unless you give it to them.

She and her husband of over forty years traveled around the world while in the U.S. Air Force. Now they're settled in rural Kentucky where Maeve writes about her courageous Highlanders and the fearless women who tame them. When she's not plotting the perfect snare, she can be found herding cats, grandchildren, and her husband—not necessarily in that order.

Printed in Great Britain
by Amazon

20882803R00149